Cat's Cradle

JULIA GOLDING

CAT IN SCOTLAND

EGMONT

Bowles's New Plan of London map courtesy of the British Library

Maps courtesy of Bodleian Library, University of Oxford: G1 A1
(1) index map, (2) survey map, (3) passage map
Reproduced by permission of the Trustees of the National Library of Scotland
Charles Ross – A map of the shire of Lanark, 1773.
William Forrest – The county of Lanark from actual survey, 1816.

EGMONT

We bring stories to life

First published 2011
by Egmont UK Ltd
239 Kensington High Street, London W8 6SA

Text copyright © 2011 Julia Golding

The moral rights of the author have been asserted

ISBN 978 1 4052 4305 6

3 5 7 9 10 8 6 4 2

A CIP catalogue record for this title is available from the British Library

Typeset by Avon DataSet Ltd, Bidford on Avon, Warwickshire
Printed and bound in Great Britain by CPI Books (Cox and Wyman)

www.egmont.co.uk
www.juliagolding.co.uk

For Peter and Ann

CAT ROYAL SERIES

❧ THE CRITICS ❧

'The British Empire need not fear going into a decline and fall while young citizens like Miss Royal bolster our national spirits!' – EDWARD GIBBON, HISTORIAN

'A perfectly framed tale – I enjoyed the extra twist' – SIR RICHARD ARKWRIGHT, INVENTOR AND MANUFACTURER

'A hairum-scarum, ramstam lassie,
May she flourish like a lily,
Now bonilie!'
– ROBERT BURNS, POET

'An unwarranted incursion into my territory – get back down south, Miss Royal!' – SIR WALTER SCOTT, POET AND NOVELIST

'Her story had me all in a spin' – JAMES HARGREAVES, INVENTOR OF THE SPINNING JENNY

'She's barking, absolutely barking, what!'
– HM KING GEORGE III

'A total counterfeit from start to finish' – WILLIAM HENRY IRELAND, ~~FORGER~~ DISCOVERER OF NEW PLAYS BY SHAKESPEARE

'My delight in her work never wanes' – JOHN CONSTABLE, PAINTER

'Her prose runs as smoothly as one of my own macadamized roads' – JOHN LOUDON MCADAM, SCOTTISH INVENTOR

'A combination of all that's best in tale-weaving' – SAMUEL CROMPTON, INVENTOR OF THE MULE

'Her Scottish tale needs no overture – on second thoughts, perhaps I should write one?' – FELIX MENDELSSOHN, COMPOSER

'She packs quite a punch – just my Fancy' – PIERCE EGAN, SPORTS JOURNALIST

'I never have to manufacture any enthusiasm when I read her tales' – JOSIAH WEDGWOOD, POTTER

'Piffle!' – WILLIAM PITT THE YOUNGER, PRIME MINISTER

INDEX

❦ NOTE TO THE READER ❦

Reader,

In my previous tales, I have journeyed far from my origins on the streets of London to the wilds of America and across the turquoise seas of the Caribbean. I have been adopted by Indians, climbed the rigging, and briefly dabbled with piracy. But I had to come home to learn that you do not need to travel great distances to come face-to-face with unfamiliar cultures and new experiences. Such things are on your doorstep if you but look.

So come with me on an adventure to a land famous for pushing forward the frontier of human ingenuity, leading us into the new age of manufactories. Can you guess where we are going yet? What if I tell you that it is also a place of rough manners and banditry; Highlands and lochs; pibroch and poets? A strange mixture indeed.

Do you know where we are bound?
To find out, turn the page and follow me.

Cat Royal

❧ Principal Characters ❧

LONDON AND CAMBRIDGE

Miss Cat Royal – orphan from Drury Lane,
your guide

Mr Billy Shepherd – reluctant travelling
companion, crime lord

Mr Syd Fletcher – old friend and admirer,
boxer, gang leader

Mr and Mrs Fletcher – Syd's parents

Mr Nick – Syd's second-in-command

Mr Joe 'The Card' Murray – street magician

Mr Sheridan – playwright, politician and
theatre owner

Mr Peter Dodsley – violinist

Mr Beamish – jolly barrister

Mr Robert Marks – Mr Beamish's hat-throwing
clerk

Miss Bridgit O'Riley – Irish girl at a loss in London

The seven O'Riley brothers – Bridgit's troublesome
siblings

The Earl of Arden (Frank) – son of a duke,
Cambridge scholar, friend
Mr Charlie Hengrave – Frank's room-mate and
Cat's former brother

NEW LANARK

Mr Jamie Kelly – trainee mechanic, unfriendly
to Sassenachs
Mr David Dale – generous factory owner
Goodwife Ross – lady in charge of the orphan
workers
Miss Martha – reluctant bedmate
Miss Annie MacGregor – helpful fellow worker
Dominie Blair – schoolmaster with a sense of
humour
Mistress MacDonald – hospitable school
teacher
Overseer Shaw – busy man in control of day-to-
day running of mill
The Moir Family (Mr Moir, Mrs Mary Moir,
Katrine, Ian, Dougie, and Jeannie) – intriguing
family living in Long Row

Dr Gordon – kindly medical man
Gillie Archibald Brown – fierce gamekeeper
Sir Charles Laud – dandified sheriff of Lanark
Lady Ross-Baillie – owner of Bonnington House,
keen on her cows

THE TOWER HOUSE
The Bruce Clan:
Rabbie – young lad who wants nothing to do
with a certain lass
Malcolm – leader of the local troublemakers
Nan – Malcolm's wife
Willy – malicious, drunken second-in-command

Rioting apprentices, noisy mill workers, outraged
duchesses etc. etc.

London, October 1792 – Curtain rises.

PROLOGUE

BOLT FROM THE BLUE

Many people are fortunate to have a family tree that stretches back hundreds of years. My friend Frank, for example, can point to a sprig and say, 'That was Great Uncle Timothy who died at the Battle of Blenheim,' or, 'That's Great Great Great Grandma Eustacia who smoked a pipe and bred rare pigs.' For him, history is a hop from stepping-stone to stepping-stone of notable or eccentric relatives all leading up to the present time – to him.

By contrast, I had always thought of myself as a lone shoot. Abandoned as an infant on the doorstep of Drury Lane theatre twelve years ago, I was the acorn dropped carelessly far from the parent plant. I had been left to grow (or not) as fate decided, with no knowledge of the tree that produced me. That was, Reader, until I arrived back in London after my adventures in the Caribbean. Out of the blue, my past caught up with me and sprouted in a most unexpected way.

The post-chaise rattled down Oxford Street, but I was in heaven. Finally, after a year of exile, I could see, hear and smell my city in all its grimy glory. I was home.

'Gawd almighty, girl, can't you sit still for a moment?' Billy Shepherd, my friendly enemy and travelling companion, gave a tug to the back of my skirt. 'You're like a jack-in-the-box.'

I ignored him. 'Look – there's the turn to Grosvenor Square! And that's the way to St Martin-in-the-Fields! And look – there's Scratch Harry.'

Billy rolled his eyes at my enthusiasm. Rumpled by months of travel, everything about him, from his limp cravat to his scuffed boots, looked weary, more than ready to exchange continual motion for a seat by a comfortable fireside.

'You know who I mean, Billy – the fake legless

beggar, the one who has his legs concealed in that cart – he's still sitting on the corner!' I called the tramp a cheery greeting and flipped him an expertly aimed penny. It plopped into his bowl with a satisfying plink. Catching sight of the donor, Scratch Harry gave a bark of laughter and doffed his cap.

'Course 'e is, you idiot,' grumbled Billy, tugging fretfully at the frayed end of a cuff. 'Works for me, doesn't 'e? 'E knows 'e 'as to put in the hours.'

I'd momentarily forgotten Billy had this part of London well and truly under the control of his gang.

'If you're going to get a cut, I want my money back.' I held out my hand and wiggled my fingers.

With a pained sigh, Billy dug in his waistcoat pocket and slapped a shilling into my palm. 'Don't carry small change,' he muttered.

'Your loss is my gain.' I smiled sweetly and turned back to my examination of the streets. After a short pause, I began drumming my fingers restlessly on the sill, beating a tattoo guaranteed to annoy Billy. 'Do you think everyone else got home safely? Frank and Syd, I mean?'

Having waved off my friends in Philadelphia, I expected them to have returned some months ago. Unless my letter to Frank had arrived before me, they would not be anticipating me landing on their doorstep so soon. They'd left me pursuing a career as an actress with a troupe touring the Caribbean. That enterprise cut short by brief spells as enslaved servant, pirate and rebel soldier,* I had finally taken passage back across the Atlantic with Billy. Our ship had carried the taint of the slave trade, having just unloaded its cargo of human captives from Africa. Mercifully, on this eastbound leg, it had only transported cotton and sugar to the manufactories of northern England and Scotland. There had been no other ship willing to take us, so we had had to make do. After a swift sailing, Billy and I disembarked with the cargo at the port of Liverpool and had spent the last few days jolting down the turnpike to make our grand entry into the capital.

* For further details of these exploits, please see my tale, *Black Heart of Jamaica*.

Billy's temper was hanging by a thread; my spirits were high. He had given me to understand that I made an infuriating fellow passenger in the close confines of cabin and carriage. Excellent news all round.

My drumming reached a crescendo.

"'Ow many times do I 'ave to tell you? Stop tappin'!' Billy ran his fingers through his brown hair, making it stick up like a bristling hedgehog. Smoky grey eyes flashed a warning – he was about to lose his composure. 'And 'ow the 'ell do I know if your friends are 'ere, Cat Royal? What you think I am? A bleedin' gypsy or somethink? With a bloomin' crystal ball?'

I collapsed back on the seat opposite him and grinned. 'The question was rhetorical, Billy.'

'What the Devil does that mean?' He massaged his temples with his long fingers. 'You've given me the 'eadache, but do you care?'

'That last one of yours was an excellent example of a rhetorical question,' I commended him as if he were a star pupil. 'It means that I wasn't expecting an answer, merely speaking my thoughts aloud.'

'Well, don't.' He clenched his fists on his knees.

'Don't what?' I wrinkled my brow in innocent puzzlement.

'Don't speak another word.' He chopped at his throat. 'I've 'ad it up to 'ere with your thoughts, rhetorical or whatever. You've done nothink but jabber on since we left Tortuga three months ago. You've driven me to drink,' he took a fortifying gulp from the flask of brandy at his side, 'as well as driven me mad.'

I smiled serenely. 'You should count your blessings, Billy. Only a few more minutes of my company then you'll be shot of me for good.'

'About time.'

Congratulating myself silently for routing the affection that Billy misguidedly felt for me, I sat back to enjoy the familiar sights. Billy had not finished; he continued to grumble.

'You snored on my shoulder all the way from Liverpool. Anyone would think I was put on earth to be your pillow. *And* you dribbled all over my best coat –'

'Did not!' I protested, though I could not

deny falling asleep on him.

'On the boat you gave me a seizure, goin' up the mast and 'angin' off the yardarm like a monkey.'

That had been wonderful: the only place on the ship I had felt free of the smell below decks. 'Ah, happy days!'

'You flirted with everyone in sight.'

'You mean I *talked* to the other passengers.'

'And the crew and every Tom, Dick 'n' 'Arry at the inns on the way down from Liverpool.'

'Jealous, Billy?'

'Course not. You just . . . just don't know 'ow to behave.'

'Thus speaks that paragon of polite behaviour Mister William Shepherd, cut-throat and slave owner.' I flourished my hand in a mock bow.

'You were brung up bad – anyone can see that.'

'I was brought up with you, Billy, on the streets, remember?'

'Yeah, but you pretend to be a lady, and them kind of goings-on will get you into trouble.'

I batted my eyelashes at him. 'I thought you liked my friendly nature, Billy dear.'

He scrubbed his hands through his hair. 'Just stop it, Cat. Stop acting like a mindless 'alfwit who'll flirt with anythink in breeches.'

I had to laugh. I'd set out on this journey home planning to push Billy past the point of endurance, playing on his misplaced feelings of ownership towards me, and five hundred yards from his door I had succeeded.

'Sorry, Billy, but this is me. Only cure is for you to jump out and leave me to meet my doom in my own way.' I folded my hands in my lap, assuming a resigned expression worthy of a martyr.

The post-chaise drew up outside Billy's grand house on Bedford Square. He grabbed his hat and was out of the carriage and on the pavement in a trice, stretching his lanky frame with a groan of pleasure. He slammed the coach door shut and shouted for his belongings to be thrown down to his footmen who were dutifully filing out of the house. While this pantomime proceeded apace outside, I sat back, arms crossed, a smug smile on my lips. I'd feared that when we reached home he'd try and persuade me to stay with him – after all, he had come all the way to the Caribbean to find me – but it now looked as if that was the last thing on his mind.

Possessions safely on the way into the house, Billy ducked his head back in through the open window.

'You'll be all right from 'ere, Cat?' he asked brusquely.

'Yes, Billy.'

'Where're you goin'?'

'Bow Street.' I could not stop a triumphant grin at his expression of relief. I suppose he was living in dread of me inviting myself in.

He gave a curt nod, turned to go, then stopped as a new thought struck him, prompted by my smile.

'You . . . you've been doin' this on purpose, ain't you? You meant to make me glad to be rid of you.'

I tapped on the ceiling and called to the coachman, 'Drive on, please.'

'You schemin' little minx!' Standing on the pavement, hands crushing the brim of his hat, Billy looked torn between admiration and fury.

The carriage surged forward.

'You could've just told me, you know!' he shouted after me. 'Spared me months of sufferin'.'

I chuckled. I could've done, but this way had been far more fun.

The butcher's shop on Bow Street was just as I remembered it: cuts of meat hanging on hooks, sausages curled on platters, basins of quivering tripe, sawdust on the floor, the sickly sweet smell of blood. Figures moved around inside but I couldn't make out who was serving. Why I thought the shop should have changed, I don't know. Twelve months was nothing really; it was just that I had lived through so much, I expected to see signs of this reflected in the places around me.

I paused on the pavement, strangely hesitant now I had reached this point. There was one old haunt that I knew would have changed out of all recognition. Just around the corner was the building site of the new Drury Lane theatre. I couldn't bear to look at it yet but I could see the clouds of dust and mason's carts rumbling in that direction. Mr Sheridan, the owner, had promised that a new theatre would rise from the ashes of the old and he was keeping his word. But there was no place for me there now.

This was a melancholy thought, but at least in Syd's butcher's shop I could be confident that he and his parents would be pleased to see me.

The shop bell rang and a customer came out.

'Mornin', Cat. I ain't seen you around for a bit, dearie. 'Ow've you been?' Mrs Peters, the cheesemonger from Covent Garden, patted me on the arm. Her full basket smelled of good strong Cheddar and onions. A ham nestled in the folds of a muslin cloth.

I bobbed a curtsey. Little indeed had changed around here – I even recognized her old basket. 'Mrs Peters! I'm well, thank you! How are Mr Peters and the boys?'

'All doin' same as ever, except the youngest. 'E's joined the Butcher's Boys.' She wrinkled her nose. 'Don't like our Jim 'avin' anythink to do with gangs but I s'pose if 'e 'ad to run with one of 'em, that's the one I'd choose. Syd's a good sort – keeps the boys in line. So, you're back, are you?'

'Yes.'

'Where've you been? I 'eard all sorts of wild rumours.' She leaned nearer and dropped her voice confidentially. 'Someone said you went all the way to Paris, but I didn't believe 'em. "Not our Cat" I said.'

'Actually, I have been to Paris – and a bit further too.'

Mrs Peters opened her eyes wide. 'Further than Paris! Well I never! I'm pleased to see you've come to your senses and are back with your own people.'

With a nod that combined reproof for my wandering and approval for my return, Mrs Peters bustled off to spread the word in the market that the prodigal daughter was among them once more. I wondered what she would have to say when she learnt the true extent of my travels. Smiling at the thought, I pushed the door open, bell ringing brightly. The shop was empty.

'Be with you in a tick!' shouted Syd from out the back. I could hear the regular thwack of a cleaver as he diced steak.

'Well, if that's how you treat your customers,

I think I'll go to the butcher on Long Acre,' I replied loudly.

Thump! The cleaver was buried in the chopping block and Syd erupted into the shop, vaulted the counter and lunged for me.

'You're back!' he exclaimed gruffly. My bag went flying as he squeezed me tight against his chest. I could hardly move my arms to hug him. Almost as abruptly, I was set apart and big hands began brushing me down.

'Fry my brains with onions – look what I've gone and done to your pretty coat!' Syd gamely tried to remove the sawdust and red smears from my light blue pelisse but only managed to make it worse.

'What's a little damage between friends, Syd?' I pushed him away and gave my coat a resigned shake. 'It's been on its last legs in any case after several months at sea.' I smiled up at him, taking in his familiar face, skin still tanned from the voyage, blue eyes shining with pleasure. He'd had a haircut since I last saw him – blond hair now cropped short. 'It's so good to see you. Is everyone well?'

'We're good. And you?'

'Fit as a fiddle – or I will be when I've had a cup of tea. Will you put the kettle on for a weary traveller?'

'Tea's on its way.' Syd ruffled my hair, then glanced behind me. 'Where's Pedro?'

My gay mood dulled a little. 'It's a long story, but he's fine, really he is.' I was trying to convince myself as much as Syd.

'Tell me when you've 'ad a chance to catch your breath.' Scooping me up with an arm around my shoulders, Syd led me into the kitchen.

'Ma, Dad, look who it is!' he announced.

Seated at the kitchen table in front of a pile of half-peeled potatoes, Mrs Fletcher gave a little exclamation of surprise. Putting her work aside at once, she greeted me warmly and called for her husband to come in from the yard. Mr Fletcher, a giant of a man with a shy manner, strode in, patted my shoulder, then gave Syd a delighted grin.

'Glad to see you back, Cat,' he said huskily – more words than he usually spoke to me in a week.

Mrs Fletcher made me feel like a long-lost daughter with her hugs and stream of questions as she bade me make myself at home in her kitchen. She was feared around the market for her temper, but underneath the sharp tongue was a kind-hearted woman.

'You'll stay with us, won't you, dear?' she said, tucking a strand of her fair hair back in her practical bun. A pretty woman with a high colour and Syd's blue eyes, she had been known as the Butcher's Belle when she first married her husband. She bustled about the range seeing to our tea, completely at ease in her little kingdom. With a nod to his son, Mr Fletcher excused himself to mind the shop.

I allowed myself to relax, charmed by the ordinariness of sitting in her kitchen. After months of the exotic and dangerous, it was very comfort - ing to be back somewhere English and tame. 'I'd like to stay if I may, ma'am.'

'Call me Joanna, dear. You're as good as family now, aren't you?' She cast a significant look at Syd who sat on the opposite side of the table, gazing at me as if he couldn't quite believe I was really there. Seeing him after months of separation, I'd forgotten just how large he was. He made his mother and me look positively doll-like.

I met the hint with a non-committal smile. There would be time to address her attempts at matchmaking later.

'Though I s'pose you might want to go and live with those fine friends of yours in Grosvenor Square,' continued Mrs Fletcher, pouring the boiled water into the pot. She waved the steam away and dabbed at her brow with a drying cloth.

'I'd prefer to stay here, if you don't mind, er . . . Joanna. I always felt I was rather out of my depth over there – all those rooms and servants watching my every move.'

'Course we don't mind.' She set out some freshly baked biscuits, slapping Syd's wrist as he grabbed two from the plate. 'Guests first.'

'I thought you said she was family, Ma,' replied Syd, giving me a wink.

'She'll think I brought you up a barbarian.' Mrs Fletcher placed a cup of her finest Indian tea in front of me.

'Perhaps you did, Ma – leastways accordin' to

the men I beat in the boxing ring you did.' Mrs Fletcher gave him a proud smile and caressed the bruise fading on his cheekbone as she passed behind his chair. Syd batted her hand away gently. 'Leave off, Ma. Cat'll think I've gone soft.' He looked at me rather sheepishly. 'Anyway, Cat, about Frank's family in Grosvenor Square – he's gone to Cambridge. You'd be on your own if you stayed there – only the dook and duchess for company.'

As much as I liked Frank's parents, it wouldn't do to impose myself on their household. We wouldn't know how to behave towards each other without Frank's presence to ease the way.

I raised my cup to my lips and blew away the steam. 'Perhaps it's best that I stay here then, back where I started.'

It took a good long while to tell Syd the whole story of what happened to Pedro and me in the Caribbean. Unsurprisingly, he was not happy to hear that I had left our friend in the middle of a war on San Domingo but he accepted that there had been nothing I could have done about it. What most concerned him was the fact that I'd spent so much time with Billy Shepherd, his old rival.

'Don't worry about him, Syd,' I laughed. 'He is relieved to get away from me – I made sure of that. You should have seen him when we got to Bedford Square: he jumped out of the carriage as if a swarm of bees were after him. I was a complete pain, a hair-shirt of a travelling companion.'

'Remind me to keep on your good side, Cat,' Syd said, his humour restored. 'But all the same, let's not take it for granted that 'e's goin' to leave you alone now.'

'Don't worry, I won't.' I knew Billy better than that. And I admit, Reader, part of me rather enjoyed our dangerous game of each trying to get the upper hand in our strange friendship. 'Did you find Mick Bailey and get back your winnings?'

Bailey, Syd's manager, had had him press-ganged rather than share the proceeds of their summer boxing tour.

Syd frowned. 'Not yet. 'E back-slanged it out of

London when 'e 'eard I was 'ome. I'll track 'im down, never you fear.'

I shivered and hugged my arms across my chest. With a quick look at me, Syd threw a shovelful of coals on to the kitchen range and rattled the embers with the poker.

'Syd! Syd! Come out 'ere – and bring Cat!' shouted Mr Fletcher from the shop.

'What now?' I placed my cup on its saucer.

Syd shrugged. 'Dunno, Kitten, but let's not keep Dad waitin'.' Pulling me up, he gestured that I should lead the way down the passage. I entered the shop to find a most unexpected customer waiting by the counter. Dressed in expensive Bond Street clothes and looking like a golden guinea among us common old pennies, Mr Sheridan tipped his hat to me.

'Well now, Cat Royal, and how are you? Far travelled, I hear.'

'Mr Sheridan!' I belatedly dipped into a curtsey, grinning at him like a fool. He had been my guardian ever since he found me, an infant of two or three years, on the steps of Drury Lane.

'Wrapped in a blanket and as quiet as a mouse' was how he had described me.

'How did you know I was back, sir?' I enquired.

'I'd asked the Avons to send word as soon as they heard from you. When I met the duke outside Carlton House this morning, he told me that you'd written to Frank when you landed. He has sent your letter on to his son by express messenger, so you can expect to hear from Frank very soon.'

Holding me out at arms length, Mr Sheridan looked me up and down, somewhat like an artist admiring a portrait he'd not seen for some time. 'My goodness, it is a pleasure to see you again, Cat! I have found the stories of your exploits among the Indians very inspiring – I'm sure there's a play in there somewhere.'

Releasing my hands, he stroked a finger along his upper lip in a thoughtful pose, his dark eyes gleaming. Stocky and flush-faced, Mr Sheridan was in appearance a strange mixture – a literary genius with the build of a labourer. No one could make the mistake of thinking him a weakling poet. His uppercut could do as much damage as his wit.

'Indeed, sir, it was kind of you to seek me out here.' I gestured to the shop, quite a comedown from his fine house in the West End and gentlemen's clubs in St James's.

'As to that, let us say that I have my reasons.' He cleared his throat. I would have said he was nervous if that hadn't been so out of character. 'I did not want to risk missing you again. You see, Cat, there is something I need to tell you.' He glanced round at our audience of eagerly listening Fletchers. 'I wanted to speak to you when I received the results of my investigation late last year; I never got the chance as you were whisked off to Bath so promptly by the Avons and then you went abroad.'

'What investigation? What did you want to tell me?'

He replaced his hat and offered his arm. 'Walk with me, Cat?'

With a slightly worried look at Syd – this was so strange – I accepted Mr Sheridan's arm. He tucked my hand in the crook of his elbow.

'Haven't grown much, have you?' he said. 'Except your hair, of course.'

I smoothed my unruly red curls: they had escaped their ribbon as usual. I knew I must look a sight, not fit to go walking with anyone, let alone a London celebrity. I fumbled for my bonnet, dangling by its strings from my wrist.

'That's my motto too: hide it under your hat and no one will notice.' Mr Sheridan tied up the bonnet ribbons for me to hasten our escape.

A little awkwardly, we exchanged news of mutual friends as we strolled down Bow Street, heading for the more genteel district of the Strand. My unease grew: Mr Sheridan had never done anything like this with me before, always treating me as part pet, part servant. Now he was acting as if I were a grown-up lady with whom a gentleman like him would promenade. It only increased the solemnity of the moment.

We stopped when we reached the Middle Temple gardens, a little patch of green amidst the lodgings of the barristers. An exclusive world of wigs and writs, I would never have been allowed in by the porter if I hadn't been with Mr Sheridan. Indeed I wouldn't have wanted to enter. Like any

Londoner with a grain of common sense, I knew better than to get entangled with the courts. The garden was beautiful though. The leaves of the trees were turning golden. With every breath of wind they scattered, tumbling on the grass like the coins poured out on fees by the unfortunate clients. Beyond the garden lay the Thames. A barge with terracotta-coloured sails floated slowly by, heading out to sea. The sun warmed the old stone of the buildings and made the dark waters of the river glow with an oily sheen.

'Sit down for a moment, Cat,' Mr Sheridan said, handing me carefully to a bench. He remained standing. 'I'm not sure how to go about this.' His eyes followed the barge downstream.

'Go about what, sir?' I was really worried now. It sounded as if he was about to announce a death at the very least.

Mr Sheridan crossed his arms, paused, and then turned to me. 'To go about telling you news of your family.'

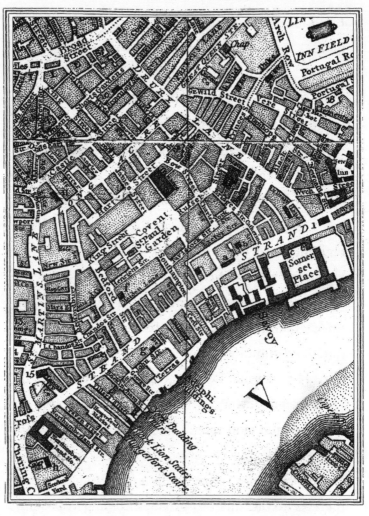

Act I – In which Cat discovers she might not be alone . . .

Act I

SCENE 1 – YOURS FAITHFULLY

Reader, I felt as if I had just been doused in iced water.

'My . . . my family? But you have always said I was abandoned – that I had no one apart from the theatre.'

He looked away. 'That's all true, I'm afraid. But something has turned up.'

My heart was pounding, palms sweating. How many times had I dreamed that someone would some day reveal the mystery of my origins! It seemed as if that was about to come true.

'You can't stop there, sir. You've got to tell me all of it.' My voice sounded strangled. *Breathe, Cat, breathe*, I reminded myself.

'You are right. I must delay no longer.' He sat beside me and took my hand. 'You see, Cat, when I found you, there were a few clues as to your identity, as you probably know.'

I wasn't sure what he meant. 'Clues?'

'Well, yes. First your appearance, carrot-topped even then – a distinctive feature. You must have wondered about that. Then there was your accent.'

'My accent?'

'You were only a little – or should I say, *wee* – thing, but the few words you spoke had a Scottish accent. I remember how you called for your *mither*. You were heartbroken at being left, and who can blame you? It took many weeks for you to settle in with us.'

My mind was reeling. None of these bits of information fitted with the image I had of myself. 'No one told me that.'

'You soon lost the accent – I doubt many remember now. I would not have recalled it if not for . . . well, never mind that now.'

'You think I'm Scottish?'

'Your mother must have been. You, my dear, are a Londoner through and through.' He gave me a bow. 'Any trace of that accent has long since disappeared.'

'And did you try and find my mother?'

I clenched my free fist in the folds of my skirt, my knuckles white.

'Of course I did. Some remembered the . . . er . . . woman with the red-headed child but no one around Covent Garden knew what had happened to her – the trail petered out. There was one more piece of evidence, however. The blanket.'

I remembered it well – I had used it on my bed in the Sparrow's Nest, the old costume store in the theatre, until it fell into holes and had been thrown out. I'd always been told that it had been found with me so I'd kept a scrap of it tucked away among my belongings.

'It was the Stirling tartan,' Mr Sheridan continued. 'I thought I'd told you that.'

I shook my head.

'Perhaps just coincidence, perhaps not.' Mr Sheridan frowned, lost in his memories of the past.

'And is that it?' I asked, feeling a gust of anger at the carelessness of great men. How like my guardian to be so casual about the few details concerning my identity, so vital to me, so unimportant to him!

'No, my dear. One more thing – and this is

where I want you to think very carefully before you do anything. Remember those pamphlets of your adventures that Mr Tweadle published last year?'

I gave a curt nod – it was still a sore point.*

'A few weeks later, while you were in France, I received a letter from a woman near Glasgow asking for more information about you. It wasn't very subtle: she wanted your address, and to find out how rich you were. I almost dismissed it as a begging letter but the writer let drop a few things that made me wonder. I'll leave you to decide what to make of it.' He passed me a fold of cheap paper. 'Even if she does have some connection to you, Cat, you must remember that she emerged from obscurity when there was a hint of money. That speaks volumes about her motives, I think. You must not delude yourself as to what lies at the end of this particular road.'

A mother only after my supposed riches: was that what he was warning me against? But could any of this be true? Could she still be alive? In my

* For details of this particular episode in my literary career, I refer my readers to *Den of Thieves*.

less fanciful imaginings, I'd decided that my mother must have died soon after she left me, of cold or disease. I'd created an image of a heroic unfortunate whose last act had been to ensure that her child survived. But what if my mother had just left me because she didn't want me? If she was still alive and only now making contact, that surely must be the conclusion to be drawn.

The paper shook in my fingers. I felt like I held a thunderbolt. If I opened the letter, it would probably scorch a painful track through all I knew about myself.

But I could not avoid it: I had to know the truth. I unfolded the letter.

29th July 1791

5 Long Row
New Lanark
Lanarkshire

Dear Sir,
I am writing to you to ask for news of the girl you called

Cat Royal but known to me as Maudie Stirling. I have just read a penny tale from London, which from the details it revealed, can only have been written by our Maudie. I pray to God that you will be able to put my mind at rest that she has not fallen into bad company as that scandalous rag suggested.

You may be wondering why it has taken me all these years to write to you. The truth is I did not know what had become of Maudie. It was only when I read about her origins in the pamphlet that I began to hope that she was one and the same with the child who disappeared in London so long ago.

If you are able to contact her, there are things she should know about her birth and the events leading to her being entrusted into your care which only I, her kin, can tell her. If you would be so kind as to give me her address and send me word of her circumstances, I would like to apply to her for sufficient money to cover my travel expenses to London. Once this arrives, I will gladly post down to fulfil my obligation to enlighten her. A sum of five pounds should be ample.

Yours faithfully,

Mary Stirling Moir

I let the letter drop to my lap, feeling strangely hollow-chested.

'Can you see why I was suspicious?' Mr Sheridan probed gently. 'It was all leading up to the request for money and I doubted that anything I sent would be spent on a journey to London.'

I nodded. The letter did not ask after my welfare, other than my reputation and fortune. No love, no affection. There wasn't even a hint of apology, only promise of a delayed explanation as to why I had been cast off in London. She almost made it sound as if it had been my fault – a child – that I had 'disappeared'. But yet that seemed in conflict with the statement that I had been 'entrusted' to Mr Sheridan. How could the act of leaving a child on a doorstep be called that? No one had bothered to look for me; no one had been interested – until now.

'Who do you think she is, this Mrs Moir?' I asked bleakly.

'I'm not sure, Cat. It could be a cruel hoax. If it hadn't been for the link to the Stirlings and Scotland, I would have dismissed it out of hand.

A relative *possibly*; your mother *maybe*.' He rubbed his throat uncomfortably.

I wasn't sure if I believed it to be genuine. I looked down again at the address. 'Where is New Lanark?'

'That in itself is very interesting: it's a cotton mill built to the latest specifications – run on water power, large workforce, benevolent owner. It's quite famous actually – people travel from all over the world to visit. It sounds as if Mrs Moir is employed there as she lives in one of the cottages. She's fallen on her feet if that is so.'

I re-read the letter and gave a stilted laugh. 'It's kind of her to write despite my scurrilous reputation.'

'Isn't it?' Mr Sheridan smiled cynically. 'Come, I didn't bring you to the Temple for no reason. There's someone I want you to meet.' He stood up and offered me his arm.

'Who, sir?'

'A friend of mine. When I received this, I could not let it rest so I asked him to look into it for me before I brought it to your attention. He has connections with that part of Scotland.'

Mr Sheridan led me over to the entrance to one of the staircases leading up to the barristers' chambers. At the bottom, names of the advocates were listed on the wall.

'Mr Beamish – that's the man,' Mr Sheridan said, tapping the nameplate. 'Top floor.'

Letting me go first, we climbed the stairs, passing the doors to four sets of rooms. The air smelled of dust and tobacco, a very masculine atmosphere. The law is serious, the reverent hush announced – not for the likes of you, Cat Royal.

Reaching the little landing at the top lit by an oriel window, Mr Sheridan knocked on an oak-panelled door. It was flung open by a scruffy-looking individual, a middle-aged man with the sharp look of a fellow Londoner. His clothes were slightly foppish, brown hair receding, a magpie alertness about his stance.

'Ah, Bob, is your master in?' asked Mr Sheridan.

Bob stood back and gestured for us to enter with a flourish of his arm. ''E is, sir.'

'Cat, meet Mr Beamish's clerk, his right-hand

man, Robert Marks. Bob, Miss Royal.'

I gave him a nod which he returned with a wink.

'I've 'eard about you, ain't I, from them stories?' Bob said affably, taking Mr Sheridan's hat and lobbing it on to the coatrack. Catching the topmost hook, it twirled there for a moment. 'A dasher, that's what you is.'

'Miss Royal was misrepresented, Bob, as I explained before,' Mr Sheridan said repressively.

'So you says, sir. So you says.'

Bob waved us on to the next room. An elderly man, head almost hidden behind a pile of books on the desk, looked up, pen clutched in one plump hand. With his curly white hair, pink cheeks, corpulent belly and innocent blinking stare, he reminded me of an aged cherub tumbled from his cloud. On the desk, a sombre grey wig perched on a stand. I couldn't imagine what the barrister would look like with it on – the two did not seem to fit together.

'Ah, Sherry, what a pleasant surprise!' exclaimed Mr Beamish, casting aside his pen with a splatter of ink over his document. Bob tutted and rushed to rescue it. 'And who is this lovely young lady?' He waggled his eyebrows at me.

'This is Miss Royal, Beamish.'

I curtseyed as Mr Beamish waddled out from behind his desk to kiss my hand.

'Sit down, sit down.' He waved us to chairs either side of his fireplace. 'Rustle up some tea for the lady, Bob; claret for Mr Sheridan.' He lowered himself into his armchair and linked his fingers across his expanse of cherry silk waistcoat. 'What can I do for you today?'

Mr Sheridan fluffed out the tails of his coat as he took a seat. 'It's about that matter in New Lanark I asked you to investigate last year.'

'Of course, of course.' Mr Beamish gave a vague look around his study until his eyes fell on a maroon document case teetering on top of a bookshelf. 'Bob!'

'He's fetching the tea,' Mr Sheridan reminded him.

'Oh yes. Mayhap the young lady wouldn't mind retrieving that red box for me. Not as young as I was, you know.'

I leaped up to get the documents he wanted, alarmed by the thought of this stout old gentleman climbing the rickety library ladder. I returned with the required case and placed it on the side table within easy reach.

'Thank you, m'dear.' With a creak of his chair, Mr Beamish rifled through the box until he pulled out the paper he sought. Feeling in his waistcoat he found his reading glasses and pinched them to his nose. 'Let me see, let me see. Mrs Moir . . . mule-spinner . . . two years service . . . good worker, though a bit of a shrew. That's your woman, isn't it?'

Mr Sheridan nodded. 'Any idea of her age?'

'Oh yes, the manufactory keeps excellent records. Thirty-five with four surviving children, three of whom are employed alongside her.'

'And Mr Moir?'

'A mixer – prepares the cotton fibres. Got lung problems though. Moved to carding. Been on and off work for a good long while now.'

'And your informant's impression of the family?'

'Solid working folk. Not well off, but neither

are they starving with five wages coming in. No known links to London and no idea why they should claim to be related to your young friend.' Mr Beamish smiled at me over the top of his glasses. I couldn't return the gesture. Was this my family I was hearing about or a group of strangers playing an unkind trick on me?

'Did they know you were investigating them, sir?' I asked quietly.

'No, m'dear, my man is the soul of discretion. I requested that our interest be kept a secret.'

'Is there a description of the woman?' asked Mr Sheridan.

'Indeed.' Mr Beamish leafed through the report. 'Medium height, thin face, a mass of freckles, red hair. Two of the children red-headed, though Mr Moir is said to be dark. Can't set much store by that though as half the workforce share Mrs Moir's colouring. That's the Celts for you.'

'But it doesn't rule her out either,' noted Mr Sheridan.

Rule her out as my mother, he meant. I shuddered.

The coward in me didn't want to hear any more.

Bob clattered in with the tea. As he handed me a cup, he murmured, "'Ere you go, dasher – drink up. You look like you've seen a ghost.'

I gave him a weak smile.

'And who was your informant, if you don't mind me asking?' enquired Mr Sheridan.

'Not a'tall, dear boy, not a'tall. It's my brother-in-law. He's gone in with Arkwright on several manufacturing speculations. It was no trouble for him to visit, he said. Came away very impressed by the enterprise.'

'You must convey our thanks to him when you next communicate.'

'Indeed I will. But the key question still remains: what is our young friend going to do about the letter writer? I hope, m'dear, you don't intend sending the woman any money?'

I delayed answering by sipping my tea. Glancing up at Bob, who was lounging on the back of his master's chair, I saw him shake his head and mouth 'no'. Sensing my interest was fixed above his head, Mr Beamish swung round.

'You want to say something, Bob?' he prompted.

'Well, sir, it's like this. Everyone knows these Scots are mean bu . . .' he changed word mid-stream, 'blighters. I reckon that this Mrs Mop –'

'Moir,' I corrected.

'That's 'er. She just wants money. That kind of family ain't worth finding. I should know, as my three brothers are all useless scroungers. If I could lose 'em, I would. Listen to me, miss: you keep away from 'em. Let sleepin' dogs lie.'

Mr Beamish turned back to me. 'Though I hesitate to award Bob any points for intelligence (that would not bode well for his hat size), it seems to me that his advice is sound.'

Bob gave a snort.

'But what if Mrs Moir really can tell me about my parents, about how I came to be left?'

'And 'ow will you know if she's tellin' you the truth?' replied Bob. 'Once she knows what you want to 'ear, she'll spin you a tale and expect you to pay for the privilege. It's like when Mr Beamish 'ere gets 'em in the dock: they'll sing any tune to get what they want.'

'But I can't just leave it. The uncertainty will torment me like a . . . a tooth that needs pulling.'

Mr Sheridan sighed. 'That is exactly why I was reluctant to tell you of the letter, Cat. How could anyone resist the urge to know the truth?'

'What do you suggest I do?' I looked up at the three men before me. My guardian looked concerned, Mr Beamish was frowning, Bob seemed lost in thought.

'I know what I'd do,' Bob ventured. 'I'd try and catch 'er out. Mr Beamish, 'e looks so soft the villains are all lulled into thinkin' 'e's easy – that's when 'e goes in for the kill.'

Mr Beamish gave me an apologetic smile. I would have to take Bob's word for it that the barrister had steel beneath the fluff.

'My clerk is right. A direct approach will not reveal the truth.'

I hugged my arms to my sides. After the happiness of my return, my soap-bubble mood had burst and I was now feeling empty and out of spirits.

'I'll have to think about it.'

Mr Sheridan rose, signalling the end of our visit. 'Indeed, I believe that is the best course of action. Any decision must be weighed very carefully.'

Mr Beamish patted my hand. 'And if I can be of service, don't hesitate to call on me.'

'Nor me,' chipped in Bob. 'Anythink for you, dasher.' With a chuckle, he showed us out.

On my return to the butcher's shop I avoided answering Syd's questions as to where Mr Sheridan had taken me, making some vague excuse about catching up on theatre news. Syd wasn't fooled but knew me well enough not to force the issue.

'I'll leave you to settle in then,' he said, setting my bag on the bed in the little box bedroom.

'Thanks, Syd.'

'I should warn you, Cat: news 'as spread that you're back. Don't think of makin' an early night of it: the boys'll be round later.'

I nodded. 'And I'd love to see them too.'

'All right then. I'll . . . er . . . I'll just go.'

He hovered uncertainly by the door, tugging at the cotton scarf knotted around his neck.

'Yes.'

He cleared his throat, his gaze loaded with unspoken feelings. 'I'm really pleased you're back, Cat.'

'I guessed.' I gave him a small, regretful smile, aware that my feelings for him did not match his for me.

With a nod to say that was settled then, he strode off down the stairs.

Alone at last, I busied myself unpacking my belongings. Guilt about my inability to feel more than sisterly love for Syd ate at me. Perhaps I should have gone to Grosvenor Square after all? That would have been fairer to Syd, and not got his hopes up.

I pushed open the little window, dislodging the sparrows perched on the ledge. They flew off with startled peeps over the rooftops opposite. Oh, why couldn't I resolve my place in the world by simply falling in love with Syd and settle down to a blameless, respectable life as a butcher's wife among the people I knew? Why did I have to make things so difficult for myself? I couldn't even shake off my foundling past but had now discovered it sticking to me like a burr carried home on the back of my skirts.

Angrily, I upended my bag and chucked my clothes around. I knew what I was looking for – the scrap of the tartan blanket. I'd been using it as a bookmark for years. I found it keeping my place in a copy of *Robinson Crusoe* borrowed from Lizzie, Frank's sister. The fabric lay limp in my palm as I mentally reconstructed the blanket it had once belonged to, the woman who had wrapped it round her child and finally the moment when she had walked away.

She had walked away.

And now, twelve years later, she – or some relative – was trying to step back into my life. That was if this wasn't all a Banbury tale made to fleece me of my supposed riches.

If only I knew.

I had to find out.

Crushing the cloth in my fist, anger surged

again, a powerful rush like the tide under the arches of London Bridge. I had been so happy to return to England and now this woman – this Mrs Moir – had spoiled it all. She had opened the Pandora's box of my past and I could not stuff it all back inside and pretend it hadn't happened. I was now desperate to know more about my mother: the elusive woman who'd rocked my cradle, fed me, clothed me – cuddled me, perhaps? I couldn't remember ever being held by a parent. A few hugs from friends and theatre folk over the years, but otherwise I had been starved of simple human warmth. An ache somewhere in the middle of my chest bloomed into a painlike hunger. I was going to find out why I had been dumped, what had been so wrong with me that my mother had decided I'd be better off taking my chances on my own on the London streets one cold night in January.

I was going to Scotland.

SCENE 2 – CELEBRATING IN STYLE

Mrs Fletcher's voice rang through the house, summoning us all to dinner. Having changed into a clean gown of blue-sprigged muslin, I jumped down the stairs, skirts kicking up with every bound, fired by my new resolve. The outline of my plan was already taking shape. All it would need was a little money and a lot of guts. Well, guts I had aplenty. That just left, Reader, my usual state of empty pockets. I was going to need a loan.

'There you are, Cat. Would you take the plates?' Mrs Fletcher gestured to the rack over the sink.

I balanced four plates on my arm, pretty white china ones from her best set.

'You'd better make that six!' she called as I set them on the kitchen table.

'Oh? Are we expecting guests?'

'They're 'ere already. Nick and Joe are joinin' us.' She stirred the pot and tasted it. 'Call 'em in for me, will you? They're out back 'avin' a bit of a wash.'

I ducked out into the yard to find Mr Fletcher, Syd and his two friends all bent over the pump, doing a fair amount of splashing at each other and not much cleaning as far as I could tell.

'Dinner's ready!'

Nick, Syd's dark-haired second-in-command in the Butcher's Boys, chucked the towel to Joe and strode over. Lifting me by the waist, he swung me round.

'Cat Royal! I was beginnin' to think we'd never see you again!' He set me down and looked me over. Long-limbed and slender, he loomed over me these days. 'I do believe . . . no, it can't be true . . .'

'What?' I looked down at myself, half expect - ing to see some fault in my clothing. 'What's wrong?'

Nick, eyes shining with mischief, beckoned Joe 'The Card' Murray. The street magician sloped over, his raggedly dandified jacket flapping open to display the ribbons he hawked. Nick nudged him, nodding to me.

'What you say, Joe?'

Joe scratched his chin. A little older than the rest of the gang, he had fine lines around his mouth and eyes; his long, brown hair fell about his face, giving him a gypsy-like appearance. I would've found him a little frightening if I hadn't known him nearly all my life.

'I can't believe it – but you're right, Nick. Stone me, but you're right!' Joe exclaimed.

Now I was getting worried. '*What?*'

'You've . . . you've grown, Cat,' Nick said with mock-solemnity, as if announcing my demise.

'At least, oh, I'd say . . . 'alf an inch?' agreed Joe.

I swatted Joe on the arm. 'I've grown much more than that, I'll have you know. I'm almost five foot.' I stood on tiptoe, hoping they wouldn't notice. My diminutive height was becoming a bit of a burden now that I was old enough to be almost my full size.

''Ave you been usin' one of Tailor Meakin's measurin' rods, Cat?' asked Nick. ''E always makes 'is stuff too short.'

'No, I haven't,' I huffed. 'I've grown – I have.'

'Course you 'ave, but you'll never see five foot and you know it,' teased Nick.

'She might – if I lend 'er me box to stand on,' said Joe.

I wondered bleakly for a moment if I had my long-lost mother to blame for all these quips about my half-pint status. I'd been quite proud of the inches I'd put on over the last year, but I'd forgotten that all my friends had been sprouting up too. It was a catch-up race I was never going to win.

Nick must've noticed my expression. 'Aw, Cat, don't take on so. You've growed up fine. No one could find a fault with you. We were just pullin' your leg.'

'Yeah, and if you let us do that, you might stretch a bit too,' mumbled Joe.

Nick thumped him in the ribs. 'Stop it.'

My lips curled into a reluctant smile at this familiar byplay among the gang. We all teased each other mercilessly; I shouldn't have let it get to me. I returned to the fray.

'So, Nick, how's the maid at Mr Gleeman's?

Fallen for your unusual sense of fashion yet?' Nick was well known for being the scruffiest lad in the market – quite an achievement.

A faint blush lit his cheek. ''Ow d'you know about Mary?'

'I know everything – don't you remember?' In fact Syd had confided this bit of gossip to me over tea. 'I'm sure she'll think you quite the original.' Giving him a wide grin, I turned to my next victim. 'And Joe, been bamboozled by any country bumpkins recently?'

'That was nothink! 'E wasn't what 'e seemed. The cards were marked. Put up to it by the boys, 'e was –'

'Yes, as a kind of birthday present to you, I understand.' I patted his arm consolingly. 'Don't worry, there's always knife-grinding if you're losing your touch.'

'Losin' my touch! Now see 'ere, Cat Royal, I'm at the top of my game, I am.'

'I'm sure you are.'

'Knife-grindin'! I ask you!'

'Someone has to do it.'

Joe began muttering about cheeky little redheads until he caught my amused expression.

'Still pleased to have me back?' I asked, leading the way into the kitchen.

'Too bleedin' right we are,' he said, rumpling my hair just to annoy me.

Nick and Joe were on their best behaviour in Mrs Fletcher's kitchen – they dared not be otherwise. Thanks to this, I learned much of the regular news about goings-on in the market. Aside from the usual gossip, I was distressed to hear that a number of the nippers had succumbed to smallpox last winter – a terrible loss.

Joe, whose skin was pockmarked from surviving the disease, changed the subject quickly.

'Seen the new theatre yet, Cat?'

'No.' I turned eagerly towards him. 'How is the work going?'

'Been a rare old scandal. Load of Irish comin' in to do the porterin' – bad feelin' all round. Caused a few fights. Your Mr Sheridan ain't the most popular man in these parts just now.'

Syd pushed his chair back from the table. 'Don't bend 'er ear about that, Joe. It's not 'er fault. So, 'ow you want to celebrate your return, Cat?'

I shrugged. What I really wanted to do was spend a night out with the gang but Syd would never let me.

''Ow about a night out with us lot?' he suggested. My jaw dropped. 'There's an apprentice ball at the Crown 'n' Anchor – a rum do, but might be fun.'

I jumped up. 'I'll get changed.'

'I'll take that as a "yes" then?'

But I was up the stairs and away.

My best gown, a green silk taffeta with gold trimming – another hand-me-down from Lizzie – was hopelessly creased from my travels but I didn't care. Pulling on a clean white petticoat and stockings, I shook it out and strained to do up the back (Lizzie, of course, had always had a maid to help her with this). It crossed my mind briefly that it might be too fine for the Crown and Anchor, but I pushed the thought aside as I put on my white slippers. Pausing in front of the mirror, I pondered whether or not to wear my cat necklace; a gift from Billy. I decided against it, not least because I didn't feel up to the debate with Syd as to where it had come from. Fresh ribbon threaded into my hair, white kid gloves on – and I was ready.

With Syd on one side and Nick on the other, Joe just behind, we made a merry party as we headed for the Strand. The Crown and Anchor had a famous ballroom, big enough to hold several thousand people. Though often hired out by the rich for fancy parties during the season, the owner allowed us common folk in when custom was sparse – like now. He knew he couldn't survive on just the few months when the blue bloods deigned to come to town – he needed us and we knew it. So it was with no feelings of inferiority that we paid at the door to dive into the festivities beyond.

A top-notch orchestra had been hired for the evening. I realized this because I could see my old friend from Drury Lane, Peter Dodsley, playing first violin. Lines of couples were already engaged in a vigorous country dance, thumping on the floorboards, making the whole building shake. Apprentices swung shopgirls around with enthusiasm provoking squeals and laughter, footmen bowed to curtseying upper-maids with all the dignity of their masters and mistresses, and a few drunks staggered through the throng, getting in everyone's way. Skirts twirling, voices shouting to be heard over the music, dust flying – this was my kind of party.

Waiters wove between those standing around the edges, serving ale and punch. One paused in front of us.

'Drink, Cat?' asked Syd.

'I'd rather dance.'

With a grin at Nick and Joe, he took my hand and we joined the end of a set. As we spun through the steps, I kept glimpsing old friends from the gang. Those I met in the course of the dance all had a kind word and welcome. After a day of upsets, it felt good to be home again.

The orchestra took a much-needed rest at the end of the second set and I made my way over to Peter. He was looking his usual, immaculate self –

a perky carnation adorning his lapel, floppy blond hair drooping artistically over one cheek. I admired his new signet ring – a gift from an admirer, he confessed – and we were soon talking nineteen to the dozen, catching up on all the gossip.

Nick appeared at my shoulder and gave Peter a wary nod. 'Cat, may I 'ave this dance?'

I glanced at Peter, only to see him picking up his bow again. 'No rest for the wicked,' he said with a smile.

But Nick had misunderstood my hesitation. 'It's all right – I checked with Syd. 'E said I could.'

I slipped off the orchestra podium. 'You did what?'

'Asked 'im if 'e minded.'

'Why would he mind?'

Nick just shrugged and led me out on to the dance floor. I didn't really need him to answer: I could guess. Without me saying or doing anything, the boys had all just assumed Syd and I were now courting. I couldn't blame Nick for erring on the side of caution – Syd had a punch that could land him in the next county – but still it was annoying to find myself wrapped up and labelled as Syd's girl. I noticed from then on that all my partners were carefully selected members of the Butcher's Boys. Syd was doing a grand job of managing my evening for me, except for my temper – *that* was simmering quite out of his control.

The dancing broke up for supper at eleven. Syd found me a table and got one of his boys to bring me a plate.

'Enjoyin' yourself?' he asked, digging into his cold meats with renewed appetite after all that dancing.

I thought it churlish to complain in front of his boys. We needed a private conversation to sort a few things out – not a public row. 'Yes. It is wonder - ful to see everyone again.'

'We can come again next week, if you like.' Syd turned away before I could answer to shake hands with an acquaintance who had stopped by our table to pay his respects. When he sat down again, I leant closer.

'I might not be here next week, Syd.'

Syd undid the top button of his waistcoat and

stretched out in his chair. 'Got another invitation so soon? Somethink to do with Mr Sheridan, I s'pose.'

'No . . . well, yes. In a way. I'm going to Scotland.'

Syd guffawed. 'That's a good 'un. Just arrived and now off to Scotland. Elopin' to Gretna Green?'

I rolled my eyes. 'Don't be daft. And I'm being serious. I'm going to Lanark.'

He snapped into his alert, fight-ready demeanour. 'You're not.'

I tilted my chin. 'I am.'

'I won't let you – not so soon after you got back.'

'You can't stop me – you've no right to stop me.'

''Aven't I?'

Oh, Lord, we *were* having the conversation despite my best intentions. Fortunately the others at our table were too busy watching a crowd of newcomers to pay much attention to us.

'You don't understand, Syd.'

'No I don't, Cat.' He reached out and took my hand. 'I thought you'd come 'ome to me.'

'I know you did. And I did, in a way – just not *that* way.'

His grip tightened. 'So what's takin' you to Scotland? Is there someone else?'

'Blimey, Syd, you've a suspicious mind!'

'Tell me.'

My hand was now protesting so I slipped it free.

'Look, Mr Sheridan got a letter.' I quickly sketched out the events of the day, sparing no detail about the dubious motives of my so-called relatives.

Syd moved his hand to cover mine again, but this time to comfort. 'Sorry, Kitten, I didn't realize. That must've been quite a shock.'

Trust Syd to understand how hurt I had been.

'Yes, it wasn't very pleasant. I'd had all these dreams, you see: perfect mothers and wonderful fathers, but the reality looks rather . . . rather sordid. Odds are they're just after money. The joke is, they think I've got some.'

'Better if they'd left you alone.'

'Perhaps.'

He gave my hand a businesslike tap. 'Then

leave it. She ain't 'ad a reply for a year. She'll 'ave forgotten all about it and you should too. You've family 'ere now.'

I looked down at his calloused knuckles. 'I know.'

He tipped my chin up with his free hand, forcing me to meet his eyes. 'I understand, you know. About you and me, I mean. You needn't worry I'm goin' to go all queer on you.'

I closed my eyes briefly then attempted a smile. 'Thank you.'

'Do you think you'll change your mind?'

With a tiny gesture that committed me for the rest of my life, I shook my head.

'Too much of a brother to you, eh?'

I nodded. 'Something like that.'

'That's not what a boy wants to 'ear. Fatal words. Can't even complain because it means you still care for me, don't it?'

'So much that it hurts like the blazes knowing I'm disappointing you. If I could make myself different, I would –'

He stopped me with a finger on my lips. 'No.

No tryin' to change into somethink you're not. I think I always knew it was a long shot. I'll just 'ave to learn to live with it.' He swallowed. 'Move on. It's just that I've always thought that you and me . . .' He stopped because he saw that he was making me cry. ''Ave a drink, Cat. Then we'll do some more dancin', all right?'

'All right.'

Nick turned round and nudged Syd in the ribs. 'Bleedin' cheek if you ask me . . .' He tailed off when he noticed my expression. 'What's wrong with Cat?'

'Nothink,' said Syd gruffly, covering for me. He was the master at coming back from a knockout blow. 'Who's got cheek?'

'Them Irish geezers, comin' into our ball as if they own the place.'

I looked over to the far corner of the supper room and saw a group of strangers clustered around the punchbowl. There were seven men and one tall female a few years older than me. I guessed that they were related because they all had the same black hair and strong features, even the girl.

Dressed in ragged finery, they were obviously not from one of the better areas in the neighbourhood.

'Who are they?' I asked Nick.

'The Paddies. Irish porters from the theatre building site. Done nothink but make trouble since they arrived. Syd, we've got to do somethink about 'em.'

Syd scratched his chin. 'Not till they step out of line.'

'But they're well out of it now – comin' where they're not welcome.'

'So where are they supposed to go?' I asked, annoyed by Nick's prejudice against them for no good reason that I could see.

'Somewhere else – with their own kind.'

One of the men moved over to a nearby table and sat down next to a girl, engaging her in conversation. It was as if he'd issued a challenge to the entire male population of the room – and from his gloating smile I could tell he knew it.

Syd stood up and took my arm. 'I think we'd better leave.'

He'd moved too late. The footman who had escorted the girl to the ball returned from the servery and found his companion being treated to some Irish charm. He grabbed the interloper by the scruff of the neck and hauled him up – not a wise move, as his muscles could not compete with that of a man who spent his day heaving stones.

Syd groaned. 'I'd better see if I can calm things down. Keep out of the way.'

I nodded and backed over to the wall.

'Now then, lads,' called Syd as he strode to the confrontation. 'Let's take this outside – there are ladies present.'

Ladies or not, the first punch fell before he reached them. The Irishman staggered back and the girl screamed. The room erupted. The Irish lads piled towards the aggressor only to find their way blocked by London apprentice boys. Mistaking Syd's intentions, one Irishman went for him. I could see Syd give a resigned shrug as he deflected him easily. That brought another brother on top of him – and another. He was going to have to fight.

What a welcome home!

As the plates flew and tables crashed over, I decided a retreat was called for. Edging along the wall, I bumped into the Irish lass: hands over her head, cowering behind the punchbowl. She was soaked in the stuff and looked plain terrified. I reached out and touched her arm. She flinched. A footman bashed into the wall beside us and slid down unconscious. I hunkered down beside her.

'Hello.'

She looked up. I found myself confronted by the most amazing violet eyes rimmed with black lashes. Briefly tempted to hate her for her beauty, I mastered myself.

'I'm Cat. Shall we escape this madhouse?'

She nodded slowly, as if not convinced that I wasn't an inmate of Bedlam myself.

'Come with me.'

I led her as we made our way on hands and knees under the tables to the door. Once clear of the ruckus I scrambled to my feet, tripping on my hem with a mild curse. 'We're making for the orchestra.'

She nodded then followed me in a quick sprint across the dance floor. The fight had spilled out here, and I could hear girls shrieking as the pandemonium spread. The manager was trying to restore order, but his attempts were futile. The cause of the altercation had been forgotten – now it was just about who shoved whom.

As expected, I found the members of the orchestra battened down behind the podium, protecting their instruments. They were in high spirits, like an army under bombardment, passing around a flask of brandy while the missiles flew.

Peter patted the floor beside him. 'What's all that about?' He jerked his head to the fight.

'It's my brothers,' whispered the girl miserably. Her husky voice had a sweet Irish lilt. 'Their idea of a good night out.' She gave an involuntary gulp of a giggle, eyes brimming with humiliated tears.

Crash! One of the mirrors in the ballroom shattered and tinkled to the floor in a musical shower.

Peter gave her a little bow. 'But no one can blame you, my dear. Take a pew.'

She sat down nervously, wiping her eyes.

'Are you all right?' I asked.

She nodded, but I wasn't convinced.

'What's your name?'

'Bridgit O'Riley.' She straightened, her pride returning.

'Pleased to meet you, Bridgit. Are those all your brothers?'

'Every last one of them.' She sighed.

'Why did they bring you if they planned to start a fight?'

She shrugged hopelessly. 'It's never stopped them in the past.'

Deciding that this was probably not a pleasant subject to pursue, I turned to Peter. 'Is there a back way out of here?'

'Of course. May I escort you two ladies home?'

Bridgit looked torn. She glanced towards where the battle was thickest; a dark head appeared from time to time only to dive right back in again.

'Where do you live?' I asked.

'The sheds on the building site,' she admitted

after a slight pause.

Peter gave her a sympathetic look.

I was not about to take her back there without her brothers to protect her. 'I think we can do better than that for tonight. I'm sure Mrs Fletcher won't mind you sharing my room when she understands the situation.'

'No, no, I can't.'

'Will your brothers worry?'

She shook her head. 'I doubt they'll be aware of anything till tomorrow.'

'Then you can come with me now. Peter, would you mind?'

'You don't understand. No one likes us –' Bridgit began.

I cut short her protests. 'I like you. And Mrs Fletcher will like the excuse to mother another girl. Peter?'

Entrusting his violin into the care of a friend, Peter gallantly offered us each an arm. 'Ladies, if you would come with me.'

Leaving the noise of the battle behind us, we slipped out the back door and headed towards

Bow Street. A party of the watch passed us at a run, heading for the ballroom. It looked like the manager had called in reinforcements.

'Mrs Fletcher!' I tapped on the back door, hoping she hadn't gone to bed yet. Mr and Mrs Fletcher appeared in the kitchen: she dressed in her nightrobe and he in his breeches, carrying a candle.

'Good gracious, Cat!' Mrs Fletcher exclaimed, opening the door to us. 'What 'ave you done with Syd?'

'There was some trouble at the ball, ma'am,' said Peter smoothly. 'Your son was unavoidably detained so I had the pleasure of bringing the ladies home.'

'It was those Irish devils again, I wager.' Mrs Fletcher beckoned us in, her eyes going to my other companion.

'Indeed so, ma'am. I won't linger. I have a violin to rescue from distress.' With an elegant bow, Peter retreated. 'I'll tell the watchman on the site where you are, Miss,' he called over his shoulder to Bridgit.

'Mrs Fletcher . . . er, Joanna, can my friend stay?' I asked hesitantly. My first day in her home and I was already bringing in waifs and strays. And I'd just turned down her son.

Mrs Fletcher took in the girl's ragged condition and pursed her lips.

'And she is?'

'Bridgit O'Riley.'

Mr Fletcher grunted. I guessed that meant he disapproved.

Bridgit hovered on the doorstep. 'No matter. I'll be leaving then.'

That seemed to decide Mrs Fletcher. 'Oh, don't be so foolish, girl. You're welcome 'ere. I won't say the same for all Irish, but you'll do for tonight.'

I gave Mrs Fletcher an impulsive hug. 'Thank you. Are you going to wait up for Syd?'

She shook her head. 'No. I've long since learned that 'e can look after 'imself. Both of you, go on up. Some of us 'ave to work in the morning.' She shooed us up the stairs.

Placing my candle on the bedside table in the box room, I gestured Bridgit to the washstand.

'You might like to get some of that punch off before you sleep.'

She nodded, still looking dazed by her good fortune to be in a proper bedroom for the night. She stroked the counterpane reverently.

'I'm afraid none of my things will fit you. I'll just run and borrow a robe from Joanna.'

When I got back, I found Bridgit had cleaned the sticky residue off her skin and brushed the worst of it out of her long black hair.

'I must smell like a drunkard,' she muttered.

'You smell like the contents of an orange-seller's basket. Not so bad.' I handed her the old nightgown and set about changing for bed.

'You're very kind.' Bridgit tugged the robe over her head, her resemblance to a dark-haired angel all the stronger now thanks to her garb and the hair tumbling around her shoulders.

'I just know what it feels like to be an outsider.'

'I doubt that,' she murmured, folding back the sheets and running the warming pan over them for us both.

I took the pan from her and set it on the hearth

to cool down safely. 'You can't get much further outside than a foundling.' I was reminded once again of my strange day. 'You're lucky: you've got brothers.'

'Lucky, am I?'

'Oh, yes. You have the luck of the Irish. Better seven problem brothers than not a soul on your side.'

She yawned and snuggled down under the blankets. 'Maybe. But you haven't met them yet.'

SCENE 3 – IRISH ASSURANCE

My chance to make my acquaintance with Bridgit's brothers came sooner than expected. It started with a thundering on the doors at three in the morning.

'Bridgit, get down here now!'

I jumped out of bed and ran to the window. In the street stood seven men, none of whom appeared to be in a good humour. It was still too dark to see them well, but my imagination supplied the blackened eyes and bruised ribs. Behind me, Bridgit had tumbled out of the blankets and was rapidly dressing. There was a whistle further up the street and Syd and the boys appeared at the corner.

'Oh, no!' I groaned.

Mr Fletcher opened the window next to us and shouted, 'Get away from 'ere, you Irish devils. She'll come 'ome in the mornin' like decent folk do.'

'What have you done with my sister?' roared the biggest of the bunch.

Mrs Fletcher decided to add her tuppenny worth. 'She's sleepin', so scat!' There was a splash as she upended the contents of a basin of water over them – at least I hope it was water.

Bridgit's brothers did not appreciate being dismissed like a pack of stray dogs. Enraged by their dousing, the thumping on the door became more violent. Syd and his gang were running now, rushing to the defence of their territory.

And it had seemed such a good idea to offer Bridgit shelter.

My new friend was having similar misgivings. 'I'd better go. Thank you for everything, Cat.' She started out of the door but I caught the back of her skirt.

'Wait a moment. Oh, this is all my fault! Look, I'll explain to your brothers and Syd that I invited you in.' I tugged an old round over my nightdress.

As we rushed to the shop door, we could see silhouettes of people grappling with each other outside and hear the grunts of yet another fight. You would have thought they'd had their fill of that tonight. I threw the door open and Bridgit dashed into the fray.

'Stop! Corny, Ody, Christy, you stop it this minute, you hear me!'

The O'Rileys were outnumbered, backed up against the wall by the Butcher's Boys. Syd had the big one caught in a headlock.

'Syd, let him go now,' I called out. 'They're not attacking the shop – they just came for their sister.'

Syd released his captive and pushed him towards his brothers. His blood was up: his normally friendly face looked positively menacing as he wiped away the sweat of battle. 'What's she doin' 'ere?'

Poor Bridgit stood wringing her hands, separated from her brothers by the ranks of the Butcher's Boys. She was staring at Syd, clearly terrified of him. I suppose he did look a mite formidable in his fighting mood; I tend to forget how he would appear to a stranger.

I moved between them. 'She's taking refuge

with me after a bunch of buffle-headed trouble-makers ruined her evening,' I replied tartly. 'Stop scaring the girl, Syd.'

Syd took a step back and relaxed his fists, taking a deep breath to regain control over his racing pulse. He then smiled at Bridgit with just a touch too much teeth to be completely reassuring. 'Don't worry, darlin', I wouldn't dare be buffle-'eaded round Cat. I'm terrified of 'er, I am.'

Bridgit gave him a wondering look, perplexed as to how the towering giant could claim to be afraid of a red-haired girl of so few inches.

'But she seems so sweet to me,' she said wonderingly, not quite sure if he was joking, but concluding he probably was.

'No, no, you've got 'er all wrong,' Syd continued, enjoying his make-believe. He put his fists on his hips, rocking on the balls of his feet, still ready to fight if called on. 'Cat's a real tiger – keeps us boys in line, she does.'

The Butcher's Boys echoed this sentiment with a chorus of agreement mixed with laughter. I realized that Syd was trying to turn this dangerous confrontation into a bit of harmless pantomime. I knew my role.

'That's right, they quiver in their boots when they see me coming,' I said brusquely, taking Bridgit's arm, 'so you've no need to worry about them. Let's call it a night, boys, and all go get some sleep.'

But the O'Riley brothers were having none of it.

'Bridgit, you come here now or feel the back of my hand!' threatened the big one.

Mr Fletcher appeared on the doorstep, a cleaver in his fist. 'Miss O'Riley is a guest in my 'ouse,' he growled. 'She only leaves if she wants to.'

But Bridgit twirled round, pulling her arm free with evident regret. 'If it please you, sir, I'll be going now. Thanks for letting me rest awhile. I'm most obliged to you. I'm coming, Corny.'

'You don't need to go, darlin' – not if you don't want to,' added Syd. 'We can 'andle those brothers of yours.'

Bridgit shook her head regretfully. 'That's very kind of you to offer, but no.' Touching me briefly on my arm, she stepped forward. Syd fell back to let her pass, sparing a bemused but appreciative look for the first non-punching O'Riley he'd met. The big brother, Corny, hooked her roughly by the elbow and dragged her off in the middle of a press of brothers. I almost called her back; I didn't trust the O'Rileys to be kind to their little sister. They seemed to regard her staying under a Londoner's roof as a kind of betrayal.

''Ow did she invite 'erself in?' asked Syd, yawning as the events of the night took their toll.

'*I* invited her, Syd, after finding her alone in the middle of a punch-up!'

'Easy now, Kitten – retract those claws. I wasn't criticizing you or 'er. I think you've done 'er no favours, though. The O'Rileys 'ave set themselves against everyone in the market. They won't let 'er 'ave no friends 'ere.'

It was as I feared. I'd dropped her into a quag - mire so I'd just have to make sure she got out.

The next day, Syd and his dad were busy out back with a fresh delivery of livestock. Making my excuses to Mrs Fletcher, I set off to check on the fate of my new friend. I didn't tell the Fletchers exactly where I was going – too much information would not be good for Syd's peace of mind – but it was not unnatural of me to wish to see my old home, was it? I mean, Reader, what was more likely than for Cat Royal to stroll around the corner and inspect progress on the new Drury Lane? It was not as if I went looking for trouble. Honest.

My pace faltered as I turned into Russell Street. The theatre had gone. The soaring walls, columns and arched windows all flattened into a featureless quarry. Men scurried over the site with barrows of rubble. New foundations were being dug, enveloping the outline of the old building like a whale swallowing a fish whole. I couldn't feel excited about the signs that the theatre was indeed rising from the dust once again; all I could feel was devastation.

I knew it would be bad – just not this bad.

The sight of a dark-haired labourer carrying a hod of bricks jolted me from my melancholy thoughts. I hadn't come here to wallow in my sense of loss. I scanned the site: here and there among the other Irishmen I spotted the O'Rileys. No sign of Bridgit. But then there wouldn't be – not among the men. I wondered if the builders employed any females. From a quick look round, it seemed not. It was then I remembered that she said they lived in one of the temporary huts built to accommodate the workers. They were in plain sight, over where the carpentry store used to be. Better quality than I expected, they made decent enough homes – many steps above the doorways where I had once slept.

Trying not to attract the attention of any of the O'Riley brothers, I skirted the site and dodged into the alley between the huts. I could see a few other women going about their chores and some grubby infants playing with rough-cut blocks – one toy there was no shortage of on a building site – but no Bridgit.

'What you be doing here, miss?' a hard-eyed woman challenged me – she had her arms up to the elbows in a tub of soapy water.

'Good morning, ma'am.' The woman seemed taken aback by my polite greeting. 'I'm looking for Bridgit O'Riley. Where does she live?'

'What you want with her?'

I smiled. 'Just wanted to call on her. We met last night.'

The woman wiped her brow, leaving a trail of suds. 'Not seen her yet this morning. Two doors down on my side.' With a curt nod, she returned to scrubbing her man's shirts.

A little further on, I arrived outside a raw plank door with a piece of string for a latch. I knocked.

'Bridgit?'

I could hear scurrying around inside as if someone was trying frantically to hide something – or themselves.

'It's me. Cat. I've come to see if you're all right.'

The door opened a crack and her amazing violet eyes peeked out at me.

'I'm fine,' she whispered. Her gaze darted uneasily down the alley. 'You'd better come in.'

She pulled the ill-fitting door open and

ushered me inside. The odour in the room was a little ripe to say the least, smelling of spirits and too many bodies packed together. I'd heard doctors claim that diseases travelled in bad air – that would make this hut a positive breeding ground for all manner of fevers. For Bridgit's sake, I tried not to show my distaste.

'Can I get you some refreshment?' she asked politely. Her manners were far better than one would expect from her surroundings. At a glance, it was clear that she kept the hut neat despite the obstacle of all those brothers. A piece with her manners, I read this as a gesture of defiance against her wretched lot.

'Can I invite you out with me?' I countered. 'I know a very good cook shop where we can grab a second breakfast.' I noted the few contents of the room. 'Or a first. My treat.'

In the gloom, she shook her head. 'I'm not supposed to go out. My brothers won't like it.'

'Why? What do they think will happen?'

She twisted her hands in the threadbare fabric of her day-dress. 'Some of the women have had trouble. It's not a very pleasant area, you know, for us Irish.'

'Believe me, I know. But with me, you'll be fine. And besides, it's only nine in the morning. The local boys won't be out looking for trouble – they'll be working.'

'I . . . I'm not sure, Cat . . .' Her voice died as she heard footsteps pounding down the alley. 'Oh Jesus and Mary, it's them!'

I didn't need to ask who she meant. The door crashed open and Corny O'Riley shouldered his way into the room, followed by two of his brothers.

'Get out!' he shouted, waving his arm at me.

Bravely, Bridgit threw herself between us. 'Don't you go shouting at my friend, Corny! She meant no harm being here.'

Ire redirected to his sister, Corny grabbed her wrist and pulled her away from me. 'You don't have no friends here, remember! They're all against us – trying to stop a man doing an honest day's work. They'd let us starve if they could.' He shook her roughly.

'Now just a minute!' I exclaimed, outraged by

his rough treatment. 'You take your hands off her!'

He gave me a scornful look. 'Oh yes? And you'll make me, I suppose, pipsqueak?'

One of the other brothers moved out of the doorway, letting light fall into the room and on to Bridgit's face. She had a bruised cheek that hadn't been there the night before. That was it.

'Oh yes, I'll make you, you big bully.' I grabbed a broom from the corner. He sneered, expecting me to take a swipe at him with the brush, but I knew better than that. I jabbed him in the stomach with the pole, producing a satisfying 'oof'. He bent double to clutch himself, freeing Bridgit. His two brothers were too busy laughing to think of retaliating.

Breathing heavily, I stood with the broom held out in front of me. 'I came here this morning to invite your sister out. She will be in no danger in my company and I certainly have no intention of seeing her starve, so you'll just get out of my way or I'll call the foreman. Get your shawl, Bridgit.'

Corny was staring at me as if he'd never seen a girl stand up to him before. Perhaps he hadn't.

But neither had he met a girl who'd sailed on a naval ship, escaped a slave master and survived an ambush in the middle of a war. His fists curled.

'Don't even think about it,' I growled.

'Let Bridgit go, Corny,' intervened one of the boys behind me. 'That's Syd Fletcher's girl you're talking to. He'd run us out of here as fast as a horse on Derby day if we touch her.'

Taking that as permission, Bridgit grabbed her shawl and tugged me away with her. Rather surprised I had got off unscathed after my explosion of temper, I stumbled after her.

'Widow King's – that's the place,' I panted, feeling rather elated by my triumph.

'What?' Bridgit was still taking worried looks over her shoulder.

'Breakfast. Best pastries in London.'

My old friend Caleb Braithwaite, formerly Drury Lane doorman, now assistant to Mrs King, found us a prime spot near the fireplace in the little dining room attached to the kitchen. He refused any charge for the mound of mouth-watering buns.

'I'll tell her they were spoiled,' he said. 'Didn't you see me drop 'em when I took 'em off the stove? She won't mind a bit – not for you.'

'Thanks, Caleb. You're a star.'

'The only payment I expect is a nice long natter when you've a moment.' He returned to his post in the kitchen watching the next batch in the oven.

Bridgit looked a trifle bemused by this kindness. She must have had a poor time of it in London so far if she'd not seen us do each other favours.

'So, Bridgit, tell me about yourself,' I said, pushing the plate of buns towards her. 'Are you liking it here?'

'Hate it.' She took a bun but didn't bite. 'My brothers get angrier each day, the place reeks to high heaven, not a green field in sight, and I've no one to talk to.'

'Other than that, you're having a swell time. Where've you come from?'

'Near Dublin.' She picked out a raisin and ate it thoughtfully. 'We were rack rented off our farm

– lost the tached cabin, the cow, the bit of land, all to keep the absentee landlord from London in fine style. Mam and Dad been dead these three year so the boys had to look for work.'

'And you had to come with them.'

She nodded. 'There was nothing else for me to do. I wanted to get a position here in London but Corny won't hear of it. Says he'd prefer me to work for the devil than a Londoner.'

'Plenty of devils here. But there are good people too.'

She shrugged. 'Good to you, but not to us Irish.' She brushed some crumbs off the table as if dismissing an unpleasant subject. 'So now, tell me about yourself, Cat.'

I chatted away, sketching out the details of my recent travels while she ate her share of the buns. I did wonder if she believed me as even to my own ears it sounded an extraordinary adventure for a girl from Covent Garden. Feeling the need to explain my background, I even told her about my plans to travel to Scotland in search of my family. Her eyes glinted with interest.

'I'd give anything to have Mam back, so I know why you feel you must find out,' she said at last. 'It's not been the same without her keeping the boys in hand. They've gone wild.'

'Thank you for saying that. Everyone else has been warning me off. I know I'm probably in for a disappointment, but I can't not know.'

'To be sure, you can't. I'd be up to Scotland in two shakes of a lamb's tail if it were me.'

Her gentle understanding was so welcome, convincing me that my decision to go was the right one. My mind turned to the practicalities. I drummed my fingers on the table – an annoying habit I knew I had to conquer now there was no Billy to provoke. 'I just don't know how to get there, Bridgit. I've not much money and I can hardly go on my own. It's impossible – the fare for the stagecoach is more than I can earn in months.' The shop bell rang as a new customer came in. I noted vaguely that there seemed to be quite a commotion out the front. 'None of my friends here have money to throw away on such a hopeless venture.'

'Er, Cat –' Bridgit tried to get my attention but I was far away pondering my predicament.

'I'll never get there – not unless I rob the stage myself.'

She nudged me, nodding vigorously over my head. 'Cat –'

Finally, I turned round. Standing in the doorway, looking every inch the noble, was the Earl of Arden.

I shot up from my chair like a rocket at a Vauxhall fireworks show. 'Frank!'

Outside in the narrow lane I could see his carriage blocking the street, his horses held by a groom in smart livery.

He hugged me with a great gust of laughter. 'Turning highwayman now, Cat? Just as well I got back in time.'

I swatted him. 'Aren't you supposed to be studying?'

'Aren't you supposed to be touring the West Indies?'

'There was a slight change of plan.'

'So I see. And who could read Pliny when

Cat Royal comes to town?'

'You make me sound like the circus.'

He grinned. 'When I heard you were home, I decided to break the record for the fastest Cambridge-to-London journey. Wagered my next term's allowance on the outcome.'

I frowned, easing back to look at him. 'And did you win?'

'Royally, I'd say.'

'Hmm. I'm tempted to tell your mother.'

'You wouldn't stoop so low.'

Bridgit, who had been looking most uncomfortable since Widow King's had been invaded by such a glittering representative of the ruling classes, made to slide out the door. I cursed myself for my lack of thought.

'Frank, may I introduce Miss Bridgit O'Riley?' Frank gave her a beautiful bow. 'Miss O'Riley, Frank, sometimes known as the Earl of Arden.'

She bobbed a curtsey, keeping her head down. 'I'll be going now, Cat; your lordship.'

'If you're sure,' I said, understanding how strange this might all appear to her.

She nodded.

'I'll see you soon, I hope?'

'If it please you.'

'Yes, it would.'

With a brief flicker of a smile, she darted out of the shop.

Frank followed her with speculative eyes. 'New friend?'

'I hope so. A stunner, isn't she? Want a bun?'

Frank grabbed the spare roll, tossed Caleb a sovereign, and escorted me to the door.

'Would Miss Royal care to take a spin in my new curricle?' he asked with mischievous formality.

'What? That two-wheeled death trap?' His matched pair of Cleveland Bays stamped their hooves, looking remarkably fresh after their dash from Cambridge. 'Are you sure you know how to drive it?'

'I passed our head coachman's test with flying colours, I'll have you know. I can turn on a sixpence and control the cattle in an emergency – Father wouldn't let me out in it until I'd proved I could drive it to his satisfaction.'

I grinned. 'In that case, I'd love to.' As he handed me up to the front seat, I assumed a puzzled air. 'And why did your father want to test you on cows in any case?'

'Cattle – Cat – are horses,' Frank replied with an air of superiority as he inducted me into the mysteries of carriage-driving.

'Is your groom coming with us?'

'My tiger,' he corrected, giving the man a nod to release the horses' heads.

'What! You've brought one of those too? Won't it eat the horses – sorry, cattle.'

'Tiger is the term for my groom.'

'Surely groom is the term for groom?' I'd known that, of course, but it was fun to needle him.

He gave an impatient flick of the whip and the horses pulled away, making slow progress down the congested street. As a cart surged out in our path, we narrowly missed a lamp post.

'This is novel,' I gulped, no longer so convinced by his skill. 'How many points for taking down a post? Three perhaps? What about running over a little old lady?'

'Little old ladies are safe from me,' he huffed.

'I think one of the boys nicked your fancy brass lamp while you were inside.' I tapped the empty bracket beside me.

Frank's face clouded. 'Damn! I promised on my Great-Aunt Veronica's honour that I'd return the curricle to Father without a scratch.'

Catching sight of a familiar long-legged man in an oversized coat threading his way through the crowds, I gave a shrill whistle.

'Oi, Light-Fingers – give it back!'

The man froze, debating whether or not to scarper.

'You know better than to pick on the Chimney Sweep Lord,* don't you? Syd'll have your gizzard made into sausages and fed to the Bow Street Runners for breakfast.'

Light-Fingers sloped over to my side of the carriage and groped in his pocket.

* For those of you who have not read my earlier adventures yet, this is Frank's honorary title in Covent Garden due to him once having disguised himself as a sweep. He fooled no one but we humoured him.

'It fell off,' he grunted, handing me the brass lamp. 'So pleased to oblige 'is 'igh-and-mightiness by returnin' it.'

Frank, fists full of reins, nodded to his tiger. 'Give the man a shilling, Jacobs.'

The shilling spun in the air for a second before being snatched by Light-Fingers. The thief was gone before Frank could repent of his generosity.

The Earl of Arden cocked an eyebrow. 'And what exactly is a gizzard?'

I laughed. 'Not sure, but it sounded suitably grisly, didn't it?'

The tale of my recent adventures in Jamaica and San Domingo, even when told in brief, took the rest of the drive to Hyde Park and then some. We were bowling down the carriage drive parallel to Rotten Row before I'd finished. Frank was so absorbed in my news that he merely raised his whip in automatic reply to his acquaintances; I doubt he really saw anyone at that moment. I drew a carriage blanket over my knees, aware that my plain dress did not compare well to the beautiful gowns of the other ladies. He'd brought me to one of the parading places of the Ton; rich folk came here to see and be seen. Every detail of my appearance would doubtless be chewed over by the mamas and their debutante daughters. Jealous of any girl sitting near one of England's most eligible young peers, they were more merciless than critics at a first night – and I certainly gave them plenty to complain about.

'You haven't yet explained why you were considering highway robbery, Cat,' said Frank as we eased round the turning circle and headed back the way we had come.

I was beginning to relax now I realized that he could actually drive this vehicle without risking life and limb. My knuckles were no longer white on the rail. 'Ah, that was yesterday's surprise.'

The news that I might not be quite as alone in the world as we had thought caused Frank to pull his horses over to the verge so he could give me his full attention.

'Are you serious about travelling to Scotland, Cat?'

'I am. I even have a plan – a good plan.'

'On your own?'

'Frank, I've been to America and back mostly on my own. I hardly think Scotland much of a challenge.'

He harrumphed – a rather impressive noise that would stand him in good stead when he eventually became a duke.

'I don't know, Cat –'

'You drive rather well, you know, for a beginner.'

I knew a remark like that would make him relinquish the subject of Scotland.

'Beginner! I'm better than that, I hope. And I don't *drive*. I *tool* the carriage.'

'I know, I know.' I waved a hand airily. 'You *tool* your *cattle* accompanied by your *tiger*. The brethren of the whip would be proud of you; you certainly have the language down pat.'

He bowed at my compliment.

'But as you are an expert, can you explain why your *cattle* are currently eating the flowers from that old lady's bonnet?'

Frank turned in horror to see one of his bays grazing happily on the brim of a hat as the unfortunate woman leaned out of her open-topped carriage to wave to an acquaintance. He jerked on the reins but the horse merely looked up, dragging the bonnet in its mouth and thus alerting the woman to the ravaging of her favourite chapeau. Her eyes fastened on Frank.

'Your g . . . grace,' stuttered Frank. 'Please accept my heartfelt apologies.'

The wrinkled countenance of the lady turned a pale puce colour. She raised her lorgnette to her eyes.

'Avon's boy, isn't it?' Her voice was so sharp it could have sawn a plank in half.

'Yes, your grace.' Shoving the reins in my hands, Frank leapt from the seat and wrestled the bonnet from his horse. He handed the mangled item back to its owner with as much aplomb as he could muster in the circumstances. I was amused to note that we were gathering quite a little audience as ladies and gentlemen paused to see what was happening.

'Your father will hear of this, you impudent pup!' She threw the bonnet on to the floor of the carriage and nodded to the coachman to continue.

'I'm sure he will.' Frank bowed as the carriage disappeared.

Trying to hide his humiliation, Frank clambered up beside me. Silently, I handed him the reins and he flicked the horses into motion, fleeing the embarrassing scene as fast as he could.

I leaned against him and gave him a nudge. 'Six points.'

'What?' he snapped, still annoyed with himself.

'Dowager Duchess's bonnet: worth at least six points.'

Torn between mortification and humour, Frank gave into the absurdity of the situation and began to laugh. Our curricle tooled once more around the park, the two occupants of the front seat near helpless with giggles.

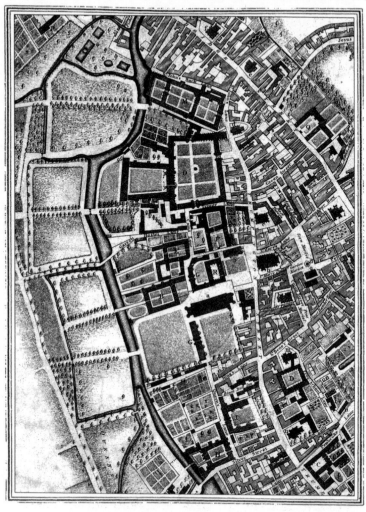

*Act II - In which seven to one proves
to be bad odds . . .*

ACT II

SCENE 1 – WAR IN THE MARKET

'I take it you are serious about going to Scotland?' asked Frank.

We had stopped for refreshments in the Crown and Anchor – Frank's treat. Signs of last night's riot had been swept away, though I thought I detected a slightly frantic air from the manager. I was currently enjoying my third breakfast in the smart dining room, served by the most obsequious waiters on God's earth.

'Would the young lady like some butter with her muffin, my lord?' drawled the attendant, prac-tically falling over Frank's shoulder in his eagerness to serve the needs of the earl.

'Yes, the young lady would like butter,' I replied brightly, determined that he should acknowledge my right to exist.

'Very good.' The waiter still had not raised his eyes to me, bowing to Frank as he departed.

My friend chuckled.

'How can you bear it?' I sighed. 'All that fawning over you as if you were some kind of demigod.'

'Only a demigod?' Frank took a bite of his bacon and chewed with relish.

'Zeus himself then. Lord knows what would happen if your exalted father graced the place with his presence.'

'I imagine the waiter would expire with excitement.'

'Still, doesn't it get on your nerves?'

'Absolutely. Why do you think I'm friends with you? A sobering dose of your insults and teasing, and my head deflates to normal size. So, Cat – Scotland. What's the big plan?'

I crumbled up my muffin, then instantly regretted wasting it and tried to stick it back together again.

Frank clicked his fingers. A waiter sprang to his side. 'Another muffin for the lady, please.'

'At once, my lord.'

A basket of warm muffins covered by a linen

napkin appeared in front of me and a fresh plate replaced my old crumb-covered one.

'I suppose rank does have compensations,' I muttered as I took a bite.

Frank met my eye and held it.

I capitulated. 'All right – Scotland. I don't think marching up and knocking on Mrs Moir's door would get me any further – she can tell me any tale that she wants. I need to slip past her defences and hear the truth without her knowing what she's revealing.'

Frank nodded. 'Good plan. So how?'

'I thought I'd get a job.'

'A job?'

'Yes, in the mill. Get to know the family and see what I can make of them.'

The cream jug arrived on a silver salver.

'How does the young lady like her tea, my lord?' The annoying waiter was back.

Frank smiled at my irritation. 'I've no idea, Herman. I suggest you ask her yourself.'

The waiter angled himself slightly in my direction but couldn't quite bring himself to frame the enquiry to such a questionable specimen of the lower classes.

'Oh, give it here,' I grumbled, taking the jug and adding a dash to my tea. 'I like it like this, all right?'

'I will remember your companion's preference in future, my lord.' The waiter backed from the table as if leaving the presence of royalty.

Frank frowned. 'He's beginning to annoy me too now.'

'I'm surprised he hasn't erected a screen around me to hide me from the other guests.'

Frank raised his hand as if to click his fingers again.

'Don't you dare!' I said in an undertone.

He gave me his sunniest smile. 'You are so easy to tease. So – back to Scotland.'

'Yes – job, get to know the Moirs, find the truth and then . . .' My voice tailed away.

'Then?'

'I don't know, to be honest with you. If they do turn out to be family then I suppose I'll have to make myself known to them.'

'Would you stay with them?'

I shook my head.

'Not even if this Mrs Moir turns out to be your mother?'

I bit my lip. 'I can't answer that.'

Frank tapped his fingers on the table for a moment – a most annoying habit.

'I can take you as far as Cambridge. You can catch a stage from there.' He felt in his pocket. 'And to prevent you donning a mask and turning highwayman, I insist you accept some money.' He placed a stack of gold coins on the table.

'Ten guineas! I couldn't. It's too much.'

He pushed the money to my side. 'Did you not hear the "insist" bit? I did it in my most impressive demigod voice especially and I don't want that wasted.'

I hesitated. It would solve so many problems but I hated being beholden to a friend – to anyone for that matter.

'You'd do as much for me if the tables were turned, wouldn't you? Admit it, Cat.'

'I would.' I touched the topmost guinea with my fingertip. 'I'll pay you back.'

'If you wish.'

'No, I insist.' Swiftly, before I could change my mind again, I tucked the coins deep in my pocket.

Frank let out a breath. 'Good. I'm glad that's over. Now tell me what else I can do to help.'

I polished off the last bit of muffin. 'You can smuggle me into the Temple.'

'Ah! It's the dasher. What might we do for you today, miss?'

Bob did not seem surprised to see me back so soon. He lounged in the doorway, his eyes sliding to my companion with amused interest.

'Is Mr Beamish at home?' I asked.

'Sleepin', I expect, miss.' Bob lowered his voice. 'Not as young as 'e was but still sharp as a tack in the courtroom.'

I nodded, as was only polite, still struggling to imagine the cherubic Mr Beamish tearing into criminals as Bob promised he did.

'Wait a 'alf a mo and I'll go see if 'e's receivin'.'

Frank leaned on the banister and inspected the oriel window above. 'Nice set of chambers. Charlie's considering the law; I'll mention it to him when I get back.'

Charlie Hengrave had been my pretend older brother during my sojourn at Westminster School.* Warm memories crowded into my mind as I remembered the lark we had had fooling the teachers that I was a boy.

'How is he?' I asked. I hadn't seen him in over a year.

'Capital. He's still sharing a set with me, but this time in Trinity Great Court. You'll doubtless see him when you come to Cambridge.'

'I'd like that.'

Bob was back. 'Mr Beamish is at your disposal, miss, and the young gentleman's, of course.'

'He's the Earl of Arden, Bob,' I explained as I stepped over the threshold.

'Blimey, miss, you do move in queer company, don't you?' he exclaimed.

* If you wish to read about my experience masquerading as Tom Hengrave Jnr, see *Cat Among the Pigeons*.

I handed him my bonnet. 'As fits a dasher.'

'Indeed, Miss.' Bob chucked my bonnet with his usual skill on to the coatrack, ribbon flying like a kite string.

'Not bad,' whistled Frank. He tried lobbing his own hat but it tumbled ignominiously to the ground.

'Takes years of practice, my lord.' Bob picked up the round-brimmed hat and skimmed it to a peg. 'See?'

Mr Beamish was sitting exactly where I'd first seen him, behind his desk, surrounded by papers. He rose on my entrance.

'Ah, Miss Royal, back so soon. Sheridan did warn me you wouldn't let the grass grow under your feet once you knew.'

Bob coughed. 'The Earl of Arden, sir.'

Beamish turned to Frank and gave him a surprisingly sharp inspection before bowing.

'Delighted to meet you. Avon's heir, aren't you?'

'I have that honour,' agreed Frank, bowing.

'How is the young duke?'

'Young?' Frank looked confused, wondering if

Mr Beamish was mixing him up with someone else.

'When you get to my age, everyone's young. A sobering thought. All my contemporaries are either six feet under or completely gaga.'

'Except you, sir,' replied Frank, taking to this jolly barrister.

'Kind of you to say so, but sometimes I wonder . . .' He waved us to take a seat. 'Now, how may I serve you?'

'I wanted to ask if you would use your influence to secure me a job.' I paused. 'At the New Lanark cotton mill.'

Mr Beamish rubbed his chin thoughtfully.

Bob nodded. 'Excellent, dasher. Blindside that Mrs Moir. No flies on you, eh?'

Mr Beamish pulled a fresh sheet of paper from the drawer of his desk and began writing. He glanced at me. 'Ever done work of this sort before?'

I shook my head.

'Thought not. Still, it's not highly skilled from what I understand. A smart girl like you will manage, I do not doubt.' He signed his name with a flourish then stamped a wax seal on the bottom.

'Just present this to Mr Dale. I imagine he will have no hesitation about assisting you. A remarkably kind man by all accounts.'

I took the letter. 'Did you explain my mission?'

'I said you were trying to trace your family but made no mention of names.'

'Thank you.'

'Not a'tall, m'dear, not a'tall. I look forward to hearing the outcome.' He glanced up at Bob. 'And I venture to say on both our behalves, that we wish you a pleasant reunion. You never know.'

It was kind of him to dress it up that way, but we all knew this was very unlikely.

Frank had already dismissed the tiger with the curricle when we arrived at the Temple. We therefore returned to Bow Street on foot, reminiscing about the times we'd shared on these streets, speculating as to what our old friends were doing now. Particularly Pedro. I could barely turn a corner without imagining I'd see him strolling towards me. He'd become so much a part of my life, it felt empty without my adopted brother.

We crossed the Strand and headed north to Bow Street. It wasn't until we were a hundred yards from Syd's shop that I realized something was wrong. An angry crowd had gathered outside. Most of the gang were there, boys rolling up sleeves and dumping jackets on the ground. Four men had picked up makeshift weapons, tools and bricks. There was no sign of Syd. I broke into a run.

'Cat!' Frank pounded after me. 'What's wrong?'

I shouldered my way through the press and grabbed Nick's arm. His face was ugly with rage, his eyes blank for a second until he recognized me.

'Nick, what's happening?' I gasped.

'Get inside, Cat. This is no place for you right now,' he replied, turning back to face his troops, for that was what they looked like.

'Where's Syd?'

Nick jerked his head to the shop. 'In there. The doctor's with 'im now. 'E'll live, we think.'

I thumped his arm to gain his full attention. 'What happened?'

Nick ran his hand through his hair. 'Look, this mornin' 'e went to check on that Irish girl.'

I groaned. It had never occurred to me that Syd would do such a thing, but of course he would have considered her his responsibility after she had stayed here last night.

''E ran across 'er brothers. The O'Rileys accused 'im of all sorts of stuff and set about him, seven to one. Even Syd can't beat them kind of odds. Bleedin' cowards! 'E's beat up pretty bad. You'd better go to 'im.'

I swallowed my sick feeling of rage. I'd caused this situation, at least in part. It was my fault Syd was so badly hurt. 'I will, but first tell me what you're doing.' I could guess. The Butcher's Boys and the people of the market would not let this pass without taking their revenge.

'Evenin' the score,' Nick said with leashed fury. He flexed his fists. 'Showin' those Irish they're not welcome round 'ere.'

I could just imagine what would happen when a crowd of angry men from the market swarmed all over the building site. It would be a battlefield, innocents crushed in their passage.

I gripped his sleeve. 'Stop this, Nick. Think

what Syd would want. There are women and children living there. You can't go marching in and let rip – Syd would hate you to do that.'

Nick shook me off. 'Get out of my way, Cat. I'm in charge of the Butcher's Boys, not you.'

Frank, who'd been waiting just behind me, stepped forward. 'She's right, Nick. You can't do it this way. This is between you and the O'Rileys – not every Irishman in London.'

'With all due respect, my lord,' Nick's tone dripped with sarcasm, 'this is none of your bloody business.'

Frank stood tall, challenging Nick with his unflinching gaze. 'You forget, Nick, I'm in the gang until Syd says different. And I say you're wrong about this.'

Nick, usually one of the kindest people of my acquaintance, would listen to no reason this morning. He was seeing the whole world through a red mist. 'Bleedin' blue blood – what do you know about anythink?'

'Don't you take it out on Frank, Nick!' I shouted, jabbing him in the ribs. 'You're just too dim-witted to realize we're right. You aren't thinking straight.' I turned to the crowd. 'Go home, all of you.'

'Shut up, Cat.' Nick seized me around the chest, stopping my mouth with his hand. I struggled, but he didn't let go. 'Don't listen to 'er. We're off!'

Thwack! With a sudden jerk, Nick's grip on me loosened and he flew backwards. Seeing his man down, Frank rubbed his knuckles and addressed the crowd.

'Joe, Tom, Mick – all of you, go home. Wait for news of Syd. Tempers are running too high. You'll regret it if you do anything now.'

Nick was pulling himself to his feet, shaking his head to clear it from the blow to his jaw.

'Think, lads: would Nick lay a finger on Cat if he was himself?' Frank continued.

A few muttered, some shoulders began to sag, taking on less belligerent stances.

I moved to Frank's side. 'Please, everyone. At least wait until Syd agrees to whatever action you're going to take,' I pleaded. I held out a hand to Nick. 'Please.'

Nick hesitated, looked at me for what felt like an age, then took my hand. 'All right, Cat. Maybe we should wait – see 'ow Syd is.' Addressing the men, he said, 'We'll meet again at six. I'll let you know the plan then.'

The crowd dispersed, leaving us three alone.

Frank gave Nick a wary look. 'Sorry I hit you, but I couldn't let you manhandle Cat.' He held out a hand.

Nick gave a gruff laugh and shook the proffered palm. 'Blimey, Frank, you can pack a punch!'

'I've had a good tutor.'

'Yeah, and 'e'd've knocked me even 'arder if 'e'd been 'ere. Sorry, Cat. I was a bit beside meself.'

'Apology accepted.' I took a breath, the full horror of what had happened penetrating now the immediate danger had passed. 'Come on – let's go see Syd.'

Syd was lying in his bed, tended by his mother. At least I think it was Syd – his face was swollen and both eyes blackened. He looked distressingly like the raw meat sold downstairs. I could better understand Nick's rage now – if the O'Riley brothers had been anywhere within reach I would have cheerfully taken a horsewhip to them myself.

'How is he?' I whispered, gripping Mrs Fletcher's hand.

Syd's eyes flickered open. 'Cat?' he croaked.

'I'm here.' I knelt by the bed. 'Frank's here too.'

'I'm not dyin', you know.'

His mother sniffed and bit her lip.

'I know you're not, you idiot. A pasting won't take Syd Fletcher down.' I swivelled round to Mrs Fletcher. 'What's the damage?'

'Busted ribs, bruisin'. Too early to say about bleedin' inside but the doctor's hopeful. 'E's got a tough 'ide 'as our Syd.'

'Tough as old boots,' I agreed, trying not to show my shock in my expression. 'You'll be up and about in no time.'

Syd beckoned me closer. 'I'm worried 'bout the Irish lass.'

'I saw her this morning. She was . . . she was all right.'

'She won't be able to stay now. She'll get 'urt – I just know it. One of my lot or one of 'er brothers. She'd be better off out of it.'

'I'll look after that. Don't worry.'

'Nick?' Syd groaned as he shifted on his pillow.

Nick took a step futher into the little chamber. 'Yeah, Syd?'

'Keep the boys from doin' anythink stupid. I'll deal with the O'Rileys in me own time. I trust you to 'ave more sense than most of them 'ot'eads.'

Nick flicked a guilty look at Frank and me. 'But if we catch 'em, I'm not goin' to let 'em get away with this.'

Syd gave a strained laugh. 'Nah, I don't expect you will. But remember, this is my battle.' He flexed his fist then let it go limp on the covers. 'Leave me at least Corny O'Riley.'

Nick gave a nod. 'I promise.'

'And no one else is to be punished,' Syd continued. 'Don't let this get out of 'and, eh?'

With some reluctance, Nick gave his word.

'Now off you go, the lot of you,' said Mrs Fletcher, flapping us from the room. 'I'm goin'

to give Syd a few drops of laudanum and let
'im sleep.'

Sobered by the interview with Syd, Frank and I sat
in the kitchen at a loss what to do now.

'How are you going to help the Irish girl?
You can't risk going over there – not with her
brothers about.' Frank stirred the kitchen fire with
the poker.

'But I promised.'

'Send her a note.'

'I doubt she can read.'

He frowned. 'True. Perhaps I could send a
footman?'

'She'd love that,' I said sourly. 'Very subtle.'

There came a timid knock on the back door
and I jumped up to answer. Bridgit O'Riley stood
on the step, small bundle in one hand, a tatty shawl
clutched at her throat.

'Er, Frank?' I said over my shoulder.

'Yes?'

'I think our problem's just been solved.'

Bridgit accepted my offer of tea with wary

thanks. She perched on the edge of her chair, eyes darting into every corner as if expecting someone to spring out and attack.

'I am so sorry, Cat,' she said hoarsely. 'I should go, but I don't have anywhere else. All I could think of was you and Mr and Mrs Fletcher and how kind you were to me. I'm so sorry. It's all my fault.'

'No, it's not.' I squeezed her hand while Frank bustled around the range looking most bemused as he worked out the feminine mystery of tea-making.

'How fares your friend?' she asked, her eyes filled with tears. 'He was so brave, standing up for me in front of my brothers. They called him – and me – all sorts of names, but he weren't having it. Told them to respect me, he did. That's when they attacked.'

I hastened to reassure her. 'He'll be all right. He's a tough one, is Syd.'

She breathed a sigh of relief, then clenched her fists and struck her thighs in impotent rage. 'I hate my brothers – hate them!'

I put an arm round her, preventing her

directing any more of her anger against herself. 'So do I right now. Where are they?'

'They have barricaded themselves in our room; they're expecting trouble. They told me to run for it.' She gulped. 'Corny told me not to come back – said it was my fault.'

I was about to protest this when I caught sight of Frank on the point of emptying half the tea caddy into the pot. Swiftly, I leapt up to stop him.

'Don't you know how expensive tea is?' I scolded, whipping the spoon from his hand. 'Mrs Fletcher will have kittens if you waste it!'

Frank shook his head. 'I don't think I've ever made tea before. Show me.'

Rather grateful to have the distraction while I worked out what to do about Bridgit, I demonstrated the art of making a pot of tea to the Earl of Arden. I think Frank was playing up his ineptitude to make Bridgit smile.

'Are you really a lord, my lord?' she asked shyly, when he presented her with a cup.

'Hard to believe, isn't it?' I murmured as I took my seat again.

'But, for my sins, I am,' confirmed Frank.

'Do you have estates in Ireland, my lord?' she asked quietly.

Frank wrinkled his brow. 'I don't think so. England, Scotland, Wales – yes. Ireland – no. Why?'

Bridgit brightened at the news, a smile flickering at the corner of her mouth. 'You see, your lordship, I wouldn't like to have to hate you.'

He gave a bark of startled laughter. 'Hate me? What have I done to deserve that? The tea's not that bad, is it?'

I had worked out what lay behind her line of questioning. 'She doesn't have to hate you because you're not an absentee landlord,' I explained. 'The O'Rileys lost their land to one of those parasites.'

Bridgit sipped and gave him an appreciative nod. 'And the tea is very good, my lord.'

An awkward silence fell. It was an odd situation – noble, commoner and Irish girl all sharing a pot of tea in a butcher's kitchen. Almost unique, I would guess. I was very aware of the gulf that separated me from Frank, something that had been nagging me all day since he first turned up in his smart curricle and had been treated like minor royalty by all and sundry. Though we might pretend otherwise, he was so far above my touch as to be almost out of sight. But Bridgit, despite her nationality – she was someone much more on my level; her path and mine could meet naturally.

'I have an idea,' I announced, putting down my cup.

Frank sat up and rapped on the table. 'Attention, everyone! Cat Royal speaks.'

'No, I'm serious. Bridgit, there'll be no fight – not today. But I believe you're right about having to get out of town. It's going to be nasty for the next few weeks. So I've thought of the very thing: why don't you come with me to Scotland?'

Her eyes widened. 'Scotland?'

'Yes. I have that family business I need to settle – and I'd like a friend to come with me. It's a long way to travel on my own.'

Frank slapped the tabletop, making the cups jump. 'An inspiration worthy of Newton!' He turned to Bridgit. 'Miss O'Riley, would you do Cat's friends the very great favour of keeping her out of trouble? I know it's an almost impossible task but we will pay you for your time.'

'Now, just wait a moment –' I broke in.

Frank silenced me with a look. 'She may not realize it, but we all suffer when she's off gallivanting on her own. With you at her side, we'll all sleep more soundly. Syd in particular will be most grateful.'

Bridgit glanced at me. 'If it please you, my lord –'

'It would please all of us.'

'After what my brothers did, I would like to repay you in some way –'

Frank waved off the subject. 'You owe no one. It is we who would be in your debt.'

'Then –' she searched my expression and I gave her a nod, 'then I agree.'

We fixed on the following day to begin our journey. There was little point delaying: Frank had to return to college and Bridgit could not go out and about. It was far better to put some miles between her and all the trouble her brothers had caused in Covent Garden. At her dictation, I wrote a note for the foreman to inform her family that she had found a position as a travelling companion to a young lady and would be gone some months. They were to leave word with the building site manager if they too moved on.

'You don't regret leaving them?' I asked as I sealed the note.

Bridgit shook her head, toying with the end of her black braid. 'No, it's time I left. Things were getting worse each day.'

I explained the plan to Syd when he woke up from his sleep. He could only manage a tired grumble at me going away but even he recognized that the journey would serve more than one purpose.

'You'll be all right, Syd?' I asked. He did look much better today, despite the rainbow of bruises.

He groaned. 'I'll mend.'

I brushed his raw knuckles. 'Try and stop the boys going too far, for Bridgit's sake. Her brothers may be a bad lot but they're all she's got now.'

He grunted. 'Don't worry. I'm goin' after justice, not revenge.'

I grimaced, thinking that after what they'd done to him, justice looked pretty serious.

'I'll see you in a few weeks then.'

He closed his eyes, drifting back to sleep. 'I 'ope you find what you're lookin' for, Kitten.'

'So do I, but I'm not sure yet what that is.'

SCENE 2 – THE GREAT NORTH ROAD

As curricles do not make a comfortable convey-ance for more than a single passenger, Frank borrowed one of the family's carriages to transport us to Cambridge. To his annoyance (and my relief) he had to relinquish the reins to an experienced coachman as his father would not hear of him handling a team of four. Bridgit could hardly believe the luxury of travelling by private coach: no foul-smelling passengers with elbows in your ribs, well-sprung seats cushioning the jolts and bumps, and room to stretch.

'To be sure, your lordship, I could take to this life,' she said, a sparkle in her eye. The further we travelled from London, the brighter she became; the spirits crushed by the misery of the past few days rising to what I guessed were their usual level.

'Don't get too used to it,' I warned. 'We've many hours on the stagecoach ahead of us.

How long do you think it will take us to get to Lanark, Frank?'

'The very fastest you can do the journey to Scotland is two days, but that's without stopping for the night and I don't advise it. I suggest you break your journey at least a couple of times – take four or five days over it.' He leaned over me to pull a map of Britain out of the side pocket of the carriage door. Spreading it out over his knees, he traced the route north for us. 'The stagecoach stops every fifteen miles or so to change horses, which means you'll have plenty of inns to choose from. When we get to Cambridge, I'll send my man to purchase tickets and make enquiries about the best inns.'

Gazing out the window to admire the golden boughs that arched over the road, I reflected how splendid it would be to have staff at my beck and call. Frank took such things for granted, but having someone else sort out the mundane details of life was a luxury worth even more than a well-sprung carriage.

After an early dinner at an inn in Saffron

Walden, we rumbled into Cambridge at dusk. It seemed an unlikely city, spiking out of the flat fenland in a crop of towers and elegant colleges. Unlike the press of traffic, beggars and working folk that thronged the streets of London, Cambridge seemed relatively empty, the lanes given over to flocks of rich young men intent on making a nuisance of themselves. The carriage rattled on the cobbles and drew to a halt outside an impressive gateway with two little turrets standing guard either side. The first thing I noticed was the statue of one of my least favourite kings, the wife-murdering Henry, over the large centre doors. With his left foot a little forward, peeking over the ledge, he looked as if he was about to cut a caper. Two irreverent stone lions guarded a shield underneath him with their tongues stuck out at all passers-by, I thought them most comical.

Frank jumped out, making the carriage rock. 'Wait here a moment. I'm just going to have a word with the porter.'

I craned my head out of the window and watched him disappear under the archway through a smaller door. Black-robed students flapped in and out of the portal like bats entering and leaving their cave. Frank came back in a trice, beaming.

'I've arranged a room for you with the porter's family. They live opposite College. If you would like to settle in, I'll fetch Charlie.'

I glimpsed through the gateway a tempting stretch of green sward and elegant wide paths. There lay hidden the forbidden fruit of male scholarship – but I was Eve's daughter, Reader, and tempted to taste. 'I've come all this way, Frank. Can't I see your college?'

Frank glanced around as if checking whether or not he could be overheard. 'I can't take a lady in without permission from the dean, Cat. It's a bit late to go and ask him now.'

I raised a brow.

He took one look at my face and groaned. 'Oh, all right, I'll think of something. I meant to show you my set of rooms; I just hadn't worked out how.'

That was more like it. I grinned my approval.

Frank ran his hands through his hair, a little

exasperated. 'You can be dashed manipulative sometimes, you know, Cat?'

I looked at him in innocent wonderment. 'What? Me? Did I say anything, Bridgit?'

The Irish girl shook her head and laughed. 'No, that you did not.'

'See!'

'You don't have to say anything,' grumbled Frank. 'You just have to fix me with those big green eyes of yours and I find myself doing all sorts of ridiculous things. I'll call to fetch you in about an hour.'

Exactly sixty minutes later Mrs Grandley, our hostess, knocked politely on the door to our chamber.

'Miss Royal, there are two gentlemen waiting for you.'

'Coming?' I asked my companion.

Bridgit was stretched out on the bed, relishing the clean cotton sheets and soft feather mattress. She shook her head.

'No, thank you. They're your friends. Mrs

Grandley has said I could have a bath in the kitchen.'

Leaving her to be pampered, I jumped down the stairs and burst into the little front parlour of this higgledy-piggledy lodging house. The two occupants seemed to fill the entire space, their heads brushing the low-beamed ceiling, long academic gowns sweeping almost to the floor. As tall as each other, the young Cambridge scholars made an impressive sight – black pillars of wisdom and learning. At least that was the appearance; reality was rather more fun.

'Charlie!' I launched myself at my old school-friend, giving him a hug before remembering my manners. I pushed back and bobbed a curtsey. He still had a mop of black hair which he now clubbed back in a ribbon.

'Tom Cat!' Charlie laughed with delight and caught me up in a second hug, refusing to go all formal. 'I can't believe how my little brother has grown into such an intrepid traveller. France, America, the Caribbean – I've been quite agog at your antics!'

'And now Scotland,' chipped in Frank.

'And I understand we only have your company for a day.' Charlie pulled a sad face.

'Unfortunately, yes,' I replied.

He reached for my hand. 'Come on then – don't you want to see our college?'

'I'd love to, but Frank mumbled something about it not being allowed.' I rolled my eyes in disgust.

Charlie smiled. 'It's not. But when has that ever stopped us?'

Frank stepped forward at this point and shook out a third robe with a flourish. 'In honour of past adventures, I borrowed this from one of the gentleman commoners – it should do the trick.'

Charlie produced an academic cap and plonked it on my head. 'Good job it's getting dark, or no one would mistake you for an under - graduate.'

Suitably disguised, I followed my friends through the hallowed portals and into the hidden world beyond. We emerged into a huge courtyard, almost as big as Covent Garden, I would guess, but without the clutter of stalls and people. The atmosphere was hushed, somewhat like a cathedral cloister. A rook cawed as it perched on one of the pinnacles that decorated the buildings like a row of Indian arrowheads. Students hugged the paths around the edge of the Great Court, leaving the perfect green lawns unsullied by their feet. I peered at a little sign sticking out of the ground. It stated in no uncertain terms that undergraduates were not allowed on the grass. How perfectly silly! I felt an irrepressible desire to do something outrageous. I recognized that feeling: it had never done me any good but I could not stop myself.

'Frank, Charlie – I'm sorry but I just have to.'

Before they could grab me, I chucked Charlie my hat and took a run, leaping the low barrier. Six perfect cartwheels later I was back on the path, still running, this time fleeing the shouts of an outraged porter. The long legs of Frank and Charlie caught up with me and they hauled me into a doorway and up a flight of stairs. I arrived outside their set, out of breath but immensely pleased with myself.

Frank pushed me inside. 'The idea of the disguise was to make you less conspicuous, Cat.'

'But where's the fun in that, hey?'

Frank raised his eyes heavenward. 'Give me strength!'

'I can't believe you just did that,' Charlie marvelled. 'You've broken more college rules in five minutes than I've managed in a month.'

'Missed me, have you?' I grabbed the cap back and skimmed it to the peg by the door. It fell perfectly in place and I applauded myself.

'Course we have,' laughed Charlie. 'Now, tell me everything while I make us some toast.'

The stay in Cambridge was all too short. After a day's rest, Bridgit and I climbed inside the Edinburgh mail in the yard of the coaching inn. Frank had insisted on treating us to this convey - ance rather than the slower stage, saying he felt happier knowing that we were travelling with the well-armed guard who looked after the mail sack. Highwaymen were known to be active on the Great North Road and Frank said he did not want to be responsible for subjecting a poor innocent thief to the experience of trying to rob Cat Royal.

Once free of city traffic, the mail set a cracking speed – about ten miles an hour from the rapidity with which the waymarkers flashed by. An astonishing pace and one our grandparents' generation would find difficult to imagine. Not as comfortable as Frank's carriage, the mail was still relatively smooth, making light work of the turnpike roads. The bugle sounded frequently to warn other travellers of our approach and we would gallop by, leaving lumbering carts in our dust. As the flat lands of Cambridgeshire and Lincolnshire fell behind, we were more frequently asked to alight to assist the horses in climbing particularly steep hills. Once, as we crossed what seemed an unending stretch of boggy moorland somewhere near York, we all had to help push when a wheel got stuck in a rut three feet deep. But all in all we made excellent progress. The hostlers at the coaching inns had horse changes down to a fine art, the swiftest being but three minutes by the pocket watch of the lawyer who sat opposite us for a long stretch of the journey in Yorkshire.

Moors gave way to rolling green dales: grazing sliced up into an uneven patchwork quilt by grey stone walls; the steep fells were home to shepherds, stubborn sheep and little else. Cottages snuggled in valleys or in the shelter of trees, hinting of harsher winters and bitter winds this far north. In Northumberland, we passed an earth bank littered with tumbled stones. Hadrian's Wall according to a friendly cleric – boundary of the Roman Empire, last bastion of civilization.

'Beyond this, they're all savages,' he joked.

After three days of bone-wearying travel and a coach change in Edinburgh, Bridgit and I finally arrived at the Scottish town of Lanark, both heartily sick of being constantly on the move. Our bags were thrown down at our feet and the coach rumbled onwards, bound for Glasgow.

Bridgit put her hands on her hips and gazed round the marketplace, crowded with people coming and going, their pattens and boots clacking on the dark cobbles. I rubbed the small of my back, feeling my spine would never be quite the same after all that jolting. In the light drizzle that was falling, Lanark did not appear very welcoming. The stallholders were packing up after a morning's business. The houses were built of sombre grey stone and reminded me of a huddle of Quakers waiting in silent worship around the square. The town was built on a slope and surrounded by steep wooded hills, giving the impression that if the houses did not hang on tight we would all slide off and land in the bottom of the valley like children spilling off a sledge.

'What now, Cat?' Bridgit asked.

Mentally giving my spirits a kick, I replied, 'We find our cotton mill, of course. Let's ask someone.'

I approached a boy of about my age lounging by a mounting block. He feigned indolence as he chewed on a straw but I'd noted that he had been watching us closely ever since we got off the coach. He had a book stuffed in the pocket of his jacket and a pair of steel-rimmed glasses hanging from a buttonhole in his waistcoat. I took these signs to mean he was educated, which in turn would hopefully mean he would have wit enough to help us.

'Excuse me, can you direct us to the mill?' Even to my ears, my voice sounded obviously and ridiculously English compared to the locals.

The boy spat out the stalk and rubbed his freckled nose as if pausing to translate my question.

'Ye'll be wanting New Lanark?'*

'Er, I think so. Is that where the mill is?'

'Aye.'

'Can you show us?'

The boy grinned, displaying his crooked front teeth. 'I can –' I opened my mouth to thank him, but he laughed – 'but I didna say I would.'

Too tired for teasing, Bridgit turned away. 'Leave him – he's no use at all.'

'Nae use? I ken the place like the back of my

---

* A note on the Scottish language: as I don't want my readers unfamiliar with the Scottish dialect to find difficulties following the dialogue, I have taken the liberty of 'translating' some of what was said to me. I've kept a few terms, with explanations in my glossary, but inevitably I fear a little of the music and colour of the language has been sacrificed. Apologies to my Scottish friends.

hand. I live there. Ye'll find nae one better to show ye.'

'Maybe, but we want someone willing,' I replied. 'And as you so obviously have an important task here today keeping that mounting block company, we'll bid you good day,' adding under my breath, '*blockhead.*'

He whipped a cap up off the stone and shoved it on his scruffy hair. 'Stop all yer bletherin' and come along wi' me.' He strutted off without pausing to see if we were following, like a master striding in front of recalcitrant pupils.

I looked at Bridgit, who shrugged.

'Seems the professor has changed his mind.' I picked up my bag. 'Let's not lose him.'

We caught up with our unhelpful guide as he turned down a road leading out of town.

'The mill – is it far?' I panted.

'Very far for sapsie Sassenachs.' He refused to look at us.

I guessed this was an insult. 'And for un-sapsie ones?'

'No so far.'

'Good.'

'What you want wi' the mill?'

'Employment. What else?'

'It's sair-work, no for soft lasses.'

'We're not soft.'

He shrugged as if he doubted my word but did not feel it worth the bother of arguing.

Bridgit gave me an expressive look and took over the interrogation.

'What's your name?' she asked, deftly diverting him from our little quarrel.

He seemed to respond well to her quietly spoken question and gave her a smile. 'Jamie Kelly, miss. And yers?'

Bridgit swiftly introduced us.

'Pleased to meet ye, Miss O'Riley.' He removed his cap then clamped it back on his head. 'I'm always happy to be o' service to a bonny lass.'

'Why, thank you, Mr Kelly.' Bridgit laughed at his compliment. He blushed, the redness creeping up his cheeks to the roots of his dark copper hair. 'And what do you do at the mill?'

'Faither's a mechanic; he looks after Mill

Number Two. It's a very important position.' He tucked his thumbs in the pocket of his waistcoat and swaggered a little. I hid a smile.

'I do not doubt it,' Bridgit assured him. 'And you? Do you work in the mill?'

He shook his head. 'Nae, I go to the mill dayschool. Faither wants me to be a mechanic wi' him so I need schooling, he says.'

I wrinkled my nose in doubt. 'So why aren't you there now, Master Kelly?'

'We had a test so I decided to troon school the day.' He met my eye in a challenge, daring me to criticize. 'And if ye tell my faither or the dominie I'll never forgive ye.' Perhaps he wasn't as devoted a scholar as his appearance suggested.

I waved his threat away. 'If you play truant, Jamie Kelly, that's your affair. Miss O'Riley and I couldn't care less.'

We walked on for at least a mile until we reached the top of a hill overlooking a wooded river valley. The air was soft with misty rain, like a gauze curtain over a stage backdrop.

'Take a keek o' that, Miss O'Riley.' Jamie

addressed himself to my companion; it appeared he had given me up as a bad lot. 'That's what ye came all this way to see.'

'Keek?' I snorted.

'That means "look", Miss Priss,' Jamie sneered.

Down below we could make out the dark slate roofs of buildings snaking along the edge of the riverbank, somewhat like the warehouses on the Thames. Nearest the water stood a vast manufactory, walls pierced by many windows in six rows. It struck me as outlandish to see such a modern building of regular lines set down in this once Arcadian spot, like a giant child's playbricks dropped out of the sky. Even from our bird's-eye view, I could hear the rumble and clank of machinery. Set a little higher up the slope were a couple of fine houses and several long rows of cottages. I could just glimpse the gardens, bright with autumn flowers and vegetables, behind the workers' homes. Everything looked neat and gave the impression of a well-ordered enterprise, but for the moment I could see no workers.

'Where is everyone?' Bridgit asked, her

thoughts travelling a similar path to mine.

'They willna be out till seven. Then ye'll see them.'

As the working day was far from over, it seemed that we would have a chance to apply to the owner today. I fingered my letter of recommendation tucked in my pocket.

'Where might I find Mr Dale?' I asked Jamie.

'Mr Dale, is it?' Jamie laughed. 'The maister doesna want to be fashed wi' the likes of ye. Ye go see the overseer if ye want work.'

'No, I want to see Mr Dale himself. I have a letter for him.'

'Ye think me a gowk? A snippie lass wi' a letter for the maister – what clamjamphry is that!'

I was beginning rather to enjoy his colourful words, particularly since I knew he would have to eat them all when I produced the lawyer's recommendation.

'Well, Master Kelly, this snippie lass intends to see the maister, gowk-laddie or no. Where is he?'

Jamie bristled at my turning of his own insults

back on him. 'This is something I must see. This way.'

He led us down a steep path to the valley bottom and up to the door of a fine house sitting in its own garden – fit for the maister indeed.

'Go on wi' ye. Chap the door,' he dared me.

I lifted the knocker and gave a smart tap. After several moments, a neatly dressed maid opened it.

'Can I help ye, miss?' she asked politely.

'I have a letter for Mr Dale.' I produced the missive with a flourish, pleased to note Jamie's mouth agape with surprise; he had not believed in its existence until that moment.

'Will ye wait a wee while in the parlour, miss? I'll enquire if the maister can see ye now.' The maid beckoned Bridgit and myself inside, ignoring Jamie. I gave him a triumphant nod as she shut the door on him. Showing us into the parlour, she took the letter and disappeared down the passage to the rooms at the back of the house.

Left to ourselves, I had time to admire my surroundings. The parlour was of modest size but comfortably furnished. Fine muslin curtains screened the view of the mill while still letting light pass through, giving the room a muted, genteel atmosphere. An embroidery frame waited by the hearth, a pansy half completed in rich purple silk. The walls held family miniatures and local views, including an impressive painting of a waterfall. I peered at the title: Corra Linn. Tiny figures could be seen on the bank admiring the rainbows in the water. If that was in walking distance, I resolved that I too would go and see it before I left Scotland. The waterfall reminded me of my time with the Creek Indians in America, a poignant memory as one of my friends had died by the banks of a much smaller fall – an incident in which I had very nearly lost my life.* But I knew somehow that if I stood where those people were standing, with the spray of Corra Linn wetting my face, I would feel happiness as well as sorrow. I wondered if my adopted Creek family still thought about me and wished me well. My heart told me that they did.

* For this painful episode, please see *Cat O'Nine Tails*.

'Miss Royal?'

So lost in my thoughts I had not heard Mr Dale enter the room. I spun round to see a rotund, bewigged gentleman coming towards me, the opened letter in his hand. Of short stature, he was at risk of being as wide as he was tall. A watch chain strained across an ample expanse of striped silk waistcoat.

I bobbed a curtsey. 'Sir.'

He turned to my friend.

'And this is my travelling companion, Miss O'Riley.'

Mr Dale gave her a pleasant smile and waved us both to take a seat while he stood on the hearth-rug, bobbing slightly on his heels. His double chin wobbled in time, making me think of a jolly pug dog begging for a treat.

'Though I have not had the pleasure of meeting Mr Beamish in person, I've heard of him – a great man,' Mr Dale said, waving the letter in the air. 'He vouches for you, Miss Royal, so I will of course be delighted to oblige him.'

'Thank you, sir.'

'Perhaps, lass, you could be a little more explicit in your needs?'

There was no reason to doubt the man, so I decided to tell him the truth. I explained about the letter and my desire to discover the truth behind the claims that I was related to the Moirs in some fashion.

Mr Dale peered at me speculatively. 'The Moirs, eh? I know the family – not well, of course – but I recognize the names.'

'I thought that . . . that if I worked alongside Mrs Moir for a while I would be able to get a sense of things.' Out in the open like this, my plan seemed so feeble. I wondered if I had not made a monumental mistake coming all this way.

'And your friend?' Mr Dale smiled encourag-ingly at Bridgit.

'I came to keep Miss Royal company on the road. I'll work alongside her too, if it please you, your honour.' She dipped a second curtsey.

Mr Dale rocked on the balls of his feet before replying to Bridgit.

'Well, miss, from the look of you, I'd say that

you are fine material for a tenter. Your friend here is small enough to find work as a piecer, perhaps in the same room as this Mrs Moir. I'll look into the possibilities. Do you have a place to stay?'

'No, sir,' I replied, wondering what on earth a tenter and a piecer were, but he seemed to expect us to know.

'Well, lass, you look young enough to stay in the girls' dormitory in Mill Four, but as for your friend, I'm afraid she's too old to be placed among the weans. I'll have words with one of the schoolteachers and see if she has room for a guest.' He tapped his watch chain, reviewing arrangements, checking he had not forgotten something. 'Report to the overseer tomorrow when work starts: he will give you your tasks. Now if that is all I can do for you?' There was a definite note of dismissal in his tone.

I bobbed a curtsey. 'Thank you. You've been very kind.'

'My pleasure.' He showed us to the door. Opening it, he spotted Jamie sitting on the stoop. 'Ah, Jamie Kelly, isn't it?'

The boy leapt to his feet, cap in hand. 'Aye, maister.'

'Show the young lass to Mill Four. She's staying with us a wee while.'

'Very good, sir.'

Mr Dale turned to Bridgit. 'I'll send you to the schoolmistress with one of my servants. You'll see each other tomorrow.'

Though I did not like being parted from Bridgit, I could find no grounds to protest the arrangement. Dipping a final curtsey, I picked up my bag, bade Bridgit farewell, and stepped outside. Jamie set off at a fast clip down the path.

'Jamie Kelly!' came Mr Dale's voice, much louder now. 'Where's your manners, lad?'

Striding back, Jamie tugged the bag from my hands, doffed his cap to the master and set off again, me lagging behind.

'I'm not your mule,' Jamie muttered mutinously.

'But you act like one,' I quipped, feeling I was definitely coming out on top of this verbal sparring match.

He headed towards the endmost building in the manufactory, stamped across the wooden bridge over the millstream and deposited my bag at the door. With two thumps on the wood, he turned back to me.

'The goodwife will look after ye from here, snippie.'

'You've been most gracious,' I replied, trying not to smile at his ridiculous bad humour. Just because I'd proved him wrong about Mr Dale!

'Ye willna be so gleg-tonguit after a day in the mill,' he said, with every sign that he relished the prospect.

The door opened and a harassed-looking woman stood in the entrance, long grey hair tumbling out of a bun.

'Another lass for ye, mistress,' Jamie declared, nodding to me. He smiled in anticipation. 'A Sassenach.'

'Lord save us, what was the maister thinking, sending her to me?' the woman moaned. 'As if I dinna have enough orphans to manage.'

Jamie shrugged and trotted away, kicking a

stone ahead of him. 'See ye later, snippie,' he called over his shoulder.

The woman jerked her head. 'Come in then, hen. I'll see if I can find ye a bed someplace.'

With a sigh, I picked up my bag and followed her.

'I should warn ye,' the woman continued, mounting a steep flight of stairs, 'the other weans willna like a Sassenach among them.'

So that was why Jamie had been so happy to leave me here. I couldn't do anything about my nationality, nor the fact that I would be staying for at least a night, so I decided it was best not to dwell on these ominous words.

'I'd just be grateful for somewhere to lay my head, ma'am,' I replied politely.

'Ye can call me Goodwife Ross.' She paused outside another door at the head of the stairs.

'Pleased to meet you, goodwife. I'm Cat.' I held out my hand.

She just looked at my grubby palm, then at my face. 'And what kind of name is that?'

'Er . . . I mean Catherine,' I amended hastily,

taking back my hand and wiping it on my skirt. It was probably for the best that I was not introduced to anyone as Cat; I didn't want the Moirs to know I was there before I was ready to tell them.

'Well then, in ye go, Catherine.'

She opened the door to reveal a dormitory filled with tiny beds. All the windows stood open, making the place feel very chilly, an atmosphere reinforced by the whitewashed walls and bare floor.

'Ye'll sleep two or three to a bed, but ye'll have to wait until this evening to find a space.'

I nodded, hugging my arms to my sides. It was no more than I expected; I'd shared beds before, if never in a room as large as this. 'Is there somewhere I can stow my bag?'

'Aye. I'll keep it for ye. It'll be safe wi' me. Mind ye remember, Catherine, we're a God-fearing community – ye need nae fear for yer goods and gear. But we willna stand for snecking. It'll be out on yer ear at the first sign o' trouble.'

I murmured my agreement, though exactly what 'snecking' was remained a mystery. But the general thrust of what she said was clear: it was a privilege to work here, a punishment to be expelled from this paradise. To my mind, raised among the colourful splendours of the theatre, this place was a cold, bare Eden.

'Supper will be at seven. Then ye'll go wi' the others to the school. Back by nine and into bed.'

'School?' I was faintly surprised by the late hours the scholars kept here.

'Aye, hen. Ye'll want to learn to read and write.'

'But I can – do both, I mean.' I did not add that I could manage this in several languages thanks to my unorthodox upbringing in the multilingual environment backstage.

My words were met with scepticism. 'Hmm. We'll see, nae doubt. The dominie will examine ye. Take yer rest, Catherine. Just follow the others at the bell.'

The goodwife bustled out, leaving me alone. She was right: I did feel desperately tired, not so much in body but in spirits. My desire to find my family no longer burned so brightly in my heart as I feared, Reader, that it was bound to end in disappointment of one sort or another. I stretched out on the nearest bed and linked my hands on my stomach, staring at the ceiling, watching a cobweb waft gently in the breeze. Having come so far, I could but wait and see.

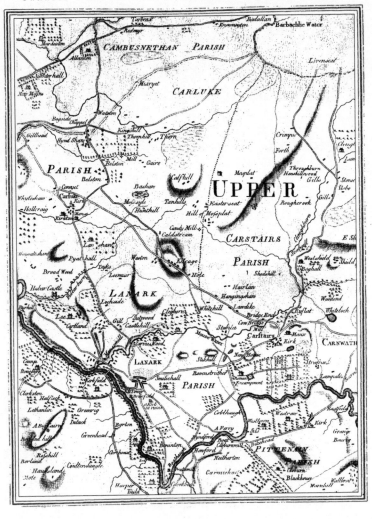

Act III - In which Cat uncovers

a secret . . .

ACT III

SCENE 1 – MILL GIRL

Two hours later, a bell rang in the yard. The rattle of the looms slowed, then muttered into silence. This layer of sound stripped out, I was now able to hear the river below the windows of the dormitory – a soothing murmur after the clatter of the machines. The reprieve was short-lived. With the rumble of approaching thunder, voices resounded outside, echoing off the high walls – shouts, shrieks, laughter. I sat up and brushed my hair with my fingers, looking expectantly towards the door. I admit, Reader, to some feelings of trepidation as to who might come through. A few minutes later, mill girls poured into the room, chatting merrily, yawning, stretching with weariness. Some pulled off long white aprons and hung them on pegs along the wall; others splashed their faces with water set out in a basin on the washstand; friends picked off cotton fluff from each other's hair. I waited, wondering when someone would notice me.

'That isna yer bed.'

I felt a shove in the shoulder blades from behind. I got up and turned to face my challenger.

'I know,' I replied, deciding to rise above such rudeness and smile in a friendly fashion at the stout, brown-haired girl on the other side of the mattress. 'I haven't been given one yet.'

She wrinkled her brow, picking her way through my words. 'Ye're a Sassenach.'

I grimaced. ''Fraid so.'

'Annie, take a keek at the new lass!'

A girl of my height with russet curls and a turned-up nose was too busy tying her laces to pay me much attention. 'What lass be that, Martha?'

'This red-topped Sassenach standing right here – in our room.' Martha put her hands on her hips and glared at me.

Annie looked up. The 'S' word was repeated from girl to girl and I soon found myself surrounded by a crowd of inquisitive but not very friendly strangers.

'What are ye doing here?' Martha asked.

I crossed my arms defensively. 'I've come to work.'

Martha's eyes ran over my well-made pelisse, dress and shoes – a mixture of hand-me-downs from Lizzie and items purchased from my meagre earnings as an actress. Though hardly the first stare of fashion, the clothes marked me out as a person of some substance. The girls, by contrast, were all dressed in a uniform of white cotton blouses and light grey skirts, woollen stockings and boots. 'Ye dinna look like ye need to work for yer bread.'

I just shrugged at that. Little did she know.

'Win off our bed, Sassenach. We dinna want any o' yer soothlan fleches biting us the nicht.'

'I don't have fleas!' I protested, having worked out her insult from the giggles of the other girls.

'We dinna believe the flech-lass, do we?' Martha appealed to the other girls.

It was an infantile way of humiliating me, Reader, but very effective. I moved away from the bed, considering my options for retaliation. I had wanted to win some friends among my room-mates, but Martha was smoothly isolating me by making me an object of mockery. She probably didn't want to share her bed, seeing as how her ample frame took up so much room.

Well, two could play at that game.

'I did not have fleas when I entered this room today. Are you telling me that I may have picked them up from your mattress?' I searched my arms suspiciously, checking for bites. I moved towards her. 'Wait a moment! Hold still.' I stared at her, transfixed by something on her head.

Martha's eyes widened. 'What is it?'

I slapped my hand down on her crown and then pretended to pick something off. 'There! Got it.'

'I dinna have fleches!' Martha exploded, pushing my hands away.

I grinned. 'No more do I. Now you know how it feels.'

A couple of the other girls giggled at Martha's blushing cheeks.

'Ye'll no last a day at our mill, Sassenach,'

jeered Martha, retreating from the battle.

'We'll see,' I replied evenly, pretending not to be ruffled by her hostility.

The girls began to leave the dormitory, heading down to supper. I tagged along at the end, wondering bleakly if there was anyone who would risk befriending me. I could sorely do with an ally or two to teach me the ropes – or threads in the case of the mill. I caught up with the girl called Annie who had lingered to put on a shawl. I'd noticed her throw me a look or two which, though not warm, had not seemed unsympathetic.

'Hello. I'm Catherine by the way.'

She gave me a reluctant nod. 'Hello, Catherine-by-the-way.'

I smiled. 'Just Catherine will do.'

The girl unbent enough to introduce herself. 'I'm Annie McGregor.'

'Pleased to meet you, Annie. Would you mind showing me where the dining room is? I'm starving.'

'Aye, I'll do that.' She beckoned me to follow her and we set off down the stairs, on the floor below, joining up with a stream of boys heading in the same direction. They were dressed in a similar plain uniform, with grey woollen breeches and jackets over their cotton shirts.

'What do you do in the mill, Annie?' I asked, trying to push past her reserves into the friendlier territory of conversation.

'I'm a piecer.'

'What does that mean?'

She gave me a funny look, astounded that anyone would not know such a basic thing, but replied anyway. 'I twist the threads together when they break on the mule.'

I guessed she wasn't talking donkeys. 'And the mule is . . . ?'

'It's the machine that spins the thread from the cotton.'

I tried to imagine such a thing – thinking it must look like some big spinning wheel. 'So how do you mend the strands?'

She laughed at my expression. 'Why, ye are an unkennin lass! Ye must crawl under the mule to fix the pieces, o' course.' I did not like the sound of this job at all, though surely it couldn't be worse than climbing a mast in a gale or emptying chamber pots? 'Ye have a minute or two to do it while the machine rests, but it is best to be gleg and keep yer head down.'

Gleg – she must mean quick. I would certainly try to be that. I didn't fancy being caught up in the machine as it set to work again – rather worse than being trampled by mules, I guessed. I stored her words of advice away for the morrow as we turned into a room set out with tables and benches. The meal was already underway, hundreds of children eating bowls of porridge and drinking from cups of milk. Almost the same meal as breakfast, Annie explained, though sometimes the cooks added bacon in the evening. At least the portions looked plentiful – my stomach was grumbling and had not been full since dawn. There was no sign of Bridgit.

'Follow me.' Annie tossed the words over her shoulder. She seemed in a fearful hurry about something. Shoving a bowl in my hand, she took me to the serving table. The big cauldron presided over by a flush-faced cook was almost empty.

'New lass, Maggie,' Annie explained, prodding me to hold out my bowl. A big spoonful of porridge landed in it.

I sniffed. 'That smells good. Thank you.'

The cook frowned on hearing my accent, then smiled when she worked out I was paying her a compliment.

'Well, hen, I dinna stint on the cream like some. Hail and happy: that's how I like my weans.'

Annie led me over to a table and set her bowl down.

'Be quick,' she warned. 'The dominie doesna like us to be late.'

Copying her example, I rapidly ate my supper and drank a good-sized cup of milk. Feeling pleasantly full, I was ready to sleep. The thought of starting school now was very unappealing, but Annie could hardly hide her excitement.

'Like school, do you?' I asked, stifling a yawn.

'Aye. I can read near all the words in the primer now,' she stated proudly.

I smiled, recognizing a kindred spirit; a budding scholar. 'And do you have a favourite word?'

She looked puzzled.

'I've always loved languages and enjoy odd words,' I explained. 'For example, right now I'm rather fond of the word "higgledy-piggledy".'

Annie repeated it slowly, savouring the sound on her tongue. 'I can see why ye like it, Catherine. It's all jummled up like its meaning. But I'm afeared I canna read such a long word. I ken "cotton" and "mill", but no much else.'

'I wager you can read far more than that, even if you don't know it. Long words are all built up of little bits, like a quilt. I imagine you could read many of them if given the chance.'

'Ye think so?' She seemed very pleased by the idea.

'I know so – or should I say – I *ken* so?'

Annie giggled.

The children were all leaving the dining room at a run, dumping their bowls in two big buckets by the door. My companion glanced around her and scraped her bowl clean.

'Come away!' beckoned Annie.

'Don't you ever get time to catch your breath

round here?' I grumbled feeling it far more suitable to sit quietly after a hearty meal than race to the next task.

'Nae, Catherine,' laughed Annie, amused by the idea. 'The maister believes that the devil makes work for idle hands. He thinks we should spend our time bettering ourselves.'

It was a commonly held view, but it seemed to me that in the rush to improve our minds we were in danger of being treated more like machines in perpetual motion than humans. At least the looms rested at seven and did not start again until the next morning. I expressed this thought to Annie as we clattered down the stairs to ground level.

'Nae, that's where ye are wrong. The mechanics oil and mend the looms the night. The mules canna keep going all the time or they'd wear out.'

'Exactly! You've made my point. Nothing and no one can work without rest.'

Annie was on the defensive now. 'We do rest, Catherine. Half an hour for breakfast at nine and an hour for dinner at two – nae other man be as kind as Maister Dale. He saved us from the orphanage – he has given us a chance for a better life.'

She was right, of course. We were the lucky ones. An hour and a half rest during the working day was almost unheard of. My friends who were sweeps and apprentices could not hope for half that. It was just that here the number of people was so huge, the work so unrelenting, I couldn't help but find it a little overwhelming. I doubted that I had the qualities that made someone a cog in such a finely crafted machine. It was just as well I was not planning to stay for long, or I could imagine the kind of breakdown I might cause.

The school – a big barn of a building set a little away from the mills – was bursting with pupils when we entered. About five hundred of us, I would guess. Despite the numbers, order reigned: the children were divided into groups and seated on benches or at desks to get on with their work. I could see at least fifteen teachers wandering among the scholars. On a blackboard one man was taking his class through their arithmetic.

A little huddle of girls sewed in one corner under the beady eye of a mistress – definitely a lesson I wished to avoid. Two women were helping little ones form letters in a sand tray.

'I'll take ye to Dominie Blair,' Annie said.

She marched me across the room to the man at the board teaching the advanced class from the look of the mathematical equations he was scribbling.

She bobbed a curtsey. 'Dominie, I have a new lass for ye.'

The schoolmaster was a tall, thin man with black hair and a pale face. Something about him reminded me a little of a raven – probably just his sharp look of intelligence as he cocked his head towards me, tapping his lip with a long, chalky finger. 'Thank ye, lass. Go to yer class. Lads, figure the sums on yer slates while I speak to the new student.'

He put the chalk down and rubbed his hands together, surveying me from top to toe.

'Mr Dale mentioned ye, lass. From London, I believe?'

'Yes, sir.'

'Have ye been to school before?'

How, Reader, could I explain that I had once attended one of the most exclusive public schools for a month?

'For a few weeks about two years ago,' I admitted.

'Ye have a long way to make up then. I'll start ye in the first form. The teacher will help ye remember yer alphabet.'

I almost choked: he was going to put me among the babies!

'I'm sorry, sir, I haven't made myself clear. I have had quite a broad – if rather odd – education from a number of excellent teachers.' By which I meant prompts, ballerinas, actors, musicians – not your usual pedagogues. 'I can read and write.'

He frowned, doubting my claims. 'Nae need to be afeared, lass, of admitting yer unkenning.'

'I'm not afraid, sir. I really am some way beyond learning my letters.'

With a slow smile, he passed me the chalk. 'Well, so be it. I wouldna like to shame ye in front of the class. Write "The cat sat on the mat" on the board.'

How apt. I blushed, thinking that he must think me a complete fool. The dominie misunderstood my embarrassment.

'I'll turn my back, lass. Just do yer best.'

The boys in the arithmetic class were watching our exchange with interest. I spotted Jamie Kelly sitting at the front, wearing his wire-rimmed spectacles. He had a full slate on his desk and I could tell he was laughing at me from behind his hand. I could hear the whisper, 'Sassenach,' rustle through the room like a breeze in leaves. Tossing the chalk thoughtfully for a moment, I decided what I should do. I wrote 'The cat sat on the mat' once in copperplate English, then translated into Latin, then French and finally, for good measure, in Italian. I wondered about doing it in Creek Indian but decided that might be a step too far. I put the chalk down with a wink at Jamie.

'Well, lass, let's see how ye have done,' said the teacher.

He turned around and stared at the board. Picking up a long stick he tapped at the bottom row.

'What is that, lass? I canna read it.'

'Italian, sir.' I wrinkled my brow. 'I think I got it right, but my memory may be a bit rusty.'

He threw back his head and gave a hearty laugh. 'By Harry, ye showed me! I dinna think I can teach ye a thing. Maybe ye would like to be a teacher instead?'

I instantly warmed to this man: he could have been offended; instead, he thought it a good joke. 'I'd like that. How can I help?'

He put a hand on my shoulder, steering me over to the smallest children. 'Ye can start here today with Mistress MacDonald and the weans. I'll have to think how to use yer talents.'

I spent an enjoyable hour helping the first form – those of five and six – making letters in the sand tray. The two little girls I sat beside were tired, having completed a thirteen-hour shift, and could hardly concentrate on their task so I decided to make it more entertaining. Rather than forming letters, we made castles in the tray. Mistress MacDonald let me do this for a while before gently shaking her head. I then made a game up where my two little friends thought up silly words and I spelt them. We were having so much fun that I did not notice that it was almost nine. Then the bell rang, dismissing school for the night.

'"P" for "pogwoggle"!' declared one of my pupils, drawing a perfect P in the sand.

'Run along now, Jeannie Moir,' said the schoolmistress.

The familiar name sent a jolt through me – I almost dropped the tray.

'Can the new lass teach me the morn's night?' Jeannie asked, looking up at me with sleepy brown eyes.

'We'll see,' said Mistress MacDonald.

Jeannie ran out, hand in hand with her little friend.

'Well, Catherine, ye are a born teacher.' Mistress MacDonald began putting the equipment away in the store cupboard. I got up to help her. 'Yer friend, the Irish lass, told me about ye – from London, she said.'

'Is Bridgit staying with you then, ma'am?' I asked.

'Aye, lass. I've a cottage at the end of Long

Row. She asked me to look out for ye the night.'

'Please tell her I'm in the dormitory in Mill Four. I'll see her tomorrow, I hope.' I shook the sand level ready for the next lesson, wondering how I could turn the conversation to the issue that had brought me here. 'Your pupils were very sweet, particularly Jeannie. Does she live with her family or is she one of the orphans?'

'Why do ye ask?'

I tried to look nonchalant as I shrugged. 'No real reason. I just hadn't noticed her in the dormitory.'

This explanation seemed to satisfy the mistress. 'Nae. That lass lives a few doors down from me.'

My throat felt dry as I blurted out my next question. 'A big family?' I couldn't get out of my head the fact that I might have just been sitting next to my sister, our fingers touching in the sand tray. But I had suspected nothing until I heard the name – no instinctive recognition when gazing into her eyes. She didn't even look like me, not with her long brown plaits and round face.

'Aye, four weans. All in mill now. Jeannie has only just started working.'

'Were her brothers and sisters here tonight?' I asked, trying to remember if there had been any faces that had caught my attention.

Mistress MacDonald gave me an odd look. 'Why such an interest in that family, Catherine?'

'I . . . I don't know.' I bent my head to brush the spilled sand off my skirts, avoiding her eye.

She relented a little. 'I expect they were here somewhere, but I see so many children go through the school, I forget. Good night to ye.'

Hearing the dismissal, I bobbed a curtsey and set off for the entrance. Annie had waited for me, but so had Jamie Kelly. He fell in beside Annie and me as we headed back to the dormitory.

'Come to check on me, professor? Seeing if the Sassenach has settled in?' I asked ironically, doubting he was here for any kindly purpose.

He gave me a hostile look, reminding me of a gang member trying to defend his territory. The professor obviously didn't like anyone rivalling him for his place at the top of the class. 'I saw, snippie – the dominie put ye on the sand tray. Ye canna fool him with yer fine ways.'

'Vous êtes un âne, professeur,' I said with a sweet smile, calling him a mule in my best French.

He frowned. 'Just because I canna speak fancy languages, doesna mean I dinna know when ye are insulting me!'

As if he hadn't insulted me first!

'Rattlepate!' I crossed my arms, tapping my foot in an angry tattoo.

'Gowk!'

'Numbskull!'

'Useless soothlander!'

But before I could set him right, Annie leapt to my defence. 'I have ye ken, Jamie Kelly, that Catherine was told by the dominie that she should be a teacher. He said that he canna teach her anything; she kens it all!'

'Not all,' I muttered, blushing.

'Is that right?' Jamie gave me a glare. 'I suppose she might ken enough – for a lass.'

'But she speaks Italian! Even the dominie canna do that!' Annie exclaimed.

Jamie tossed his head contemptuously. 'What use is Italian round here?'

'Well . . .' Annie seemed lost for an answer so ended up giving a feeble shrug.

I rolled my eyes. Thanks, defender. There seemed little point flogging this particular dead horse.

We had reached the door to the dormitory building. Annie bade Jamie goodnight and went ahead. As I made to go past, he caught my arm and held me back.

'Listen, Sassenach, ye dinna fit in here,' he announced, as if his word was final. 'Ye should get yerself back sooth.'

Infuriated by this unearned hostility, my temper snapped. 'What is your problem, Jamie Kelly? Why does it matter to you if I speak Italian, French or . . . or Greek?'

His eyes widened at this latest claim, looking somewhat like an owl whose last tail feather had just been plucked.

'For the record, I don't – speak Greek, I mean.' I scrubbed my hand through my hair, feeling very weary all of a sudden. 'Look, professor, I'm here to work and you've done nothing but try and make me feel unwelcome since you set eyes on me.' I had a sudden, unbidden memory of the angry O'Riley brothers, resorting to violence in response to the cold reception they had received in London. I now knew how they felt. 'If you don't like me, just leave me alone. I won't bother you, I can promise you that now.' I shook my arm free. 'Buonanotte!'

The goodwife was waiting in the dormitory for me to come in. On my tardy entrance, she tutted and shook her head.

'I expect my lasses to be back on time – nae dawdling.'

Feeling tired, longing for my bed, I had no appetite for a battle with another Scot. 'I apologize, ma'am. I stayed to help the school - mistress clear away.'

She gave a nod, letting the matter drop. 'I have yer cloots here; ye'll want to keep yer others for Sunday.' She gestured to my London clothes. 'Too fine for the mill.'

'Thank you.' I took the bundle of cotton and wool from her.

'Now to yer bed. There's room here wi' Martha.'

I stifled a groan. My stout enemy – she of the flea insults – was in sole possession of the bed I had dared rest on earlier. A great round mound of blankets, she was lying in the centre, pretending to be asleep. The image came to mind that Martha was like some rampant form of weed who had gained control of this particular cot by crowding out all other forms of life.

'Hurry up, hen. I want to douse the light.' The goodwife gave me a little push towards the bed.

Placing my new clothes on top of my boots, I quickly stripped down to my shift and climbed in. Martha made no concession to my presence so I found myself clinging to the edge with the blanket flapping halfway down my back. I was sorely tempted to pinch her to make her move over but instead opted for the path of least resistance. Burrowing to the other end of the blanket, I lay down, top to her tail. The goodwife blew out the last candle and left.

'I dinna want yer smelly feet in my face,' growled Martha, giving me a kick.

Little did she know it but she'd picked the wrong person to bully. I'd stood up to Westminster schoolboys, sailors and slave-owners; one mill girl would not bother me.

'If you do that again, I'll punch you,' I growled.

She snorted and moved her foot back in preparation for another strike. I caught it in my fist and squeezed her ankle.

'My best friend in London is a boxing champion and he's shown me a trick or too. Do you want to find out how we English lasses fight?'

That gave her pause. 'I'm no scared o' ye.' But her voice was thin and her foot moved further back.

'Good. And I'm not scared of you. Understood?'

Silence.

'Well, then. Sleep tight.'

SCENE 2 — CROMPTON'S MULE

A bell rang while it was still dark, summoning us to work. With practised ease, the girls rolled out of bed and donned their clothes without the aid of a light. The dormitory was chill; no place to linger. I had a little more difficulty dressing, not having put on the uniform before, but Annie came to my rescue, untangling apron strings and helping me find my boots which had mysteriously migrated under another bed. A morning gift from Martha, no doubt.

'I'll take ye to the overseer,' Annie told me, dragging on my hand to make me hurry. I was still tucking my hair under my cap so that not a strand was showing. Annie had explained it could get caught in the machines. 'He'll tell ye where ye are to go. We must be gleg though, else I'll be in trouble wi' my spinner.'

With a quick splash of icy water on my face, I followed her down the stairs once more. We passed the dining room but the fires were not yet lit – hours yet until we could break our fast. My stomach grumbled at the thought.

Out into the soft grey damp of a late autumn morning, the workers were hurrying to their tasks. The overhanging trees on the opposite bank of the river looked rusty brown in the drizzle; they were gently dropping leaves on to the indigo silk water, releasing them to bob away like tiny ships of the line bound for the sea. That wood belonged to a different world to the cobble and iron of the mill yard where we were on our way to work. Annie marched me to an office in Mill One and abandoned me, scurrying off to her duties with a hasty farewell until she too was swallowed by the unseen mechanical beast that lurked behind the blank facade of the buildings. The great human machine of the cotton mill was swinging into action again, each cog turning in his or her place – I longed to see what this looked like, finding the boom-clatter noise of the looms both terrifying and enticing. I felt rather like Saint George waiting outside the dragon's cave, listening to the rumbles and groans of a beast made all the more fearful for being out of sight.

The overseer had not yet arrived but I didn't have to wait on my own for long as Bridgit joined me. She looked annoyingly well groomed and rested, thanks to her stay in a proper bedroom at the home of the kindly teacher. I snuffed out the spark of jealousy before it could make my got-out-of-the-wrong-side-of-bed morning temper worse. But then, there was no right side to a bed shared with Martha.

'Cat, my dear!' Bridgit gave me a sisterly hug. She looked genuinely pleased to see me, which went a long way to improving my temper. 'How are you this morning? Was the dormitory comfortable?'

I returned her hug.

'It's not so bad. The food's good, my bed mate is learning fast not to kick me, and I've been promoted to teacher already.'

She laughed as she absent-mindedly straightened my collar. 'So I heard. And I have hopes that you will be impressed to hear that I've not been idle either. I think you'll be fair proud of me.'

I smiled at her cat-in-cream expression. 'Oh, yes? What wonders have you performed, Oh So Clever One?'

'Last night I made the acquaintance of my neighbour, one Mrs Moir.'

'Gracious!' I hadn't thought that Bridgit could do my job for me. In many ways this was so much better as there was no chance of Mrs Moir guessing our interest. A little trill of anticipation thrummed through me like a flute tuning up for the overture. 'How did you manage that so quickly?'

'Oh, I went to borrow a hot coal for the fire, claiming I'd let ours go out.'

'And?'

Bridgit shrugged. 'She gave it to me – a little grudging but she did stir herself to help me eventually.'

'That's not what I meant!' I was almost beside myself to hear her verdict.

'Then what did you mean?'

'*Could she be my mother?*' The words were out

before I had a chance to recall them. I hadn't wanted to state my question so baldly, but of course that was what I was thinking.

Bridgit took my hand sympathetically. 'I don't know. How could I so soon?' She squinted into my face. 'She looks a little like you, I suppose. Her hair is no longer such a flaming red, but it might have been when she was younger. I didn't really get much of a chance to study her – she was busy with her ironing. I'll say one thing for her: she keeps a tidy house.'

My spirits swooped down to my boots. It had been unreasonable of me to expect an answer. Mrs Moir was hardly likely to throw into the conversation, 'Oh, by the way, let me tell you about the child I abandoned in London.' But I was starving for a family, eager for any crumbs Bridgit could feed me. 'Anything else you can tell me?'

'I found out that she's got four children – a girl of seventeen, boys of fifteen and thirteen and a little girl of six.'

'Fifteen and thirteen.' I rubbed my hand over my brow.

Bridgit guessed the direction of my thoughts. 'How old are you, Cat?'

'I've never been sure – no more than fifteen, I guess. Mr Sheridan said I was an infant, not a tiny baby, when I was found – a toddling two-year-old or thereabouts. I suppose that rules her out as my mother.'

'Not necessarily.'

I cocked an eyebrow.

'Twins. Or you might fall between the two boys.'

I shook my head. 'The chance of that is very slight. She never claimed to be my mother in her letter after all. And I'm not sure I'd want her to be if she's managed to keep all her other children with her except me.'

Bridgit squeezed my hand comfortingly. 'Still, it is a possibility.'

Our discussion was brought to an end by the arrival of Overseer Shaw. A large man in a brown suit, he walked with the air of someone with much to do and too little time to accomplish it – a busy bear with a pocket watch.

'Mr Dale's new lasses?' he asked us briskly.

'Yes, sir.' We both bobbed curtseys.

'Follow me, then.' He strode towards Mill Two with us jogging along at his heels. 'The maister explained that he wanted ye to start in this mill. The wee lass will be a piecer – always need of nimble fingers in the spinning room. And ye, lass,' he nodded at Bridgit, 'are to be placed in the carding room, working as a tenter. Mr Dale suggested Moir look after ye – he's one o' our most experienced hands.'

Mr Dale had not forgotten our quest – this would give Bridgit a chance to get to know another of the family.

'The carding room,' announced the overseer.

He had opened the door on to a chamber filled with rumbling machines that resembled nothing more than two-humped iron monsters, the inner workings hidden by their metal casing. I'd never seen anything like it, not on this scale – the room seemed to stretch on and on. At one end of each beast stood barrels of raw cotton with women feeding the white fluff into the steely mouth of the carding contraptions; at the other, children were gathering the straightened fibres into containers to take them to the next stage in the spinning process. Stray cotton wafted in the air like dandelion seeds, catching on clothes and machines in an indiscriminate snowfall. Strange to think that this ghostly stuff came from fields on the other side of the world worked by slaves. Black slaves, white workers – we were all linked by the same thread.

Once the first shock of seeing the vast scale of the factory passed I studied the machinery more closely, trying to fathom what made it all work. Stout straps linked the wheel turning the mechanism to a revolving pole that ran the length of the room.

Seeing my interest, the overseer pointed upwards. 'There lies the secret of New Lanark. The waterwheel outside turns that shaft up there and that in turn powers all the machines on this floor.' He rubbed his hands for a moment, enjoying the spectacle of the world's most advanced technology. 'Nature harnessed by man – an inspiration to us all.'

'And what do these machines do, sir?' asked Bridgit.

'Have ye used a carder at home, lass?'

'Yes, sir, but they were two little paddles with spikes on – nothing like this.'

'Believe it or no, lass, but these machines are just a big version o' that. The cotton is tumbled inside until it comes out all combed straight and ready to turn into thread.'

He led Bridgit over to a man on the second machine. 'Moir, I have a new lass for ye.'

A skinny brown-haired man with an unhealthy pallor nodded at Bridgit. 'Pleased to meet ye, lass.' His attention immediately returned to his machine like a chef fearing his sauce might burn if he spared a moment to look away.

'I'll leave her in yer capable hands, Moir.'

'Aye, sir. Here, lass, I'll show ye where to put the raw cotton. It's simple enough.'

Leaving Bridgit to get accustomed to her new role, I followed the overseer up to the next floor. This room was also filled with machines, but these looked very different from the hump-backed carders, being made of open iron and wood frames suited to the delicate spinning of such fine threads. I tried to find something to compare them with and decided they were a little like giant pianofortes with a front section that moved out to transform them to a grand before retreating back to more modest proportions. Rows of bobbins sat on the top like a cluster of white doves watching the musician at play.

As we stood in the doorway, the front part of the loom rolled forward again, drawing out hundreds of white threads from bobbins of combed cotton, twisting as it went. Once it reached its limit the process reversed, but this time the threads were wound on to spindles, neatly combining the two processes of spinning and winding in one action. I found the sight mesmerizing; it looked like a vast game of cat's cradle played over and over by the machines.

Only then did I notice the people. Men and women tended the machines with anxious care, watching each bobbin and spindle. Occasionally one would shout over the din to a child-worker, pointing at the threads. The child would dive under the machine and next their fingers would be seen twisting together a broken thread from beneath. Work had to pause while they did this, but as soon as they were clear the machine would trundle back. No wonder Annie said you had to be quick.

The overseer took me to a woman standing with her back to us.

'Mrs Moir, I have a new piecer for ye.'

I gulped, my thoughts stunned as if I'd just been clubbed over the head with one of those bobbins. I hadn't been expecting to be working with her. Mr Dale was nothing if not direct in his approach.

The woman turned round and bobbed a curtsey to the overseer. I stared at her face, drinking it in, trying to memorize the details for later contemplation. Her hair was hidden by a cap, her nose freckled, skin pale. She turned her eyes on me and I swiftly dropped my gaze. For a moment, it had been like looking in a mirror: green eyes rimmed with my own reddish-blonde lashes.

'Get one of the other lasses to show her what to do,' the overseer continued.

'Aye, sir.'

'Good luck, lass.'

'Thank you, sir.' My words came out hoarsely, but I couldn't blame the cotton dust for that.

Once he had left, Mrs Moir beckoned over the little girl I had taught her letters. 'Jeannie, show the new lass her duties. What's yer name?'

'Catherine,' I murmured, trying to return Jeannie's delighted smile, but my face felt stiff, like the time I'd sneaked into the theatre dressing room and applied too much of Mrs Siddons' egg-white skin cleanser.

The little girl tugged on my hand. 'Dinna fret, Catherine; it's easy – easier than school.'

'Well then, let's set to.' I crouched down beside her, leaning against a pillar to regain my composure.

Mrs Moir had already forgotten us as she was busy replacing the bobbins on her loom. I watched her back, the flexing of her shoulder muscles as she worked. Slender, not tall – could she be?

Jeannie nudged me. 'Wake up, Catherine – the mule is moving again.'

The front of the loom began its glide across the floor. Jeannie spotted the break before I did and dived under the stretched cotton. I followed quickly. Above us the white threads vibrated like piano strings. Two ends sagged to the floor. Jeannie grabbed them and with a deft pinch and twist pieced them together.

'Now out we go,' she sang happily.

I scurried after her – we'd completed the move before the loom had begun its retreat, allowing the machine to work uninterrupted.

'Well done, Jeannie,' called her mother.

'So that is being gleg,' I muttered, my heart racing. Dodging the loom reminded me of trying to beat the waves on a beach; I had got my feet wet too many times to be confident of avoiding the mechanical mule.

'Ye'll get used to it,' grinned Jeannie with all the wisdom of her six years.

And she was right. By the end of the day I was able to spot a break, dip in, mend it and be out in thirty seconds flat. Yet despite the rest time at breakfast and dinner, by seven I was exhausted, my back aching, my knees sore. I had not thought of myself as being particularly soft, but these mill girls were tough if they could survive a day at the looms and still have energy for classes. Only my pride stopped me from complaining; I didn't want word to get back to annoying Jamie Kelly that I had found it at all difficult. And, of course, the thread of my attention was snagged on Mrs Moir, trailing after her as she paced the mill floor like a dangling end forgotten by the seamstress, but she was oblivious to my desperate interest. Several times little Jeannie had to nudge me in the ribs to remind me to watch the loom, not the spinner.

The rest of the week followed a similar pattern. The noise of the machines prevented much talk in the mill so I learned little about Mrs Moir except that she was attentive to her work, rarely smiled and took pride in her children, particularly Jeannie. The little girl was respectful to her mother, a touch afraid when she thought she had made a mistake but delighted at any praise. From this I deduced that Mrs Moir was a strict but loving parent. Comparing notes with Bridgit, it appeared that Mr Moir had a pale character to match his complexion. Not unkind, not loud, not in good health – he was the kind of man easily forgotten. Putting together what we knew, Mrs Moir seemed the last person one would expect to do anything so outrageous as to run off to London, have a child and dump her there.

So what then did she know about the circum - stances of my birth? And, Reader, how to get her to tell me the truth?

Sunday arrived – our day of rest. As the chapel was too small to contain all the workers, the children were expected to attend Sunday school instead. I was asked to read the Bible to the little ones – a task I thoroughly enjoyed as I had always loved the odd stories one can find tucked away in the Old Testament. I read them the tale of sulky Jonah and got them to act it out, resulting in some graphic retching as my whales pretended to cast up their accounts on the beach. I was half-expecting to be reprimanded for unsabbath-like behaviour but was told by the dominie that Mr Dale would approve of anything that encouraged us in our faith, even play-acting.

At the end of our performance, or should I say, lesson, I walked with Jeannie to the door. She was still bubbling over with excitement.

'Thank ye, thank ye! I so love making up plays!' she exclaimed. 'But Mither thinks they are evil. She dinna like it when I play make-believe.'

'Why not?' I asked indignantly, finding it hard to imagine anyone taking against dramatic entertainments.

Jeannie leaned towards me conspiratorially. 'She says they turn people bad, make them do wicked things.'

'They do not!' I huffed. 'I think your mother is mixing up *Macbeth* with real life!'

Jeannie slipped her hand in mine. 'What's Macbeth?'

I was deep into my explanation when we reached a gaggle of boys standing on the foot-bridge over the millstream. They were racing paper boats down the rapids.

'Mine's the winner!' crowed Jamie Kelly, clapping his hands over his head in celebration.

It would have to be him, of course.

'Look, Catherine – there are my brothers,' Jeannie said happily. 'I'll take ye to meet them.'

She had no idea that every small step of intimacy with the Moir family was a giant stride for me, something I needed to prepare for to protect my raw feelings. Before I could stop her, she was pushing her way through the gang and hooked a tall, handsome red-headed boy by the arm. He looked down and ruffled her hair.

'What do ye want, chuckie?'

'Ye have to meet Catherine, Ian – the lass I was telling you about.' Jeannie pulled me forward.

'Och, aye, the Sassenach.' The boy gave me a hostile inspection. 'Jamie's been bellyaching about ye all week.'

'Pleased to meet you too,' I said coldly.

He elbowed his neighbour in the ribs. 'See, Dougie, she dinna have two heads like Jamie said.'

Dougie, who was shorter, much stouter compared to his brother's thin stature, and topped with a mop of dark curly hair, placed a protective hand on Jeannie's shoulder. 'Ye're right, Ian. She doesna look so bad. I suppose she canna help being a soothlander.'

My temper was pricked by their thinly veiled scorn. I crossed my arms. 'And I suppose you can't help being ill-bred louts.'

Cat, Cat, what are you doing? my more sensible side berated me. This was a fine way to make their acquaintance: an exchange of insults.

A new voice broke into our conversation. 'I see ye've met Snippie.'

I groaned. Jamie Kelly had sauntered over to see what was happening. I let my hands drop, clenching them at my sides.

'Good morning, professor,' I said with barely a snarl.

'Aye, an hallockit lass as you said,' pronounced Ian with all the dignity of his year or two of seniority.

Jeannie felt for my hand and squeezed it. 'She is nae such thing, Ian. Ye are an ill-deedie brother for calling my friend names.'

Jamie took off his glasses to clean the lens. 'And are ye hen-hertit too, Snippie?'

'Actually, I've always considered myself brave as a lion,' I snapped back.

'Some of the lads and I are off to Corra Linn. Will ye come?'

I was instantly suspicious. 'Why do you have to be so brave-hearted to go on a little country walk?'

He folded his arms and smirked. 'Well, there's the wee matter of the estate wall and the ghillie with his gun. His dogs are worse – great scary beasts with a taste for man-flesh. The lady doesna like us trespassing.'

He was baiting me. He wanted me to refuse so he could laugh at me with his mates. But as you now know, Reader, I'm the kind of girl who takes up the bait, regardless of the consequences.

'I'm not afraid and I had already decided I wanted to see the falls. I'll come, and gladly.'

Jamie's face fell.

'Don't tell me *you* are too hen-hertit to go?' I mocked.

He straightened up and nodded to the Moir

brothers. 'Nae. We'll go now, before ye change yer mind.'

'Before *I* change *my* mind?' I protested.

'Run along, Jeannie.' Ian gave his sister a push in the back. 'And dinna say a word to Mither.'

Jeannie gripped my hand tighter. 'Nae, I want to come too.'

Dougie knelt down beside her. 'Ye ken ye canna do that. Ye're such a wee lassock that ye'll never get over the wall.'

Grumpily, with a curse on all over-protective brothers, Jeannie relinquished my hand and ran off in the direction of her home. Feeling the need for more support, I looked hopefully around for Bridgit, but she had gone to church with some workers of her Catholic faith and would not be back till dinner. I also doubted that she would be as game as me to go on such a foolhardy expedition. But I was eager now I had committed myself; a week confined inside the mill and I was ready for a challenge outdoors. And I had just been handed an opportunity to get to know the Moir boys – the Beau and the Boxer as I'd nicknamed them in my head.

'Right,' I said, rubbing my hands together. 'Where's this wall?'

Jamie had not been lying when he said that it was difficult to reach Corra Linn from the mills. The owner of the Bonnington estate clearly did not want the thousands of workers at the end of her garden tramping over the grounds: poaching the game, invading her privacy; so she had barricaded her lands off from New Lanark. Not that this stopped us. Having located a suitable tree near enough to the wall, I was up and over in no time – the first to reach the other side. The boys went very quiet when they realized I was no simpering Miss in need of their manly assistance.

'Where did ye learn to do that?' Dougie asked once he'd swung himself down with a hefty thump.

'In the navy,' I replied, straight-faced.

'Shh!' hissed Jamie. 'Do ye want the ghillie to find us?'

Following his lead, we crept along the bank of the Clyde. In places it was very steep and slippery and soon my hands, skirt hem and stockings were smeared with mud. I didn't care: it just felt so wonderful to be outside, though undoubtedly, Reader, it was a shame that I was wearing my Sunday best. My lace-edged petticoats would never be the same again. Yet, despite Jamie's dire warnings, the hint of danger only added spice to the adventure, well worth the sacrifice of a little trimming. The wood was a patched harlequin cape of green, gold, crimson and brown, dazzling in the sunshine. All around us the trees were shedding their leaves, a celebratory shower at autumn's wedding. Red squirrels darted along branches, launching themselves across the gaps in the canopy with the ease of rope-walkers at the fair; the rustle of the breeze applauded their antics. Nut husks crunched underfoot.

Climbing steeply, we rounded a bend and emerged out of the trees to a ledge overlooking the river. There before us was Corra Linn. The waterfall was more impressive than I had imagined: two great veils of white water tumbling over a ledge, kicking up spray from the pool beneath. As I gazed, the sun came out from behind a cloud; rainbows shimmered in the mist. I was caught in the spell, enchanted by how the falls could be always in motion yet still the same. The water roared, exultant at being free of the riverbed for one glorious moment of flight. I could almost feel what it might be like to tumble heedless over the edge, out of control . . .

A hand gripped my arm as I swayed forward.

'Watch out, ye glaikit Sassenach!' Jamie glared at me. 'I dinna want to have to dive in after ye!'

I laughed at him, sensing for once that his harsh tongue was due to his fear for my safety. 'Don't worry – I know from experience not to jump into a waterfall.'

'Ye are a strange lass. I dinna ken what to make o' ye.'

I sat down on a rock to enjoy the prospect in greater comfort. The Moir brothers had taken off their hats to collect nuts from a bush a little further up the slope, Ian doing the high branches, Dougie scrabbling around at his feet.

'I thought, professor, you'd decided I had two heads – a regular spawn of Satan.'

Jamie leaned against the rock beside me. 'Ye dinna fit here.'

I was reminded of Nick's insistence that the Irish labourers were not welcome in his patch. It seemed this territorial streak ran in us all. But still, it was odd in a manufactory with thousands of people from all over Scotland and further afield.

'Why don't I fit in? The mill employs all sorts. Bridgit says there are other Irish, people from the Isle of Skye, Edinburgh, Glasgow – what's wrong with me?'

'Ye speak funny.'

'*I* speak funny! Most of the time I don't even know what you are saying! Half your words probably never made it into Dr Johnson's Dictionary.'

Jamie chucked a stone over the edge into the river below. 'Who's Dr Johnson?'

'Only the greatest man of our century – with the possible exception of Mr Sheridan.' I thought for a moment. 'And Mr Wilberforce.'

'See! Now I dinna understand a word *ye* are saying!'

I scowled at him, but then realized how ridiculous it was to squabble about an accident of birth. After all my travels, surely I should know better? I'd learnt that we didn't live in one world, but lots of different ones where we all thought our concerns were the most important, no matter if we were a Creek Indian, Jamaican planter or London waiter. Unable to contain my laughter at his indignation, my shoulders began to shake.

'What's the matter with ye?' Jamie asked in exasperation. 'Are ye laughing at me?'

'At us both,' I gasped, wiping my eyes. 'You've taken against me for something I can't help, and I'm reacting like a prickly hedgehog whenever you challenge me. Don't you think that silly?'

He glared at me, making my laughter redouble. Then his mouth twitched. 'A hedgehog, ye say?'

I nodded.

'That's true. Then what does that make me?'

I had regained enough breath to wave towards him and gasp: 'Your choice. I don't want to be charged with insulting you again.'

He thought for a moment, biting his lip. 'A dog in a manger,' he declared, referring to Aesop's fable where a dog sat on food it could not enjoy rather than see others eat it.

'Very apt. So, pax then?'

'Aye, pax. Take my paw.'

We shook hands.

He tugged at his waistcoat and stood up, staring out at the falls. 'That still doesna mean that I like ye.'

'No, of course not, professor. But I thank you, kind sir, for disliking me for myself rather than for my place of birth.' I rose and bobbed a curtsey.

He snorted, whether in amusement or disgust was difficult to say.

A dog barked behind us. Startled, I dodged behind my rock. Jamie spun round, then went very still, like prey that had been cornered. The two Moirs hared off into the trees. I peeked out from my refuge to find Jamie confronted by a tall man dressed in green tweeds, a hat decorated with fishing flies. His eyebrows flourished like some rust-coloured plant life on his craggy face, a long moustache drooped over his lips. He carried a rifle which was now aimed at Jamie's belly. A black Labrador waited at his side, watching Jamie with unfriendly intent, teeth bared.

'Give it up!' growled the man. 'Show me what ye've poached!'

A sickly white beneath his freckles, Jamie stuttered: 'I s-swear to ye, Mr Brown, I havena taken a thing.'

'I ken ye too well, Jamie Kelly, to believe that. Ye are a wudscud in need of a skelping, that's what ye are.' He raised his hand in a thrashing gesture. 'And it's a skelping ye'll get the day by my hand. Show me what ye've snecked!'

Thinking fast, I smoothed down my skirt, now thanking my lucky stars that I was wearing my London clothes rather than my mill uniform. I stepped out from behind my rock and fixed the ghillie with my best duchess glare.

'I say, my man, why on earth are you pointing your gun at my guide?' My tone was the most arrogant aristocratic drawl I could muster. I lifted my chin, staring him down; the rifle barrel sagged as he gaped in surprise at my appearance. I forged on.

'I really cannot abide such loutish behaviour. This boy was showing me the falls. Is there a law against one of the master's guests walking in his grounds?' I crossed my fingers, hoping that the ghillie would not call my bluff. I didn't even know if the master of the estate was at home.

'Mistress,' Jamie hissed.

'Of course, I mean the mistress,' I corrected, kicking myself for forgetting that the Bonnington estate was owned by a lady.

'Ye know the mistress?' marvelled the ghillie.

Oh dear. I suppose I did push his credibility to the limit in my mud-stained clothing, not quite the fine lady I was trying to be.

'But of course.' I gave a gay laugh. 'My parents are her good friends. We are here for the . . .' I gazed around for inspiration, saw the ghillie's hat, and improvised, '. . . for the fishing. And hunting of course. Not me, you understand, but my father. I thought I'd . . . er . . . embroider this view so I asked the boy here to show me the way.'

I have no idea what he made of my explanation, but I had confused him enough to make him feel unsure of his grounds of complaint against Jamie.

'The lady rarely has visitors from England,' murmured the ghillie.

'Well, today she does – unexpected ones. Our carriage broke down not far from here and she was kind enough to invite us to stay.'

Jamie shook his head a tad, a warning that I was giving too much detail.

I changed tack, choosing a direction I hoped would push the ghillie further into bewilderment. 'You cannot deny this is a fine view. I've seen little to match it in my travels, not even in Paris. I can't wait to get out my embroidery hoop and begin. My governess was right when she said it was one of the wonders of this part of the world.'

I could see the ghillie's eyes begin to glaze over. I continued.

'Yes, I think chain stitch for leaves. See, over there.' I pointed to the forest. 'And satin stitch for the river.' I tapped my lip, a gesture borrowed from

Mr Sheridan. 'If only I can find silks to do justice to the magnificence of the scene. I don't suppose you know a good supplier of embroidery threads in the district, do you, Mr Brown?'

The ghillie flinched as if I'd poked him with a needle. 'Me?'

I frowned. 'No, you don't look the embroidering sort. Your wife perhaps?' I added hopefully.

Jamie stifled a snort of laughter in an unconvincing sneeze.

'I dinna have a wifie!' growled the ghillie.

I wasn't surprised, not with eyebrows that had a life of their own and grizzly bear manners.

'What a shame. I shall have to return to the house and consult my dear mother, Lady . . . er . . . Siddons. Yes, that's what I'll have to do. Good morning to you.'

With a flounce of my skirts, I swept past him.

'Boy, are you going to show me the way back or not?' I snapped with sublime arrogance.

My question unfroze Jamie. He tugged a fore - lock in my general direction and jogged after me.

'This way, my lady,' he called, passing me on

the path and heading off into the trees.

Once out of sight we both broke into a run, keeping going until our lungs felt as if they would burst. We reached the point in the estate wall where we had come over and found the Moir brothers waiting for us. I collapsed, hands on my knees, chest heaving. Jamie rolled on the ground, looking as if he were in pain.

'Are ye hurt?' Dougie asked Jamie, patting him to find his injury.

Jamie sat up, pushing Dougie away. 'Nae, but nae thanks to ye hen-hertit laddies.' He gulped a couple of breaths and then the laughter escaped in great gusts. 'Ye should have seen her, Dougie! She asked Ghillie Brown for embroidery tips, just like a fine lady. He was so bumbazed, he let us go.'

Ian joined in the laughter and thumped me on the back. 'Ye saved Jamie's hide, that ye did. Lady Ross-Baillie is very fierce about trespassers. She's so proud of her grounds and cattle, she's given the ghillie orders to chase us all off – told him shoot if he has any doubt. That was well done o' ye, Catherine.'

I straightened up, my stitch beginning to ease. 'It was fun. The ghillie was such a flat.'

Ian frowned. 'Flat?'

'Gullible.'

'Ah, ye mean a daftie?'

'I suppose I do.' I glanced over my shoulder, wondering if the soft-footed ghillie was still stalking us. We had relished our victory for longer than was wise, making no effort to be quiet. 'But if it's all the same to you boys, I think we should get back over this wall.'

'Let me help ye,' said Jamie, stooping by the wall and forming a cup of his hands to give me a leg-up. He saw that I was about to refuse. 'Nay, Snippie, dinna make us lads feel so useless.'

He needed to display his gallantry now I had rescued him from the fire-breathing dragon of a gamekeeper.

'In that case, professor, I'll accept your help.' Putting my muddied shoe into his grip, I hauled myself to the top of the wall, trying not to display my ankles in the process. Once up, I helped Jamie and the Moirs climb, then we swung down on a well-placed branch and back to the safety of New Lanark mill.

Jamie bowed, cap clutched to his breast. 'I hope my lady enjoyed her excursion to Corra Linn?'

'I am much obliged to you all,' I replied, dipping into an elegant curtsey. 'I am now going to retire to my couch and begin my tapestry. Good day, gentlemen.'

'Dinna I get paid for my trouble?' Jamie asked, his lips twitching.

'In your dreams, professor. In your dreams.'

I swept away, hoots of laughter ringing in my ears.

SCENE 3 – REVELATION

Over the next few weeks, my mission to find out more about my origins appeared to be going nowhere, like a carriage axle-deep in mud. I felt I knew no more about Mrs Moir than I had at the end of the first day. It was the punishment of Tantalus – the grapes of knowledge dangling just out of my reach.

Perhaps I failed because the working week passed in a haze of exhaustion and on the one day when I had any free time (Sunday) I had no opportunity to see her, busy as she was with the household tasks. I must admit to a grudging admiration: like the majority of women employed in the mill, she never stopped trying to eke out a respectable existence for her family from meagre resources. A fierce little competition ruled in Long Row for the cleanest doorstep, prettiest window boxes and tidiest children (though admittedly Mrs Moir was never going to win that one with Ian and

Dougie at home). As I walked past the cottage trying to find a natural excuse for my questions, she was perpetually busy, having no time for anything but a nod in my direction.

I confided my frustration to Bridgit. We were sitting on the slope by the waterwheel one dinner hour. The wheel was turning slowly, water pouring from the paddles, tumbling from the millstream back down to the Clyde. You could become mesmerized if you stared at it for too long. Bridgit, however, had her eyes fixed on my frowning face as she laid out our picnic of bread and cheese. For weeks now she had counselled me in her gentle way to be patient, told me we had made progress, warned me not to expect too much.

I didn't really want to hear such sensible words – I'd always been more inclined to rush my fences – but I knew she was right.

'But how can I find out the truth?' I asked, wrapping a shawl more tightly round my shoulders against the nip in the air.

Bridgit smiled, her violet eyes taking on a fond

expression as she looked at me. 'You could always knock on the door and introduce yourself – put an end to all this uncertainty.'

I groaned and rubbed my knees. 'If I did that, then what would be the point of all this time spent working with her?'

She laughed at my indignant expression. 'Don't tell me, Cat, that you can't do an honest day's work without complaining?'

I picked a bit of cotton off the hem of her skirt. 'Course I can. I just find it so . . . so boring.'

'I thought boredom was the privilege of fine lords like your Earl of Arden. The rest of us are too busy earning our living to worry about being bored.'

I laughed at myself. She was right: I sounded ridiculous and self-pitying. I was pleased I'd brought her along; her good sense had helped keep me on track on more than one occasion.

'What about you, Bridgit? Do you regret coming with me?'

She shook her head. 'No, not at all. My brothers were pleased to see the back of me and

I . . . to be sure, I had no reason to stay.' She couldn't hide the note of regret despite her brave words.

I touched her arm lightly. 'I'm sure your brothers love you in their own way.'

She shook her head. 'I think not.'

'They do.'

'Then they have a strange way of showing it.'

'They're just bitter. Remember what it was like here at the beginning? I felt like thrashing Jamie for his snide words, but I didn't, and now we're friends.'

Bridgit shook her head. 'I doubt my brothers have escaped a thrashing, not with all the trouble they were stirring up.'

'I'm sure they are safe. Syd knows what they mean to you. He won't let justice be taken too far.' I had received a letter from Frank just the day before, telling me Syd was mending well. There had been no mention of further trouble in the market, which suggested Syd had been able to keep a lid on things.

Bridget passed me a wedge of bread topped

with cheese. 'He sounds a fine man, your Syd.'

I chuckled. 'Yes, he is – but he's not mine.' I took a big bite.

And then, like the turn of the waterwheel, my thoughts spun into a new pattern in my head. Syd needed a new sweetheart; Bridgit needed someone to love and look after her. And I'd always fancied myself something of a matchmaker . . .

I cast a sideways look at my friend, sitting at peace as she admired the trees on the far bank of the river, wisps of her long, dark hair waving in the breeze. Could she guess my thoughts? I hoped not, as it would only spoil my lovely idea if she suspected what I had in mind. I just knew she and Syd would suit if they gave each other a chance. And a match between them would have the added advantage that, like a marriage of state, it would be a way to reconcile the two communities, Londoners and Irish. Covent Garden could declare an end to hostilities. All I required was a little time to put my skills to work. That thought made me even more impatient to finish my task here in the north.

The bell rang, summoning us to return. I brushed down my skirt, folded the empty napkin and tucked it back in Bridgit's basket. 'Come on, Bridgit.'

Bridgit choked on a laugh at my unaccustomed enthusiasm. 'So eager now?'

'Why not? I've got work to do.' I tugged her towards the mill, joining the stream of workers heading back to their looms. 'Did I ever tell you how Syd saved me from a murderous sea captain?'

November passed in a procession of cheerless, dank days. I rarely saw the sun, except for a fleeting glimpse at dinner time, as we now rose in the dark and returned to the dormitory after nightfall. Colds and snuffles passed from one girl to another like a baton in a relay race, and soon all of us were sporting unattractive red noses and teary eyes. Martha, who had still not warmed to my presence in her bed, complained that I kept her awake with my sneezing. I pointed out that her icy feet were chilling my back. I think that made it a stalemate.

One frosty morning, I woke with a sore throat and aching bones. For one moment I considered the possibility that my malaria (caught while in the Caribbean) had returned, but then discarded that idea for the more likely chance that I had succumbed to the influenza doing the rounds of the mill. Annie reported my condition to Goodwife Ross and I was allowed to remain in bed. Despite feeling wretched, it was a luxury to have the covers all to myself and sleep the day away. Bridgit came to visit after work, the Moir boys and Jamie sent a basket of chestnuts to cheer me, even the dominie sent a note wishing me a speedy recovery.

Fortunately, I did not have the illness too badly and shook it after three days. Allowed Saturday off to recuperate, I was expected back at work on Monday.

I emerged on Sunday afternoon to take a breath of air with Bridgit, walking somewhat wobbly like a newly birthed foal. She had invited me to eat with her rather than in the hubbub of the dormitory dining room. Giving me the warmest spot by the fire in the kitchen of the two-roomed cottage, Bridgit set about cooking a hearty stew for us and her landlady.

'This is lovely.' I stretched my hands to the grate, pausing to admire the neat arrangement of the kitchen. A little pot of geraniums sat on the windowsill; one late flower in bloom. An alphabetical sampler decorated the wall. By the other chair, the schoolteacher had a shelf of books – copies of *The Rambler*, Richardson's *Clarissa* in many volumes, a collection of Shakespeare's plays. I could imagine such a future for myself: a little cottage furnished with the belongings I had paid for out of my own earnings. A proper home.

'So, tell me what's been happening while I've been in bed,' I said, stretching my toes out to the fire.

Bridgit put the pot on the stove to stew and sat opposite me, wiping her fingers on her apron.

'I've some bad news for you, I'm afraid.'

I sat up straight. 'What's happened?'

'The Moirs have gone down with the flu.

Jeannie is very bad, they say. Mr Moir – you know he's not healthy at the best of times – he's seriously ill. The worst is that Mrs Moir has developed pneumonia.'

Pneumonia. That was often a killer.

I mentally chided myself when I realized my first thought had been fear that if Mrs Moir died I'd never find out the truth. So selfish. I gave my better self a shove to the fore.

'What about Dougie and Ian?'

'They are helping look after their parents. Their older sister, Katrine, is in charge. Have you met her yet?'

I shook my head.

'She's about my age. Red-headed.' Bridgit paused. 'She looks a lot like you, in fact, except she's much bigger.'

My heart did a clumsy flip-flop like a badly trained acrobat. There it was again – the hint that there might be substance in the claim that the Moirs were related to me.

'Can we do anything to help?'

'I was going to offer some of the stew. You can

take it along if you like.' Bridgit knew I had been looking for a chance to meet the Moirs at home for weeks now.

I gave a jerky nod. 'All right. Thank you. I'd like to do that.'

An hour later I knocked at the door of Number Five. The door was pulled open abruptly and I found myself face to face with the oldest sister, Katrine. She gave me a hard look.

'Do I ken ye?' she asked, wiping a weary hand across her brow.

I fumbled for an answer, too busy ticking off the points where I resembled her – freckles, eyes, curling red hair . . .

'Um, yes. I mean no. I know your brothers and Jeannie. I work with your mother in the mill.'

She nodded. 'Och, aye, the wee Sassenach. Can I help ye?'

'Sorry, I meant to say – I've brought you some stew if you would like it. Bridgit cooked it – she's Irish so it must be an excellent stew.' I was blabbering but I couldn't seem to stop myself.

She stepped back and waved me in.

'Thank ye both. I could do with some help, if the truth be told. Ian's caught the fever and I'm no feeling so good myself.'

Now she mentioned it, she did look unnaturally pale. This family needed rescuing.

Perhaps my family.

'My name's Catherine,' I said as I placed the stew on the stove to warm through. I spotted Jeannie lying on a little truckle bed by the hearth. Her eyes flickered open and she gave me a wan smile. Kneeling down beside her, I brushed her hair off her forehead.

'How are you, sweet pea?'

'Getting better, Catherine,' she whispered hoarsely, slipping her hand into my palm. 'And ye?'

'Fit as a fiddle now, just like you will be in a day or two.'

She nodded, though I didn't like the hectic flush on her cheeks. I raised my eyes to Katrine who was swaying by the kitchen table, a pile of vegetables waiting to be chopped. She shook her head slightly and sighed.

'I dinna ken what to do, Catherine,' Katrine

suddenly burst out, a sob in her voice. 'Faither's mortal sick, Mither is worse, and now Ian.' I could almost hear the snap as she broke under the weight of responsibility for so many sick people.

I stood up, my duty clear. 'I tell you what you should do, Katrine: go to bed. There is no point you getting sick as well. I'll make broth and see everyone gets some.'

Katrine fought a feeble rearguard action – really she was desperate to go into full retreat. 'The doctor said I must bathe Jeannie to keep the fever down.'

'I'll do that. Just let me tell Bridgit where I am and I'll then be back to stay.'

As soon as Bridgit heard that Katrine was sickening she, of course, wanted to help too. Refusing further argument, we took over the kitchen, ushering Katrine up to her rest. Not long after, Dougie came down from getting Ian into bed, a tough task despite his stocky strength because Ian had been adamant that he should look after his parents and sisters. Wrestled into submission, Ian was now asleep. Relieved to have our company,

Dougie insisted on helping Bridgit with the soup, grabbing the little paring knife and setting to on the carrots. He said he welcomed the distraction from worry for his family. Together they prepared enough for the following day while I tended the little girl. Then, leaving Jeannie slumbering, I went upstairs to find the rest of the patients. In the back bedroom Ian was fretful, blankets tossed on the floor. I covered him up and left a cup of water by his bedside in case he woke with a thirst. Katrine was lying quietly in her bed behind a curtain on the other side of the room. I wondered if her problem was exhaustion more than anything as she had dark rings under her eyes. She did not seem unduly hot when I touched her.

Finally, I ventured into the front bedroom. In the double bed I found the most serious cases. I could hear Mr Moir's pained breathing, the rattle of each gasp. By contrast his wife was very still and for one ghastly moment I thought she might be dead, but no, she was taking shallow breaths. Gingerly I touched her wrist, stroking it gently. What was she to me? That question would have to wait until they were better. I left the bedroom, deciding that they needed sleep more than soup.

'I'm going to stay until they are recovered,' I announced on my return to the kitchen.

Bridgit nodded, accepting my decision without protest. Dougie, however, was quick to object.

'But ye canna do that, Catherine: ye'll get into trouble with the overseer! He'll dock your pay.'

'I don't care. Your family needs a nurse.'

Dougie frowned. 'I'll do it.'

'You might be next to fall ill. I've had this flu already – I won't get it again.'

'But ye're a stranger. Why do this for us?'

That was the question, wasn't it? Was I really a stranger or one of their blood? Would Dougie know the answer? I had to speak to his mother first; I'd only ask him or Ian as a last resort.

'I'm doing this because I want to,' I replied firmly. 'So let's not argue about it, please.'

That night, I slept in a chair by Jeannie's truckle bed. The little girl passed a quiet night and I began to hope that she really was improving. The next morning, she ate a little soup before falling asleep again. At least I could give over bathing her as her temperature had fallen back to normal. That was just as well as I was now required to sponge Ian whose fever had soared. I got several cuffs from him in his delirium as he objected to the tepid water trickling down his neck. On his way out to work, Dougie told me I was welcome to save up the blows and hit Ian when he got better. I said I would look forward to it.

'And tell the overseer I've had a relapse,' I added.

'Ye'll lose another day's pay, Catherine.' He was obviously having second thoughts about handing over responsibility for his family to me.

This had never been about wages as far as I was concerned. 'That's no matter, Dougie. You've got five people relying on you – you've got to work.'

Fortunately, Katrine was well enough to tend to her own needs but I soon became familiar with the mechanics of bedpans for the other members of the household. When I had wished to become better acquainted with the Moirs this wasn't quite what I had in mind.

I suppose you might say, Reader, that the reward for my labours came mid-morning as I tried to get Mrs Moir to take some broth. Sitting her up against some pillows, I gently eased the spoon between her lips. She sipped it, not even bothering to open her eyes, until a spasm of coughing shook her.

'There, now,' I said softly, wiping the soup off her chin. 'When it's passed I'll give you some more.'

'Who is that?' she whispered.

'It's Catherine – from the mill.'

She opened her eyes a crack. The room was in half-light, curtains drawn, so she could only see me in silhouette against the window. Reaching out she took my wrist in her feeble grip.

'Nae, it's Jesse: ye canna fool me, lass. Ye never could.'

Rather than annoy her, I agreed. 'Yes, yes, it's Jesse. Now take another spoonful for me.'

Mrs Moir's brow furrowed in confusion.

'What ye doing here, Jesse? They said ye were dead.'

'Well, I'm not. I'm here with some lovely soup. I didn't cook it so it's bound to be good. You need something to eat, Mrs Moir. You need your strength.'

She batted the spoon away, more interested in the puzzle I presented than the offer of food. Her cheeks were sunken; so frail, she looked as if a puff of wind would blow her away.

'Ye canna be her. But ye look like her wi' yer hair all wild.'

I touched my head self-consciously, realizing for the first time I was in her company without my cap.

'Who are ye?'

My heart was turning over and over like cotton in the carding machine. The moment to tell the truth had arrived.

'I'm Cat Royal, Mrs Moir. Maudie Stirling if you like,' I added, remembering the name from the letter.

Mrs Moir's hand dropped back on the cover. 'Ye came then,' she said in a flat voice, not really surprised. 'I would have come to ye – it was my duty. It would have been better that way. I didna want ye here bringing the shame with ye.'

'I know. You asked for money to do so.'

She shifted on the pillows uneasily. 'Ye see how we live, Maudie. There is nae money to chase after Jesse's mistakes.'

Was she saying that I was one of those mistakes? Her coldness left me empty. This was not the rapturous reunion for which I had once hoped – an outpouring of tears, hugs and joy.

'Who is Jesse, ma'am?' My tone matched hers in coolness though inside my feelings were tumbled, scraped and buffeted.

'*Was*, lass. Yer mither's dead. Buried in Stirling where the family came from.'

My hand was shaking. I put the spoon down and clutched my fingers together in my lap. I had been foolish to hope that my mother might still be living. Of course not. Life wasn't like a fairytale.

'Will you tell me about her?'

Another bout of coughing racked Mrs Moir's body. I waited for it to pass. Mr Moir turned over in the bed, mercifully still deeply asleep. I wanted no interruption to this conversation.

'I've never told anyone the whole story,' Mrs Moir said in a wisp of a voice.

'I think you should tell me.'

Her eyes locked on my face and she half-lifted a hand to touch my cheek before thinking twice and letting it fall back. 'I must protect my weans from the disgrace.'

I would swear to anything to get this story from her. 'I will not endanger you or your family if you would just tell me what I need to know.'

She took a breath. 'Ye are my wee sister's first child.'

'Jesse was your sister?'

She nodded.

'That makes you my aunt?' My mind clutched on to this wonderful news: I did have family! Real, proper blood family! 'And – and Jeannie, Dougie, Ian, Katrine: they're my cousins?'

She nodded again. 'But they're no to ken about ye – they mustna know what wicked things Jesse did.' Her face looked quite bitter as she spoke these words. 'I must have yer word on that.'

'You'd keep my family from me because of something my mother did?' I asked incredulously.

'Aye, I would. Ye've gone the same way. I read the stories. I ken ye, Maudie. Ye're just like Jesse.'

Those wretched pamphlets! A rogue publisher had stolen my manuscripts and then sensationalized them, making me out to be a thief, queen of London's underworld, to improve their circulation.

'I'm nothing like that. You shouldn't believe everything you read, Aunt.' The word tasted strange on my tongue – uncomfortable.

'Dinna call me that!' Her hand made an angry swipe towards me, as if she was wiping my words out of the air. I flinched, feeling as if I'd been slapped. I grappled for my self-control, reminding myself she was sick and weak.

'All right, Mrs Moir, I give my word. Tell me about your sister, please.'

I could hear the sound of the mill in the distance, spinning, spinning without pause. How I wanted to draw out the threads of my life story from this woman, but unlike those looms she was broken, exhausted, offering only bits and pieces, not enough to weave a whole cloth. 'Please.'

Mrs Moir sighed, her breath wheezy. 'She was a wild lass, Jesse Stirling. In love with the pleasures of the town, theatre, dancing. She couldna settle to a quiet life and a douce home. Ran away wi' an actor when she was sixteen. Our faither disowned her for the shame she brought on the family.' Distressed by the memory, she struggled for breath, her chest heaving. I waited as patiently as I could for her to be well enough to continue. 'She went to London. Sent me word secretly from time to time.'

'The actor? What was his name?' I asked eagerly.

'It doesna matter, lass. He left her. She never said he was yer faither. I dinna ken how Jesse lived – poorly, I've nae doubt – but she had ye and managed for a year or two. Then she met someone else – a countryman from these parts. She got with child again, reckless lass. She had to choose – go with him to have the baby or stay with ye. She said she kenned ye'd be well looked after at the theatre – that it was best for ye. Her man didna like her wee by-start. Wanted to marry her, he did, but nae wi' the evidence o' her bad behaviour hanging on her skirts. His family wouldna accept her wi' ye in tow.'

Mrs Moir fell silent again, the tale proving too much for her strength. So I'd been just a millstone round my mother's neck that she cut free to take the second chance she'd been offered.

'But she left me on the theatre steps on a cold winter's night,' I said hoarsely. 'I could have died.'

'Nae, she watched ye being picked up and taken inside. She said yer faither's people would look after ye. She regretted the necessity of leaving ye, but she had a new life, a countryman to look after her, and a new baby to think of.'

'My father's people?'

'Aye, ye were begotten backstage, lass. A true child of the theatre, Jesse said.'

'Did she tell you who my father was?'

'Nae. With Jesse, there was always more than one possibility. She was a wicked lass – nae morals at all.'

So the truth about my father was forever lost to me. Whoever he was, he probably never knew I existed.

'And then what happened?'

'The Scotsman – his name was Kenneth Bruce – didna seem to mind her ways. She married the man, came back to Scotland and had a wee lad. She died a few days later – God's judgement nae doubt on her ill deeds. Her husband passed away a year or two after.'

I squeezed my knuckles until they hurt. 'And the boy – did he live?'

'Aye. He came to us for a while but couldna settle – just like his mither. Ran off with some o' his faither's kin – cattle thieves the lot o' them. Last I heard they were living in an old tower house in the hills.'

We sat in silence for a long while. I had an aunt who didn't want to know me, a brother who lived with thieves, a mother who had chosen her security over her own child, abandoning me to who knows what fate in London.

I smiled with sour self-knowledge. Pop, pop, pop: that was the sound of my soap-bubble fantasies breaking at the pinprick of truth.

'What is his name?' I asked softly.

'Who? Yer brother?'

I nodded.

'Why, Rabbie o' course.' She gave a throaty chuckle that turned into a pained cough.

'Why "of course"?'

'Robert Bruce – wee Rabbie Bruce. My sister always had a hankering for drama so she named him after a Scottish king.'

'And she named me Maudie. Was I christened?'

'Nae, I doubt it, lass. That ramstam sister o' mine never went to kirk in London. She likely forgot.'

Of course, my feckless mother would be so careless. I didn't even have a legal name. At least that left me free to choose my own. Maudie Stirling? Who on earth was that? No one anyone wanted.

Mrs Moir rubbed at her throat fretfully. I offered her a sip of water and then she sank back on the bed. 'I'm tired, Maudie. Leave me be now. I've told ye all I ken. I'm sorry about Jesse – about yer mither. Some people canna be saved.'

Despite my desire to pick over the information and draw out every last thread from her memory,

I knew it would be cruel to push a sick woman any further. I stood up, taking the unfinished soup with me.

'Thank you for telling me, Mrs Moir. I'll let you sleep now. But I'm not Maudie. I'm Cat Royal.'

Between my nursing duties, I spent the rest of the day pondering Mrs Moir's tale. For the moment my emotions were frozen, my brain struggling to comprehend the facts. The gap that had once held the imaginary mothers of my dreams had been filled by a red-haired Scottish lassie on a collision course with the tough world of the London streets. That particular carriage-crash had produced me. She'd hauled herself out of the wreckage, found a husband, grasped a new life and then promptly died.

But none of my relations had bothered to find me until evidence of my continued existence had been thrust upon them. That hurt, driving home just how unwanted I was.

But at least my cousins were blameless. The news that Jeannie, Katrine and Ian were so closely related to me made the task of caring for them even more poignant. I wanted to whisper to them who I was as I cooled their faces with a cloth; I longed to ask for their love in return for mine; but my promise to Mrs Moir held me back. And if I had spoken, would they have recoiled in horror as she had done and assumed I was a bad apple in the family basket, just as their mother warned? But they at least knew me for myself, and had become my friends. If I could persuade Mrs Moir to acknowledge me, would they be happy to accept me as their cousin?

And I hadn't promised not to make myself known to my half-brother, had I, Reader? Wee Rabbie Bruce, living with cattle thieves – but still my kin. Was he aware I even existed? I wondered.

Bridgit and Dougie came in from work soon after seven.

'How are they?' my cousin asked.

'All quiet. Ian seems much better this evening. I'm most worried about your mother –

she's not roused since this morning.'

I was secretly afraid I'd overstretched her strength; her condition had gone downhill since our conversation.

Dougie clattered up the stairs. Jeannie sat up in her little truckle bed, looking sweetly tousled.

'Where's my mither?' she asked.

I crouched at her side. 'Still in bed, sweet pea. How are you feeling?'

'Much better, thank ye.'

I gave her a hug: at least there was one of the family back from the brink.

Bridgit stroked my shoulder. 'What's the matter, Cat?'

I stood up and put my back to the little girl. 'You can tell?' I gave Bridgit a rueful smile.

'Yes. You look upset.'

I lowered my voice. 'I feel I've been through the wringer today. Mrs Moir told me what I came to find out.'

Bridgit's eyes widened. 'And?'

'She's my aunt – can you believe it? According to her, my mother was a lightskirt who left me in

London to marry a Scotsman. I have no father –
or at least no one who knows he's my father – but
I do have a brother.'

Bridgit's frown turned into a radiant smile. 'A
brother? How wonderful!'

'But he's gone bad and joined a band of
thieves.'

'Oh.'

'So I'm from excellent stock, you see. So good
that Mrs Moir has banned me from making any
claims on her or my cousins. I'm not even to
announce my presence.'

Bridgit looked indignant on my behalf.
'She's a narrow woman. How can she treat you
that way?'

'Quite easily. She's tried with my brother, you
see, but he ran away. She probably thinks I'd bring
some similar scandal down on them all.'

Bridgit pulled me into her arms and gave me a
much-needed hug.

'If she persists in thinking that, then she's a
foolish woman. So now you know, what now?
Home?'

I shook my head. 'I thought I'd go brother-hunting.'

The quiet of the house was broken by the clatter of boots on the stairs. We both turned as Dougie staggered into the kitchen. One look at his face and I knew something was badly wrong.

'What is it?' I asked, holding out a hand to him.

He took it blindly. 'It's Mither. She's dead.'

'What!' exclaimed Bridgit, dashing from the room.

I couldn't move – I'd killed her with my questions. But no, that was a stupid thought – she'd been ill. It wasn't my fault.

'I sat with her for a moment,' Dougie continued. 'She knew I was there because she squeezed my hand. Then her breathing got quieter and quieter – and then it stopped. I tried to wake her but I . . . I couldna.'

'Oh, Dougie!' I hugged him. I could hear Bridgit's light footsteps overhead as she checked the front bedroom.

'Mither?' whispered Jeannie.

Dougie burst into stormy, gasping tears. I gathered Jeannie into our hug so the three of us stood together, rocking the pain away.

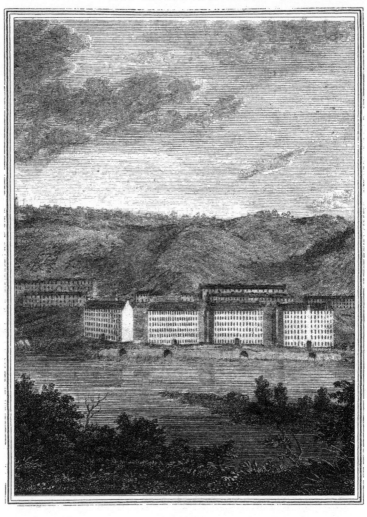

*Act IV – In which Cat is tempted to
eat her words about brothers . . .*

Act IV

SCENE 1 – BROTHER-HUNTING

My aunt's funeral took place three days later in the dreary graveyard of the parish church. Leafless trees edged the plot, a permanent guard of forked-limbed mourners presiding over us mortals doomed to be buried at their roots. The rest of the Moirs had recovered enough to attend but from the look on their faces it was clear that the emotional blow had taken all strength from them. They were sinking like a tent with the centre pole removed. They clung together at the graveside, finding what comfort they could in each other. Katrine had a stoic expression as she watched her mother's coffin being lowered into the damp soil; she seemed to be silently assuming the burden of caring for the family, steeling herself for stepping into Mrs Moir's shoes. Mr Moir, still weak, leaned on Dougie's broad shoulder, his face grey. Ian cuddled Jeannie in his arms while the little girl sobbed.

As for me, I felt I had no right to stand with them. Held by a promise to a dead woman, I could not now make myself known to my cousins without dishonouring her memory. So I stood outside the family group, just another neighbour come to pay her respects. Awash with confusion, grief and hurt, I tried to feel as I should for my cousins but struggled with selfish regrets.

'Cat, if we are going to leave the mill, I think we should go soon,' said Bridgit in a low voice at my side. 'This place is doing you no good. It's written all over your face. And I promised your friends I'd look after you.'

She was right: I was suffering the torment of seeing within my grasp what I'd always wanted but had promised not to seize. It would be so easy just to cross the muddy ground and announce, 'Hello, I'm your Aunt Jesse's mistake, Cat Royal.' I was secretly hoping that the truth would out without me having to break my word, but thus far none of the Moirs had displayed any leaps of intuition as to my true identity. My soulful, meaningful stares were doubtless just taken as sympathy; little did they know I was mourning not only my aunt but the biggest missed opportunity of my life.

I turned from the funeral party as the Moirs and their neighbours filed back to the house. With a sigh I took a final glance around the churchyard, at the gravediggers spading the soil on top of the coffin. I felt as if they were burying my past along with my poor aunt.

'Yes, you're right,' I said. 'We should go. There's nothing more I can achieve here.'

'Leaving so soon, Snippie? Just when I've decided ye're no so bad.' Jamie Kelly emerged out of the crowd to hook me by the elbow and offered his free arm to Bridgit.

He wasn't used to seeing me in anything but a combative mood so I snapped into it, despite my depressed spirits. 'Playing the gentleman now, professor?'

'Aye. I want to hear about yer daft plans. I thought ye had more gumption than to give up now. Too soft after all, are ye?'

His ploy to goad me into staying was transparent. Sweet really.

'Yes, Jamie, I'm so weak and feeble I've decided to slink off down south, tail between my legs, awed by the superior staying power of you braw Scots.'

He shook his head. 'I dinna believe it! I ken you now: ye wouldna run away!'

I gave him a smile. 'I believe, Mr Kelly, that was a compliment. You'll have all the girls swooning at your feet if you carry on this way.'

He flushed and glanced sideways at Bridgit. I already suspected that he nurtured tender feelings for my companion despite her being several years his senior. But he would have to cure himself of his admiration for Bridgit: I had other plans for her, God – or should I say, Syd – willing.

Jamie adjusted the woollen scarf dangling around his neck. 'Perhaps it was a wee bit o' reese – but it's the truth,' he said defensively.

I turned my head to hide my amusement. Buttery-lippit – that's what they called a flatterer round these parts, but Jamie would never find the role easy as he was as sharp-tongued as me in his own way and a touch clumsy with his compliments.

'Jamie, do you remember a little boy called Rabbie Bruce, kin to the Moirs?' Bridgit asked, deftly changing the subject.

Jamie searched the crowd at the graveside. 'Aye, Ian and Dougie's cousin. Did he come then? That was brave o' him.'

Bridgit shook her head, tugging him further away from any listeners. 'No, we don't think he was here. But we need to find him.'

Jamie frowned. 'Why do you want him? He's gone wild – a briganer skulking out at the tower house with a pack o' Bruces. He's set to be one o' the worst when he's full-grown. I'd say ye best stay away from the likes o' Rabbie Bruce.'

We had reached the same spot where the three of us had looked down on the mill on that first day. The funeral party unfurled down the path like a spool of black ribbon, heading for the cottage where a wake was to be held. I'd promised Jeannie I would be there but I could not face it just at the moment. I let go of Jamie's arm and leaned on the top bar of a fence, rubbing away a headache. It would not be breaking my word to confide in someone outside the family, I decided.

'I'm afraid we can't leave Rabbie Bruce alone, Jamie,' I said. 'Mrs Moir told me just before she died that he's my brother.'

To my surprise, Jamie's reaction to my earth-shattering revelation was to chuckle. 'Nae, lass. That canna be true. Ye're a Sassenach; Rabbie's a Scot.'

I sighed. 'All the same, we had the same mother.'

Jamie took his glasses out of his pocket and pinched them to the end of his nose to get a clear view of my face. He looked the earnest scholar in this pose. 'Is this a jest?'

'No. I have a brother.' I then proceeded to tell him the reason for my journey north, my last conversation with Mrs Moir and my promise.

'That isna fair,' Jamie announced when I'd finished. 'I have nae wish to speak ill of the dead, but she had a heart as hard as three-inch ice in the well bucket.'

'But still, I gave my word.'

Jamie was thinking fast. 'Aye, but the Moirs ken that Rabbie is their kin. If ye bring him back and he says ye are his sister then all will be out and ye'll nae have to break yer promise.'

I'd been thinking this myself but couldn't help wondering if it was breaking the spirit, if not the letter, of my oath to Mrs Moir.

'Nae, Catherine, dinna look at me like that: Ian and Dougie will be glad to find out that ye are kin, wee Jeannie too. They wouldna forgive me if I kept it from them and let ye slink off back to London.'

I hadn't thought of that. Was it possible that, if they ever found out, my cousins would feel cheated if I left without telling them? Would they want to know me as much as I wanted to know them?

Decision made, I tapped the fence like an auctioneer closing the bidding. 'Whatever I do about the Moirs, I think my next step is clear. I must find my brother.'

'Aye, ye must, but it willna be so easy,' Jamie replied sagely – an annoying stance seeing how he had just been encouraging me to make myself known to Rabbie. 'Ye canna go to the tower house and demand to see him. They dinna take to strange folk. And think what yer brother will make o' ye, a Sassenach lass claiming to be his long-lost sister. If I remember one thing about Rabbie, it's his ill temper. I doubt he'll take kindly to the news.'

I took a deep, steadying breath, determined not to be put off. 'So I have a crosspatch of a brother locked in a tower with a bunch of bandits? That sounds like the sort of quest to appeal to a brave-hearted sister. I'll just pack my bag and you can point me in the right direction.'

'Wheest, lass, ye are nae listening! Ye canna do that and think to come back in one piece.' He took my shoulder and actually gave me a shake. 'The Bruce clan are raucle, ill-likit and kittle –'

I held up a hand. 'Stop! Translation, please.'

Jamie scrubbed his hand through his hair in frustration.

'I think he means they are ill-mannered ruffians who would as soon slit your throat as speak to you,' offered Bridgit mildly.

Jamie nodded his thanks. 'Aye, that's it. Ye would be daft to seek them out by yerself.'

He clearly hadn't heard the bit about me being determined to go. He had no idea what a brother meant to someone without family – it was everything to me.

I crossed my arms stubbornly. 'I've proved I'm not hen-hertit once and I'll show you again.'

'But, Catherine, this isna a walk to the Linn we're talking about – ye take yer life in yer hands when ye tangle wi' the Bruces.'

'Strangely enough, Jamie, I think I understood that,' I said sarcastically. 'But that changes nothing.'

He groaned. 'Aye, it does.'

'How so?'

'It means I have to go wi' ye and keep the pair o' ye alive.'

With no reason to delay, we left the next morning. Being a Sunday, we were the first up and about so very few people saw us head out of the valley. My goodbyes had already been said. Martha rejoiced to have her bed back; Annie wished me well. I'd already told the Moirs at the wake that Bridgit and I were off to find work in Glasgow. Jeannie had cried in my arms, distressed that she was losing a friend so soon after the death of her mother, but I couldn't find it in my heart to promise her that I'd be back when I wasn't certain of it. And I hoped I could soon reveal myself to her as something rather better than a mere friend. I did give her a very unneighbourly hug – a real squeeze – hoping that she could sense more than I could say.

Dougie, Katrine and Ian were still too stunned by grief to pay much attention to our departure, though Ian did tease Jamie a little for agreeing to set us on our way. None of them thought it strange that we were to walk to Glasgow as it was a well-travelled road. With all the cotton wagons passing to and fro from the port, there would be plenty of opportunities to beg a ride.

But, Reader, we had no intention of going that far; our destination was nowhere so civilized. We were heading into bandit country.

On Jamie's advice we carried only a small bundle each, strapped to our backs to leave our arms free for the rough terrain. Following his lead, we did not stay on the Glasgow road but struck off north-east up a track that was little more than a muddy trail. We climbed a steep wooded slope, pulling ourselves up by root and limb, until we emerged on to moorland. I stood still to regain my breath, marvelling at the view spread out before me. An icy wind cut through my thick shawl and pelisse and I tucked my hands under my arms to keep them warm. In the distance, I could see the faint outline of dark blue hills capped with white – the beginning of the true highlands, according to Jamie, many miles away. Here in the lowlands the countryside looked much kinder – a network of rivers hidden in wooded valleys, open hilltops where sheep grazed, villages and farms. It was amazing to think that the largest manufactory in the country, if not the world, was just a few miles behind us. Step away from the Clyde valley and it was as if New Lanark did not exist and the old country life carried on undisturbed. I was already missing the clatter of the looms that had become a comforting noise to me, like the rumble of traffic in London. I'd never been entirely at ease in the quiet of the countryside.

A sheep bleated on our left, setting off the whole herd as they ran for no apparent reason across our path, little hooves thudding on the ground. Not that quiet really, I thought with a smile.

'How far is the Bruce place, Jamie?' I asked as we strode along the track, weaving our way between clumps of dead bracken that were the colour of cinnamon. A sugar-coating of light snow lay in drifts on the higher ground, making a stunning contrast to the iron-grey satin of the sky. The hint of sweetness was misleading: this was a poor man's landscape, a treacherous place where the bones of the earth showed through the thin skin of grass.

'The tower house is some ten miles from Lanark, in a wee valley, very hard to approach wi'out the Bruce lads being aware o' ye.'

I hopped over an ice-crusted puddle. 'But we don't want to creep up on them, surely? I want to meet my brother, not kidnap him.'

Jamie stopped to take a stone out of his boot.

'Ye didna listen to a word I said, did ye, Catherine?'

Bridgit sat down on a rock and folded her hands patiently in her lap, anticipating another of our spats.

'I did too,' I protested.

About to begin his lecture, Jamie waved to the north. 'The Bruce clan are hard-handed reivers – or thieves as ye would say.' He gestured to me. 'Catherine, a soft-headed Sassenach. Put the two together and what do ye get? Trouble and an empty purse. They'll take every last thing ye have on ye. Ye'll be lucky to get away wi' yer life. Is that clear enough for ye?'

I folded my arms, standing apart from my two companions on the far side of the puddle. 'Yes, yes, I heard all that when you told me yesterday. I didn't ask you to come with me, remember.'

'And what about her?' Jamie nodded at Bridgit.

'She doesn't have to come either. It's my brother, my risk.'

Bridgit shook her head. 'I can't believe the Bruces would be worse than my brothers, Cat, and you faced them all for my sake.'

━ 253 ━

Jamie rolled his eyes. 'No another soft-headed lass! I was counting on ye to make yer friend see sense before it's too late. These are reivers – I canna believe yer brothers are anything like them.'

Bridgit gave a hollow laugh.

'So why did you come with us if you only wanted to turn me back?' I asked.

Jamie scuffed his boot in the dirt. 'Rabbie willna take so badly to me. He'll remember me from his time in New Lanark. I thought I could go and get him for ye.'

Words failed me for a moment. Jamie Kelly was planning on playing hero.

'I can't allow you to do that, Jamie,' I said finally. 'If anyone goes in alone, it will be me.'

Bridgit stood up and brushed down the seat of her skirt. 'No one is doing anything on their own. We'll go together or not at all.' Her authoritative tone announced that she was the eldest there and had decided to assume command. As I looked around our little circle, it was apparent that we had three officers and no foot soldiers. The thought made me laugh.

'What's so funny?' snapped Jamie, still on edge.

'I was just thinking that in our army we need some more followers.'

Bridgit smiled, but she showed no signs of backing down. 'Cat, Jamie, why don't we just go forward and see what happens? We don't need to decide now.'

'We canna put it off much longer. We'll be entering Bruce land soon,' grumbled Jamie.

'Then let us think of a plan while we walk.' Bridgit looked to the north. 'This way, is it?'

'Aye.' Jamie surveyed the looming clouds ahead. 'And from that dreich sky, I can tell ye that snow is on its merry way.' He tapped his forehead. 'I must be daft to be out here wi' ye.'

'If you can tell us where we need to go, you can still head back and be home in time for dinner and before the storm hits,' I called over my shoulder.

'Ye canna get rid of me so easily, Snippie!' he shouted back, leaping the puddle.

Even from our distant vantage point, I could see that the Bruce tower house was every bit as difficult to approach as Jamie said. It was getting dark but there was just enough light to see the old building crouched midway down the valley on a flat-topped hillock by the river. At least five storeys tall, the house looked like a little grey castle keep, with walls that promised to be several feet thick. The pitched roof was protected by square-cut battlements like a fancy brim on a pointy hat. From the number of missing slates it appeared that the tower itself was in poor repair, but someone had been tending the land around. There were signs of a vegetable garden dug into the flat ground in front of the main door, and the trees had been cleared to give the inhabitants an unobstructed view in all directions. I felt very disheartened by the prospect. They just do not build them like that any more – at least not where I come from. This was the kind of home meant to deter Viking invaders or provide protection from wolves, not something that belonged to our modern age.

'Er, Jamie, I don't suppose there are wolves around here?' I asked in a whisper, glancing fearfully over my shoulder.

'Nae, none that I've heard,' he replied carelessly.

Good. One less worry.

Bridgit touched my arm lightly. 'Time for us to put our plan into action.'

'Yes.' I dug out of my bag a piece of paper, a quill and the little bottle of ink I always carried with me. 'I need somewhere flat to write.'

Jamie gallantly offered his back. A snowflake fell on the page, leaving a damp smudge. Bridgit held the ink while I scrawled the note, briefly announcing my aunt's death and the fact that the bearer could take Rabbie Bruce to someone who had something of value for him: a bequest from his aunt.

Well, it wasn't really a lie, was it, Reader? My aunt had left me the knowledge of our kinship; I hoped my brother would value it.

'There.' Before I could think better of it, I folded the letter and handed it to Jamie. He had finally persuaded us that he should make the first approach in the guise of messenger boy. Hopefully, the Bruces would think him of no account and leave him alone. 'My brother did go to the mill school while he was with the Moirs, didn't he?'

Jamie frowned. 'I think he did. I saw him being sent to stand in the corner a few times.'

'That doesn't exactly mean he knows his alphabet.'

We looked at each other, aware of the wrinkle in our plan. We'd have to chance it – or at least hope that Rabbie had the sense to ask someone he could trust to read him the letter.

'I'll go now,' Jamie said, tucking his glasses back into his pocket. I wondered if he was afraid of getting them smashed.

'Please hurry,' said Bridgit with a worried look at the sky. 'We can't stay outside tonight. Either Cat's brother offers us shelter or we'll have to find it ourselves. Maybe that barn we saw a mile back?'

'Aye, I'll be gleg. If I dinna come back in an hour, find yerselves a roof and wait till morning. I'll meet ye at the barn.'

'Good luck, Jamie.' I gave him an impulsive hug. He looked hopefully in Bridgit's direction.

'Be careful,' she warned, giving him a sisterly peck on the cheek.

Much emboldened by his own gallantry, Jamie squared his shoulders and set off down the valley. He was soon swallowed up by the shadows under the trees.

'You've made a conquest,' I said teasingly.

Bridgit shook her head as she slipped her bag off her back and sat down on a rock to wait. 'Puppy love, Cat. Haven't you ever seen it before?'

I nodded, remembering the devotion I had once felt for my friend Johnny. If that was puppy love, it was nothing to be mocked; the feelings were as acute and real as any I knew.

'I remember being in love with the priest in our village in Ireland,' Bridgit continued, laughing gently at her memories. 'Mother Mary, talk about a hopeless affection!'

'Why?'

'Our priests don't marry.'

'Ah yes, of course.'

'And if it had been otherwise, half the girls in the parish would have been in line to be his wife.

He was a fine-looking man – and kind.'

'Is that what you want in a husband?' I asked, mentally ticking off these two on the list of Syd's attributes.

'Don't we all?'

I shrugged. 'I don't think I'll be getting married.'

'Maybe you are just too young and no one's caught your eye yet.'

'Perhaps.' That was what she – and the rest of society – expected me to say, but it wasn't what I felt inside. Every time someone made a comment about me marrying, I felt like the ugly sister trying on Cinderella's shoe, toes crammed to pretend I could be the conventional bride.

'But surely, Bridgit, there is more to life for us than marriage and babies?' I asked.

Bridgit tucked the ends of her shawl more snugly around her body. 'Yes, there is: there's poverty,' she counted points off on her fingers, 'being an outcast, unhappiness. That's the future for a woman on her own.'

I wanted to protest but was held back by the

thought of my mother. Jesse Stirling had found all three when she had me.

'Would it be too much to ask for adventure, for work that I liked – without the unhappiness and poverty bit?'

I could tell Bridgit was smiling even though it was now too dark to see her face properly. 'Perhaps not too much for you, Cat.'

We waited in silence. Snow continued to flutter through the tree canopy, settling on our skirts in damp drifts. I could feel it beginning to soak through my shawl.

'How long do you think he's been gone?' I wondered, my teeth chattering.

'Almost an hour, I would guess.' Bridgit reached out and took my hand. She was trembling from a mixture of cold and anxiety, her fingers chill.

'Do you think something's happened to him?'

How could she answer? We didn't know. All we could do was wait in the dark, watching the snow.

An owl hooted down in the valley. At least, I hoped it was an owl.

'Sh-shall we go to the barn?' I stuttered. My feet felt like blocks of ice.

'I think we should,' murmured Bridgit.

'I don't like to leave Jamie. What if he's in trouble? He might need us.'

We stood irresolute for a few more minutes, staring into the night. A light twinkled at the top of the tower, a lighthouse warning of trouble.

'We should've had a better plan,' I burst out in frustration. 'I thought he'd come straight back. I'd never have agreed if I really thought he would be in danger.'

A second owl hooted, this time behind us.

'But what can we do?' whispered Bridgit uneasily. 'We'll freeze if we stay. At least in daylight we will be able to come back and see if he's all right. And if he gets away he'll expect to find us in the barn, not here.'

'You're right.' I blew on my fingers. 'Sorry. I'm just worried.'

'So am I.'

We picked up our bundles and turned to head up the track to the barn. We had not even taken three paces when a man jumped out of the trees in front of us, landing on the ground with a heavy thud. Bridgit screamed, hands to her mouth to muffle her cry. I spun round only to find we had company behind us too.

Reivers.

'Get them!' said the first man with soft-spoken menace.

Silently, the men took our bags and bound our wrists behind our backs. The only sound was Bridgit's soft whimpering. I held my tongue, though in my mind I was swearing a blue streak for having fallen into their trap so easily.

'Welcome to Bruce land, my bold lasses,' said the leader with a mocking bow. 'Sadly, ye'll soon wish ye hadna trespassed.'

Guided by rough hands down the track, we stumbled into the clearing by the tower house, shoes sliding in the slush. I frantically tried to free my wrists but only succeeded in rubbing the skin raw. Led up a flight of wooden stairs on the outside of the building, we entered the tower through a low door on the first floor. On my right, stone steps ran upwards within the thickness of the wall, the top lost in the darkness, but we were shoved straight forward and into the well-lit main chamber. The first thing I saw was Jamie kneeling, hands and feet trussed together in a most uncomfortable position. He looked distraught to see us there.

'It wasna my fault!' he called, before being pushed over by a kick in the back and warned to hold his tongue.

I couldn't watch my friend be mistreated without protesting.

'Leave him alone!' I shouted, giving his attacker, a burly old man with a scrawny grey beard, a kick in the shins.

With a swipe of his hand, I found myself on the floor next to Jamie, my cheek on fire. Unable to break my fall, I lay still, momentarily winded.

'Damn and blast!' I huffed, shuffling on to my side. 'That hurt.'

Jamie met my eyes. 'I think our plan's gone agley.'

'I think it has.' I closed my eyes, waiting for him to say it. 'Go on.'

'What?'

'Say, "I told you so." '

'I'll save it until we're safely out of this fix.'

Behind us Bridgit was talking fast, seeing what negotiation could do to improve our situation. I listened carefully, though I could not see her through the forest of legs that surrounded us. She was pleading for our release but receiving scant encouragement. I pulled myself up on to my knees and surveyed our surroundings, hoping to see a way out. The room was large and square-shaped. A fire crackled in a vast stone hearth some feet away. The floor was covered in dirty mats and benches lined the walls. Above, I caught a glimpse of a painted wooden ceiling. Weapons hung in place of portraits. No luxury here, just the belongings of a bunch of fighting men. Little wonder the room smelled of mud, whisky and unwashed bodies.

'Have you seen my brother?' I whispered to Jamie.

'Aye. He's by the fire.'

I crouched lower, trying to peek through the

men. My eyes met those of a boy sitting on a stool, an open letter on his lap. Large for his twelve or so years, he bore absolutely no resemblance to me that I could see. Dark hair, brown eyes, mean-looking: he was the sort of boy I would normally cross the road to avoid. Was this truly my brother?

I glanced back at Jamie, a question in my expression. He nodded.

Rabbie got up and pushed his way through to stand before Bridgit; his passage cleared a space so I could now see her. She looked scared but resolute, standing up to the big man who had jumped out at us. He was dressed in tattered plaid and had a long mane of brown hair tied back in a leather thong.

'Malcolm, ask her where my money is,' Rabbie said, tugging at the leader's sleeve. The big man looked down at him and gave my brother a mirthless smile.

'There is no money,' Bridgit replied, trying to keep her tone soothing. 'There never was. That's not why we are here.'

She was ignored.

'Search the bags,' ordered Malcolm Bruce.

Our things were unceremoniously emptied out on to the floor, our change of clothes picked over by calloused fingers. Bridgit flushed in anger and embarrassment to have her shifts on display; I cursed as they found my dwindling stock of Frank's money. Malcolm threw it to Rabbie.

'That isna much, but then my aunt wasna a generous woman,' said Rabbie, shoving the purse into his pocket.

I could not help myself: I was taking an instant dislike to my own kin.

'Hey, that's mine!' I struggled to my feet. 'Give it back! Of course Mrs Moir didn't leave you money. And why should she? You ran away!'

The room fell silent as my southern tones registered on the audience. A lick of fear crept up my spine.

'A Sassenach?' sneered Rabbie. He jingled the purse in his pocket. 'Thank ye for yer donation then.'

'That is my ticket home,' I replied staunchly. 'Hand it over.'

'Nae.'

'I'll tell you what Mrs Moir left you if you give it to me.'

'As if I care.' He turned his back.

I saw red. 'Damn you, Rabbie Bruce – you're my brother! You shouldn't steal from me!'

Believe me, Reader, that wasn't how I intended to make myself known but my anger had run away with my good sense.

'Cat!' squeaked Bridgit.

Rabbie shoved past everyone to confront me, raising a fist between us. 'Brother! Ye are naething but a dirty liar!'

'Jesse Stirling was my mother, same as yours.' I flinched, half expecting him to strike, but he let his hand fall. It was unnerving to find my younger brother had quite a few inches on me. That didn't seem very fair.

'Do we have to listen to these lies?' Rabbie asked his cousin.

'Nae, lad. We'll put her downstairs.' Malcolm waved to one of his men and I found myself picked up round the waist and hauled out before I could protest. Bounced down a flight of steps, I was dumped in the cellar, wrists untied and the door locked on me.

In the pitch darkness I kicked the wall, only to find my foot connect with a sack of potatoes. Stupid, stupid, stupid! I berated myself. If I had set out to muck up my reunion with my brother, I could not have done a better job. Caught unawares, blurting out the truth in front of a room full of hostile witnesses – I had failed miserably. And now I was far down the path to hating my own brother – and after only a few minutes of acquaintance. Unfortunately, I suspected that the feeling was mutual.

SCENE 2 — KIN

Some time later I heard a scratching at the door.

'Cat?'

It was Bridgit. I knelt on the cold flagstones, pressing my face to the crack between door and frame. It was so dark I couldn't see it, only feel the draught flowing through against my cheek.

'Yes?' I whispered.

'I haven't got long. I told them I was going to the privy. Jamie is trying to talk your brother round.'

'Don't call him that.'

'What? Your brother?'

'Yes. He's nothing to me. He doesn't know me. Doesn't want to listen.'

I could hear Bridgit huff in frustration. 'So quick to give up on him? You hardly broke the news in the best fashion.'

I groaned and thumped my head on the door. 'I know. I'm a prize ass. But still, he doesn't seem to have much use for a sister – not with all those cousins.'

'Give him a chance.'

'Why?'

'Because you once told me that it was better to have problem brothers than no one on your side.'

'I said that, did I?'

'Mm-hmm.'

'Then I was wrong. Give me bread and butter and I'll spread my words on top and eat them.'

'No, you will not – and you know it. You are just angry at the moment. We've come all this way – don't waste the opportunity.'

I shivered. 'How are they treating you?'

'All right so far. They aren't really interested in Jamie. They just want to know about the valuable thing we claimed we were carrying.'

Another groan. 'Perhaps that letter wasn't such a good idea.'

'As we feared, your brother can't read. If he could, he might have kept it to himself, but instead he showed it to Malcolm Bruce. All the Bruce boys now think we're hiding something, especially since you as good as told them it wasn't the money you had in your purse.'

'Can you think of any more mistakes I've made today? I might as well hear them all in one go.'

Bridgit tapped the door to get my attention.

'Hey, we all made that one together, so don't feel too bad about it. It could've worked.'

'But it didn't. What chance do you think we have of convincing the Bruces that we had in mind the news about me?'

'Very little, I'm afraid. It's a bit too much of a stretch for them – they like gold and silver. I'd better go back.'

'Try to get them to send Jamie on his way. He was only the messenger after all. No need for all of us to be stuck here, and he might be able to fetch help.'

'That's why they won't let him go. They aren't bothering to question him – it's only you and me they're interested in. I expect they'll come for you soon.'

'Anything is better than sitting in this hole.'

Alone again, I settled back on my sofa of

potato sacks. At least I wasn't going to starve, no matter how long they kept me locked up.

In the darkness, my thoughts revolved around Rabbie Bruce.

My brother.

What did that really mean? I'd been blessed with many good friends in Drury Lane. Syd, Pedro and Frank had always stood in for family. They made exemplary brothers, looking out for me, encouraging me when I was low, laughing with me during the good times – and there had been plenty of those. Lizzie and Johnny had opened their home to me. Bridgit was fast becoming an honorary older sister, as were my friends across the Atlantic – Kanawha, Jenny and Georgie. I'd told myself I had no one on my side when all the time I'd had legions of people behind me. Why had I followed up this link to Rabbie against all warnings, even knowing that our relationship was no more than an accident of birth? I had made a romantic nonsense about the importance of kinship, and look where it had got me.

And yet, they say blood is thicker than water . . .

My turn to be questioned was not long in coming. I had barely had time to doze off when the door opened and I found my brother, candle in hand, looking down at me.

'Come along,' he muttered. 'Ye're wanted upstairs.'

Stiffly, I got to my feet and shook out my wrinkled petticoats. He stood back to let me pass as if even the merest touch of my person would sully him. But we were on our own: I wouldn't have a better chance than this to try to get through to him. I turned on the bottom step, blocking the way up. We were eye to eye this way, which suited me.

'I'm sorry I blurted out the news just now, but that doesn't change the fact that I am your sister –' I corrected myself, 'your half-sister. That is what I came to tell you. There's no bequest from Mrs Moir unless you count me.'

'Get out the way,' Rabbie said brusquely. His

voice was still as high as mine, reminding me for all his size that he was only twelve, and I had just blown his mother's reputation apart with my cannonball of news. I could understand him being angry. 'I dinna want to hear nae more of yer blethering.'

'Even if it's the truth? Our aunt told me about Jesse Stirling just before she died – that's why I haven't come before.'

He pushed me aside. 'Ye lie. My mither was a good woman. She wouldna have had any by-starts.'

His refusal to listen set light to the fuse on my anger again. I was furious he was making me out to be the villain of this piece when I had been the victim. It was time he acknowledged that. I dodged in front of him again.

'For your information, our mother left me on a doorstep in London in order to marry your father and have you. If that makes her a good woman, then I'm an eight-foot giant.'

I regretted the words as soon as they left my mouth, spoken partly through jealousy as all along

I'd been acutely aware that he was the child she had chosen over me. Rabbie looked fit to explode, red in the face, fists clenched.

'Sorry, sorry, I didn't mean that,' I said, holding my hands out in front of me to keep him away. 'She must have been trying to survive the best she could. Good and bad don't really come into it. I don't remember her either so we'll never know.'

Rabbie stabbed me in the chest with a finger to emphasize each word. 'I . . . dinna . . . believe . . . ye.'

He took off up the stairs, leaving me to follow or not as I liked. Trailing after him in the dark, I wondered if I could make a run for it, but the entrance to the tower house was barred for the night when I checked – no escape there. I couldn't think of another way out, windows on the lower floors being no more than arrow slits, nor could I stomach the idea of leaving my friends.

So, choosing warmth over my cold cellar, I entered the main chamber. The Bruces were seated around the fire, empty plates witness to the fact that they'd just finished eating. Bridgit perched in a window niche with Jamie. They both looked up on my entrance and I gave them a brief smile to signal all was well.

'Well, if it isna the wee Sassenach!' crowed Malcolm. 'Rabbie's sister from London!'

All the Bruces with the exception of Rabbie seemed to find this very funny.

'So kind o' ye to pay a family visit. Why dinna ye tell us where the bequest is and be on yer way?'

'You'll let us go?' I asked doubtfully, rubbing my arms to stop shivering.

'My word as an honest man.' Malcolm Bruce's smile was chilling.

The big grey-bearded man who had knocked me down earlier was sitting on a bench opposite Malcolm. He now laughed meanly, 'Aye, we'll let ye go – we'll set ye loose on the moss in the middle o' the blizzard. But it seems to me ye might just choose to stay here the night.'

'Wheest, Willy! Keep yer tongue between yer teeth,' chided Malcolm.

The big man just laughed the louder and took a gulp of his drink.

I moved a step closer to the fire. Rabbie was again sitting on a stool by the hearth but he wasn't looking at me. Instead he was toying with a knife, stabbing it in and out of its scabbard.

'The truth is –' I cleared my throat. This was a more hostile audience than even the one that had thrown rotten eggs at me in Kingston.* 'The truth is, there is no bequest. I came only to tell Rabbie that I had discovered that we were brother and sister. The note was bait, to get him alone to give me a chance to explain.'

'I told ye there wasna money in it for us,' grunted Willy to the chief. 'Ye should get rid of her – she's trouble, she is.'

Malcolm did not reply to his adviser but narrowed his eyes at me speculatively. 'Ye still claim to be Jesse's wean?'

'So I've been told. Jesse Stirling left me behind in London.'

Malcolm crossed his legs at the ankles, his muddy boot nudging a big black lump of a dog

* For that pungent moment I refer you to *Black Heart of Jamaica*.

lying on the hearthrug. It growled softly but did not shift. 'My uncle, her husband, didna mention a lass from an earlier marriage.'

'Well, he wouldn't. There wasn't a marriage. I was a . . .' I shrugged, '. . . a mistake, I suppose.'

'Dinna listen to her,' interrupted Rabbie, digging the knifepoint into a log. 'She's speaking ill o' my mither who canna answer back.'

Malcolm poked his little cousin in the arm. 'Yer mither speaks through the lass, Rabbie: she is the spit o' Jesse. I ken the lass spoke true the moment she made the claim.'

What! He knew?

Rabbie leapt to his feet, fist clenched around the knife hilt. 'Nae. Ye always said my mither was a fine woman.'

Malcolm smiled, unperturbed by his cousin's warlike stance. 'Aye, that she was. So she kept quiet about her by-start? That only means she was a canny one. Are ye no going to greet yer sister now ye ken the truth?'

To my horror, I realized that Malcolm was taunting the boy, pouring oil on his fiery temper.

Rabbie said nothing, just glared at me. I tried a smile but my lips would not cooperate. Why was Malcolm purposely stoking up Rabbie's anger? Was he hoping to see him lose his control?

'Look, there she is. Come all this way to see ye.' Malcolm gave him a little push towards me.

'I want naething to do wi' her.' Rabbie sheathed the knife and stormed out, disappearing up the stairs. I couldn't believe it: my brother didn't even want to know the truth!

I swallowed down the tears that had gathered at the back of my throat. 'That was cruel,' I said, 'telling him like that.'

Malcolm laughed and beckoned me closer. 'Aye, life is cruel, lass. Now the lad has gone away, tell me where the bequest is hid.'

I sat down heavily on my brother's abandoned stool. I felt chewed up and spat out. Rejected again.

'I told the truth. There is no bequest.' I shook my head wearily. 'The Moirs are poor. What could our aunt possibly have left Rabbie?'

'Ye tell me. Ye had the letter.'

'I've explained that already. What could be

more valuable than finding out you had a sister?'

'I believe Rabbie can think o' a rickle o' things he'd rather have.'

I crossed my arms on my knees and bent my head forward to rest on them. It must have been past midnight and I felt exhausted.

'What do you intend to do with us, Mr Bruce?' asked Bridgit from her corner, stepping in to draw attention from me.

'I havena made up my mind. Ye might still have something for me –'

'I swear that we don't,' I interjected.

'Maybe, maybe not. Either way, I canna let ye go and make trouble wi' the law. I'll tell ye before noon what I've decided. Willy!'

The old man sat up with a jolt from his daze. He'd been cuddling a jug of whisky like a child would a rag doll. 'What now, man?'

'Take our guests to the upper room and give them some blankets. We dinna want them freezing the night.'

Grumbling, Willy grabbed a lantern and beckoned us to follow him. We followed him in silence, saving our discussion until we were alone. The old man led us up the uneven stone steps, his vast shadow like a cloak of darkness at his heels making it hard for us to see our way. Jamie stumbled once or twice until he finally succumbed to putting on his glasses. He gave me an embarrassed smile when he saw that I had noticed.

Passing a number of closed doors on the steep climb up, we emerged on to a narrow rampart at the very top of the tower, at the level of the pitched roof. A few yards away, a door opened off the battlements into another storeroom. From the gentle cooing and acrid odour of bird droppings, I could tell we were also near the dovecote.

Entering the attic, Willy took three blankets out of a large chest and threw them towards us.

'Make yerselves at home,' he said, managing to make it sound a sinister offer. 'I'll leave ye the lantern but dinna forget to blow it out before ye sleep. Naebody will come and save ye if ye set light to the place and ye'll be the first to burn.'

With that he left us, his boots ringing on the

stones outside. Out of sight, his strong voice bellowed a song to the echoing passageway:

'Gie him strong drink until he wink,
That's sinking in despair . . .'

The rest of the words were lost in the night.

'What a horrid man,' Bridgit said when the noise of his departure had faded. 'He hit you earlier.'

From my kind friend, this was a serious insult.

'Yes, horrid,' I replied, clutching my shawl closer to my shoulders. 'There's a razor-edge to him, unlike Malcolm who seems half-decent, apart from his stubbornness about the bequest and a cruel desire to taunt his cousin. I can't understand Malcolm. Doesn't he like Rabbie?'

'I expect he sees him as a rival,' explained Jamie as he listened at the door for a moment. 'Before his death, Rabbie's faither ruled the roost. Malcolm is worried your brother will grow up and try to take his place. He's trying to keep him down under his boot-heel. Nae wonder Malcolm was so pleased to meet the by-start sister. Ye've given him a weapon to use on the lad.'

'Lovely. That explains why my brother is so delighted to see me.'

No noise from the battlements, Jamie tried the door. To our surprise it opened, but before we could get too excited about this we discovered that the door to the stairs down was bolted from the other side. Unless we jumped off the snow-covered roof and flew away like the doves, we were trapped.

'Rope?' suggested Jamie.

We searched the stores by lamplight but found none. I turned my examination to our blankets, wondering if we could tie them together, but we were at least forty feet off the ground and I doubted we had enough cloth to make a decent rope ladder.

Bridgit was the first to give up this idea. She sat down on her blanket and wrapped it around her.

'I don't know about you, but I think we should wait till morning.'

Jamie yawned and nodded. 'Aye.'

I showed my agreement by grabbing my blanket and cuddling up close to Bridgit. The storeroom was freezing and full of draughts.

Jamie noticed my shivers. 'It's going to be cold the night wi'out a fire. We must make the best defence we can. I'll drag some o' these boxes around us. Maybe that will help.'

Bridgit and I got up to assist him in sliding the chests and barrels into place. Soon we had constructed a little castle within a castle with just enough space for three cold inhabitants. We settled down once more, with the lantern by our feet.

Bridgit slipped her arm around my shoulders. 'All right?' she asked.

'Everything's just fine and dandy.'

Jamie nudged my foot in a friendly gesture. 'I tried to talk to Rabbie, Catherine, but he wouldna listen. Maybe tomorrow he'll feel different about it all.'

'Perhaps. But I'd save your breath to cool your porridge – he's not going to change so quickly.'

'What do you think they will do with us,

Jamie?' Bridgit asked. She was trying to sound brave but her voice shook a little. We all pretended not to notice.

Jamie shrugged. 'I canna say. I think if they were going to kill us, they would have done so. Even the Bruces do not like to murder in cold blood. And ye heard the man: one o' us is a sister – that does mean something to Malcolm. He willna harm his cousin's kin wi'out good reason.'

'So we should just sit tight?' I asked doubtfully.

'Aye. We have nae choice, do we?'

'True, Socrates. Very philosophic.'

Jamie snorted. Bridgit looked confused. 'Who is Socrates and what's he got to do with anything?' she asked.

'An old Greek who liked asking questions.' I scrubbed my forehead, finding it hard to believe I was stuck at the top of a tower discussing ancient philosophers when we weren't even sure whether a bunch of ruffians were going to let us live on the morrow. 'Never mind. Let's go to sleep.'

Summoned the next morning to hear Malcolm's

judgement, we stumbled wearily into the main chamber. None of us had slept very well, thanks to a combination of anxiety and cold. The Bruce clan were gathered, including some females who hadn't been present the night before. A tall woman with a square jaw and thick black brows stood behind Malcolm's chair, declaring her status as his wife by her stance. Her eyes widened when she saw me and she stooped to whisper something in her husband's ear to which he nodded in reply. Rabbie skulked in the window niche, an empty bowl on his crossed knees. That reminded me how hungry I was. Would the Bruces feed us? Perhaps I should do something to get put back in the food store downstairs?

Malcolm stood up and the chatter in the room died away. He tossed a plaid blanket over his shoulder, treating it like a badge of office or Roman toga.

'I have decided,' he announced, 'for the sake of our wee Rabbie,' here he cast an insincere look of concern at his cousin, 'I need to find out what bequest his aunt left him. So the morn, I'll go with the Kelly lad to New Lanark and talk to Rabbie's kin.' There was a general murmur of agreement in the room. 'His sister will stay here the while until we uncover the truth.'

My heart sank. It seemed I would have to endure yet more of the Bruces' cold hospitality.

'What about Bridgit?' Jamie chipped in bravely.

Malcolm shrugged. 'The Irish lass can stay or go as she likes, as long as she realizes that any trouble she brings upon us will fall first on her wee friend.' He resumed his seat. 'Help yerselves to some breakfast.' He waved us to a cauldron over the fire. 'I want to leave as soon as ye're done.'

We quickly filled three bowls with porridge and retired to a corner.

'What do ye think?' whispered Jamie.

'Better than I expected,' I admitted. 'You and Bridgit will be out of here and when he finds out there's nothing he's bound to let me go.'

'I'm not leaving you,' Bridgit muttered staunchly. 'I promised his lordship I'd stick by you.'

'Of course you're going!' I protested. 'You'd

be foolish to miss this chance. You can be far more help to me on the outside than stuck in here. And as Jamie said last night, I'm the last one the Bruces are likely to hurt, seeing how I'm kin to one of them.' I was no more eager than she to be left on my own but it was so obviously the best choice in unpleasant circumstances. 'Besides, I need you to contact Frank for me. When we get out of here we'll be penniless and we still have to get home.'

Bridgit was not about to jump to my orders. She looked at me, then at Jamie, worrying her bottom lip with her teeth. 'What do you think I should do, professor?'

Jamie frowned at my determined expression then turned back to Bridgit. 'I think Catherine is right: better for ye to be in New Lanark than here. If they dinna let her go, we can find a way to persuade them. It will be easier to do that if ye are away wi' me.'

'And though Rabbie may not like the fact that I'm here, he's not likely to harm me, is he?' I was not entirely sure of this myself, but it seemed a reasonable argument to make to Bridgit.

She nodded slowly. 'I'll go back with Jamie. But Cat, if we don't hear from you after seven days, we'll come back and get you – bringing help this time.'

'Agreed – but I doubt it'll come to that. If they're reluctant to let me go, I'll just slip away. I've had some practice at that.'

An hour later I watched from the battlements as my two friends trudged through the snow in the wake of Malcolm Bruce. The grey tower house thrust from the valley slope like an island from an icy sea, and I felt like the lone inhabitant on lookout, watching the last boat leaving for safety. It was a quiet morning for such desperation. Everything was beautifully still, woods frozen in a white tableau, tree-dancers holding a pose for our applause. In the pale blue sky the moon lingered late, hanging like a curled feather on a satin counterpane.

Once the three travellers had disappeared, I went back down the stairs, at a loss as to what to do with myself for the next few days. Most of the men had left to tend the livestock and haul in firewood while the women were chattering in the main chamber, preparing dinner and minding the smallest children. I peeked in, aware of being an outsider to their daily activities. But, fortunately, Malcolm's wife spotted me hovering by the door.

'Well, if it isna Jesse's by-start. Come in, lass.' She beckoned me to the trestle table where she was chopping root vegetables for the pot. 'Ye have the look of yer mither as I told Malcolm when I first saw ye.'

It increased my feeling of strangeness to know that I was surrounded by people who knew my mother better than I did. By rights she should belong to me, but in truth she was always going to be theirs in ways I could never match.

'Can I help?' I asked, gesturing to the paring knife.

'Aye, everyone in the tower pulls their weight. Take a bench beside me.'

'Thank you, ma'am.'

'Och, ye do have fancy London ways! That

would make Jesse cackle if she could see ye now. Ye can call me Nan.'

I nodded and picked up the knife to set to on a bunch of carrots.

'Would you tell me about my mother, Nan?'

The woman's lips bent into a smile. 'She was a lively one. Had her man – old Kenneth – running like a fox with a torch tied to his tail; that made us women laugh. She wasna wi' us long before she died, but she came like a comet streaking across our heavens, lighting up our world for a while.

'We all mourned her when she didna survive the birth. And Kenneth wouldna marry again after she were dead, even though he had the wean to think o'. I always thought it was a love match.'

But one that did not include the inconvenient child left in London. Nan's words unwittingly painted a picture of a heedless woman who drove everyone to distraction, leaving chaos in her wake.

'Did she ever mention me?'

'Nae, but the midwife told me Rabbie wasna her first wean. I thought that meant Jesse must have lost one, but it were too late to ask. The last thing I expected was for ye to show up on our doorstep. She left ye to be fostered, did she?'

'Something like that,' I mumbled in reply. And I suppose from my mother's point of view, Drury Lane theatre was a safe foster parent in uncertain times – loving and generous, always there, not likely to abandon one of its own no matter what the provocation.

'Och, dinna fret, lass, about yer mither. Have ye no thought that maybe she meant to come back for ye when she'd had the wean? Giving Kenneth a lad would have made her the apple of his eye – he would have done anything for her after that,' Nan suggested, correctly reading my melancholic expression.

Her words penetrated my gloom. Perhaps my mother had intended to reclaim me once established in her new life here – it was a comforting thought. My mind whirled, imagining how different my upbringing would have been. My goodness, I would've been Scottish! Can you imagine that, Reader? And I would have had blood relations, a rough-and-tumble family all of my own. A family of bandits admittedly.

Well, no one's perfect.

Rabbie didn't know how lucky he was. He may have grown up in a clan whose way of life seemed like something out of one of Bishop Percy's collection of ballads rather than our modern age, but at least he'd known where he belonged.

Rabbie chose that moment to stump into the kitchen with his arms full of logs. With one look at me, he dropped them by the fireplace and turned on his heel.

'Nae, ye dinna treat yer sister like that, Rabbie Bruce!' scolded Nan. 'I was just getting acquainted with the lass and I think ye should take the trouble to do so too.'

'I dinna want to be fashed wi' her,' he grumbled, tugging at the frayed end of his scarf.

'Well, hard luck, my wee man. Malcolm left orders that ye stick to her side like her shadow so she canna escape. My daft husband thinks she's hiding gold from him. He willna be pleased if she disappears before he can settle it one way or another.'

Nan was evidently not a person to disobey. Rabbie sat down at the table but did not offer to help. I could feel his eyes examining me surreptitiously as I chopped up the carrots. This was progress – at least he seemed a little curious.

'Ye've asked me before what yer mither looked like, Rabbie,' continued Nan cheerfully. 'Well, take a keek at the lass and ye'll see.'

Rabbie snorted in disgust and toyed with a discarded carrot top, winding the feathery leaves around his index finger.

'Dinna ye have a hankering to ken where yer sister has spent all these years?' asked Nan.

'Nae, I canna say I give a fart.'

If I hadn't been convinced that we were kin, his bad language would have given it away.

Nan sighed. 'Like that, is it, lad? As thrawn as yer faither, ye are. It's nae fault of Catherine that she was born. Take the lass and shew her around the place. Ye can do that, can ye no?' She took the knife from my hand – perhaps to stop me using it on my grumpy brother – and ushered us out of the room.

'I'll shew ye the cows,' Rabbie muttered grudgingly.

He pushed open the outside door and jumped down the wooden stairs. I followed more slowly, not caring for the patches of ice on the treads.

'I suppose ye fine London ladies have never seen a cow before?' he sneered.

'Once or twice perhaps,' I replied dryly. 'And I'm hardly a fine lady.' I felt tempted to shake him; he wasn't giving me a chance.

Crossing the clearing that surrounded the tower, he led me to a barn set back in the trees. I could smell the cattle from many paces – a stench that caught the back of the throat, reminding me of Smithfield market. Rabbie pushed the door open and beckoned me inside. I stepped in, to be immediately confronted by an enormous shaggy red head topped with curved horns. I couldn't stop myself – I gave a shriek of alarm and backed off.

'Scared of a wee cow?' mocked Rabbie, skirting the beast and climbing on a cart stationed by the door. I quickly scrambled up beside him.

'That is not a wee cow; that is a monster.'

'Aye, our Highland cows are nae built small and dowie like the soothland cattle. They have to survive our winter.'

'For your information, I've yet to see a cow that could be called small, even down south. I was just taken by surprise, is all,' I replied defensively. 'You could have warned me they were loose in here.'

'Why?'

'Why? Because it would have been the kind thing to do, that's why.'

'I dinna have to be kind to ye.'

I rolled my eyes in exasperation. 'Obviously. But, Rabbie, doesn't it mean anything to you that I'm your half-sister?' I nudged him in the ribs with my elbow. 'Why are you so angry with me? All I've done is come and find you.'

He frowned and threw a pebble at the barn door. It ricocheted and disappeared under the cows' hooves. 'Ye should've left me alone – no come stirring up stories about my mither.'

'About *our* mother. She was mine too . . . or was for a while.' It was useless. He didn't need or want me – he had made himself perfectly clear on that point. He was only annoying me and I suppose I was irritating him. Time to change the subject.

I waved to the twenty head of cattle wandering in the straw-strewn barn. 'So, do these cows all belong to your cousin Malcolm?'

Rabbie sniggered. 'Ye can say that.'

Which meant 'no'.

'So they're stolen – like my money.'

'We're reivers – that's what we do.' He crossed his arms, defying me to criticize – which is exactly what I did next, of course.

'Reivers is just a fancy name for thieves. Where I come from, it's nothing to be proud of and will likely lead to the gallows.'

Rabbie jumped down from the cart. 'That's one reason I dinna want a sister – clashing on wi' yer everlasting clack. I need none of yer preaching.'

'And I thought I was being sensible.'

'If ye had any sense, ye'd never have come here.' He made for the door.

I held up my hand, determined to get this said before he scurried off again. 'No, just stop a minute, Rabbie! Listen for once. How could I have known not to come? I wasn't even aware of your existence until a few days ago. I hoped then that you would be as eager to see me as I was you.'

His back was to me but he hadn't left the barn. Braving the cows, I slipped from my perch and approached him.

'Unlike you, I've never had a single person in this world who was mine. Do you understand what I mean? Of course you don't: you've had cousins and aunts and uncles around you even after you lost your parents. I came because I just wanted to see – to touch someone who belonged to me.' Tentatively I reached out, daring to do what I had longed from the first moment I saw him. I touched the back of his head, feeling the softness of his brown hair.

My brother.

He stood very still, neither encouraging nor rejecting my light caress. I dropped my hand. 'I'm not planning to stay around and spoil things for you but I would be grateful if you could find a little bit of brotherly feeling for me while I'm here.'

Rabbie let the silence stretch between us almost unbearably.

'Dinner will be ready,' he announced abruptly, choosing to ignore my plea. 'Let's go back.'

He pulled the door open and trudged away, taking the path of crushed snow to the tower.

SCENE 3 – REIVERS

That evening I was invited by Nan to remain in the main chamber with the family to enjoy the fire.

'It's too cold to put ye up in the attic. Ye'll freeze yer wee toes off,' she explained.

I was grateful for her kindness. I curled up in the window niche, half listening to the Bruce boys as they celebrated their most recent acquisition of cattle from an estate to the south of their land.

'I say we take them to the Highlands the morn,' proposed Willy, sitting in Malcolm's chair during his absence and clearly enjoying his elevation in rank. 'Their markings are too clear to risk round here.'

Accustomed to the thieves of London, I found the discussion of their fencing arrangements for stolen goods very familiar. It might be cows rather than silk wipes but the principle was the same: shift it before someone could trace the theft.

'Aye, the MacDonalds might give us a good

price,' agreed another. 'They're fine beasts – the best the lady breeds.'

My attention was drawn to an owl hooting outside. The window was shuttered so I could not see the bird, but the call was insistent and repeated rapidly. I was just beginning to wonder if it were a signal of some kind when one of the younger Bruces burst into the room.

'Sheriff's men!' he shouted.

The response was immediate and showed all the marks of a well-rehearsed drill. Willy began firing off orders.

'Neil, Gordon – take two men and drive those cows out of the barn. Head north when ye've lost the sheriff. Nan, ye take the women and weans to the top room and dinna come out until ye get the signal. Nae lights.'

The women started to evacuate the room, picking up sleepy children, hushing those who made any sound. I started to follow.

'Nae, ye stay here, Sassenach. I have nae doubt it were yer friends set these men after us. As Malcolm said, the trouble falls on yer head first.

Guard her!' He pushed me towards Rabbie who took my arm in a firm grasp. 'We're away!'

With barely time to grab a shawl to protect me from the cold, I was forced along with the Bruce boys as they rushed out into the night. Last to depart, Willy closed the door. I heard the bolt being drawn on the inside as Nan secured the tower. I wished I could be with her, as I did not trust Willy or his cohorts to care much what happened to me in this mad flight. The women had the better part as they were unlikely to be disturbed tonight. With fire dampened and all lights extinguished, the tower looked empty.

Willy cursed softly as he spotted the tracks the boys made in the telltale snow.

'We'll have to split up and meet at the way-stone,' he muttered to Rabbie. Blowing softly between his fingers, Willy let up three short owl calls, signalling the news to the rest of his kin. 'I'll fetch yer pack, Rabbie. Ye get the lass out o' here before the sheriff arrives.'

Down in the valley, I could now see a line of flaming torches coming closer. If I could give

Rabbie the slip, I'd be able to seek sanctuary among the sheriff's men.

'If ye lose her, or let her go, I'll skin ye both alive,' Willy warned, giving me a sharp look.

'I willna lose her,' promised Rabbie, tugging me away from the lights.

But I had no intention of being dragged off into the unknown with my unloving brother and a bunch of bandits. I took a breath to scream for help; Willy thrust a palm over my mouth, mashing the inside of my lips against my teeth with the pressure of his hand.

'Nae, ye dinna want to do that,' he hissed. 'One squeak from ye and I'll slit yer throat, Rabbie's sister or no. Understood?'

I nodded because I believed him. His eyes had that cold glint that I'd seen in Billy and his gang in London. He was out to protect his own neck and that of his brothers; he would not think twice of disposing of an inconvenient girl.

'Get on wi' ye!'

With a shove, he pushed us towards the trees. Half-stumbling, half-running, I followed Rabbie past the barn. The doors stood open, cattle gone, but the lingering stench and cowpats steaming on the snow bore witness to recent occupation. We plunged into the trees, brambles snatching and snagging at my skirts.

'Where are we going?' I panted.

'Hold yer tongue!' Rabbie snapped. 'Willy doesna make idle threats. Do ye really want us to be caught?'

To be frank, yes, I did. But I didn't want my brother to hang for cattle-rustling. I kept quiet, trusting he knew where we were headed and could see better than I could in the darkness. I spent the time hoping for a more favourable turn of events that would allow me to get free. The desperate plunge through the woods was making me miserable, my hands scratched, my ankles and feet soaked in snow-melt, my ears and nose blue with cold. I flipped the back of the shawl over my head, trying to stop the leeching away of all body warmth. And to think I'd believed the woods so pretty with their snow covering!

After what felt like an eternity since our flight

from the tower but was probably only an hour, Rabbie slowed.

'We're nearly at the way-stone,' he said in a low voice. 'The others will bring the horses so it'll get better from here.'

That was the closest he had come to a caring comment.

'G-good,' I stuttered through chattering teeth.

'Ye're cold?'

I gave a bark of laughter. 'You could say that. I've just come from the Caribbean – they don't make weather like this there.'

'I canna see ye well in this light but ye no going to faint on me, are ye?' He sounded very unsure of himself. I had to remind myself that he was only twelve. His bravado, learnt no doubt from relatives like Malcolm, was not fixed and signs of a younger, more vulnerable boy occasionally peeped through – like now, when he thought I was going to keel over and leave him the problem of what to do with an unconscious girl in the middle of snowy nowhere.

'I'll endeavour not to make a complete cake of

myself, little brother, but I can't help being frozen.'

'Little! I'm bigger than ye.'

I felt smug to have finally provoked a normal brotherly response from Rabbie. This was more like it. He couldn't help himself: he was beginning to think of me as his sister, even feel a grudging responsibility towards keeping me safe. It was a moment I wanted to treasure – and would have done if my extremities weren't in danger of freezing into icicles.

I blew on my fingers. 'Let's keep going while I still can.'

We reached the waymarker, a granite pillar by the side of the track. Willy and three other men were already there, mounted and leading a string of horses. Without needing to say a word, Rabbie picked up his pack from Willy and untied a small grey horse from the line. It was the last one with any tack – the rest had only a rope bridle each.

'The lass can ride wi' me,' said Willy, scanning the road behind for sign of pursuit. 'We had nae saddle for her and nae time to find one. But we must be gleg; thanks to the snow, the men can follow our trail as easily as a fly to the midden.'

'I'll take her up wi' me,' countered Rabbie. 'She'll only slow ye down.'

'No need, gentlemen,' I announced. 'I can ride quite well without a saddle, thank you for asking.'

I had no desire to spend the rest of the night jogging behind someone else, not when I was perfectly capable of riding without the paraphernalia of tack. Choosing a sable mare from among the remaining horses, I swung myself on to her back.

'Ye'll fall!' warned Rabbie.

'Don't worry, squirt – I learned to ride bareback with Indians. This is child's play.' I gathered the reins in my frozen fingers and patted my mount's neck.

It was far from child's play, of course: the horse was not used to having a rider with no saddle and took a few minutes to settle down. She jigged on the track like a nervous girl dancing her first cotillion. When I had her under control,

I found that the Bruces were all staring at me as if I'd just fallen from heaven in front of their very eyes. I felt inordinately pleased with myself.

'Ye've surprised me, lass, I'll give ye that,' said Willy. With a click of his tongue, he gave the order to ride out. Unfortunately, the late hour had not dulled his wits any and he wedged my mare between his horse and Rabbie's, in position to stop me making a run for it.

There went one grand plan.

'Where are the rest of your cousins?' I asked, noticing that we were short of a face or three.

'Driving the cows across the moss,' Willy explained curtly. 'We are the decoy to keep the sheriff's men distracted, so I hope ye can ride fast at need.'

'Like the wind,' I declared, aware that I was trying to impress my brother of my horsemanship at the expense of the truth. I might well end up arsy-varsy on the ground if we tried a canter.

'Is it true? Did ye really learn to ride from an Indian?' Rabbie asked, the first time he'd shown any interest in me.

'Yes,' I replied.

Willy snorted. 'Course it isna true, ye fond laddie! How could a wee lass go to America and do all that?'

How indeed. But I had. Blowing on my fingers, I decided it was not worth arguing, not when we were riding through a snowy landscape with the law on our tail and I needed all my concentration to remember the skills taught me by my Creek Indian friends.

We spent a few daylight hours camped out in an old cottage well known to the Bruces.

'Do this often, do you – up sticks in the middle of the night and flee?' I muttered to Rabbie as we stretched out blankets on the beaten earth floor to grab a few hours of sleep.

'Aye, from time to time. We go into the Highlands to shake off the sheriff and come back when his attention turns to some other poor man. It's the way for us reivers.' He sounded proud of the admission.

'I suppose it's a bit like my friends in London –

they disappear into the Rookeries if they get in trouble,' I said thoughtfully as I finger-combed my tangled hair.

'Rookeries?' Rabbie lay back and yawned.

'Lawless places full of desperate types – too dangerous for decent folk to venture in, even the Bow Street Runners.'

He snorted. 'The Highlands are unchancie for some, but no for us Bruces. We've friends there who'll hide us as long as we have need.' He yawned again. 'Maybe we never should have struck on Lady Ross-Baillie's cows; it's well known the sheriff's a family friend of the lady. We've never hit on her land before because o' that.'

Rather too late to mention that now. If I was not mistaken, my brother had stolen from the lady who guarded her lands with Ghillie Brown and his gun. If she minded a few bent blades of grass from the feet of mill trespassers, I imagine she would not let theft of her livestock go without revenge. I hoped we would not find out how far she would take it.

I lay down on my side on the dirt floor of the

cottage and watched Rabbie's profile relax into sleep. My brother was at home in this country just as I was in Covent Garden, managing the twists and turns of fate with confidence. Perhaps this part of our character was something we'd both inherited from our mother. As Nan had told me, Jesse had had people dancing to her tune – that suggested she was by no one's estimation a shy, retiring violet. As I fell asleep, I wondered what she would have thought of her two children sharing a floor together for the first time.

We remounted in the twilight and pushed on for the Highlands, taking tracks across country rather than risking the roads and towns. I had plenty of time to speculate as to what purpose my presence among the reivers was serving. Willy had made no further mention of me being to blame for this pursuit and I had come round to the view that it was far more likely cattle-stealing lay at the root of their problems. But I'd had more than I could stomach of tagging along with them – every step took me further north and further from my home.

At daybreak, we reached the top of a hill and looked down upon a shallow scoop of a plain that suddenly opened out at our feet before the ground climbed again. The hills opposite were ranged like an opposing army against us. Scree littered their sides like grey crocodile skin – it would be tough going for the horses over there. A smudge of a day after yesterday's bright morning, low clouds drifting like smoke, grazing the summits. Melting snow formed black puddles in the low-lying bottoms of the fields, green reclaiming the ground surrendered to the white.

Taking a breath, I broached the subject of my future with my brother. 'Look, Rabbie, why don't you persuade Willy to let me go? I could ride into one of these towns we're passing and make my own way back; wouldn't that be more sensible than keeping me with you?'

He gave a non-committal grunt.

'Surely the sheriff will have stopped tracking you by now?'

'They willna stop till we reach the Highlands,' he corrected me.

'But even if they did find me, I wouldn't be any help to them. I've no idea where you're going.'

He shook his head. 'Willy wants ye wi' us. He has promised Malcolm that he willna let ye go.'

'And you all do what Malcolm says even if he's got some stupid idea in his head that I'm sitting on a crock of gold that belongs to you? Makes me sound like a leprechaun – and about as likely.'

At that moment, the rearguard gave a whistle. As one, the Bruces urged their horses into a gallop, plunging recklessly across pasture, scattering sheep in their passage. It took me a moment to cotton on to the fact that our pursuers had been spotted but my mare had followed the lead of the other horses and already picked up her pace. Now my full attention was given to gripping with my knees to stay on. Skirts flapped as I bent low – pointless to wish for my Creek leggings which had made the whole business of riding astride much easier but I did so anyway.

Crack! A shot rang out behind us, spooking my mare. We were approaching a stone wall that the men were taking at a leap. This was not good, not good at all. My skittish horse refused the jump, dancing sideways. I struggled to control her, turning her in a tight circle and brought her head round to take the wall at the lowest point.

'No there!' I heard Rabbie shout from the other side – but too late. We landed in the muddy puddle where a spring bubbled up in the grass. My mount struggled to gain her footing, slid and surged up. I went backwards, landing with a splash in the icy water, colliding with a stone at the base of the wall. With pain like a sword thrust, I felt something give – and it wasn't the stone.

'Are ye all right?' Rabbie leaped from his horse and waded towards me.

I rolled on to my stomach and groaned.

'I'll take that as a nae.' He pulled my arm, eliciting another protest from me.

'My arm – shoulder,' I moaned. 'If you don't want me to be sick on your boots, don't touch.'

'Leave the lass!' shouted Willy, doubling back. 'There is nae time to get her on a horse. Leave her!'

Rabbie looked at his mount, at my fleeing

mare, and then at my white face. Another shot, much closer, crackled overhead. Willy turned his horse's head and spurred onwards.

'You'd better go,' I urged my brother. I felt close to passing out – the pain in my shoulder was making stars bloom in my vision.

He swore a vivid phrase, damning all sheriff's men and stupid Sassenach girls and casting doubt on our collective parentage as he dragged me into the shelter of the wall just before our pursuers could leap on top of us.

'Very good,' I said in a hoarse voice. 'You have a fine way with words.'

Continuing with his curses, he deftly made a sling from my shawl. With no rider to control it, my horse had taken up the race across the field with the sheriff's men, bumping into the front-runners.

'One's fallen!' shouted the leader. He grabbed the reins of Rabbie's horse and turned back, easily spotting us huddled at the base of the wall. 'There they are.'

Half the pack continued on after the fleeing

Bruces, leaving the rest to confront us.

'It's two Bruce whelps!' the leader announced, pointing a crop at us. He was a finely dressed gentleman, well mounted, with only the softest Scots burr, suggesting an English education. Enter the Sheriff of Lanark. 'Stay where you are!'

'I'm not exactly going anywhere like this,' I muttered for Rabbie's benefit. His grip on my arm increased a fraction; I could feel that he was shaking but trying valiantly not to show it. 'Don't worry – I'll get us out of this,' I promised.

'Well now,' said the man, pushing the brim of his hat further up his forehead. 'If it isn't the Bruce lad. Rabbie, isn't it? Poor taste of your mother to give such a thief a noble name. The girl's your sweetheart, is she?'

Rabbie glared up at him but said nothing.

'No sir, he is not. He's my brother,' I said in the firmest voice I could manage. 'As you can see, I've taken a spill from the saddle and am in need of assistance.'

'Assistance!' The man laughed. 'A Bruce girl talking like a London lady! That is a first.'

A second man approached wearing a battered tweed cap decorated with fishing flies. He squinted at me thoughtfully.

'The lass looks very familiar,' he pondered aloud, rubbing his beetling eyebrows. With a sinking heart I recognized my old enemy, the ghillie from Corra Linn. He snapped his fingers. 'Aye, I have it! I met her trespassing on my lady's land, sir. Spun me a tale, she did – lies from start to finish, though I didna ken it then. Dinna believe a word the lass says.'

The sheriff tapped his crop on his boot, assessing the pair of us. 'Boy, where are Lady Ross-Baillie's cattle?'

Rabbie's face was a blank. 'I ken naethin about any cattle.'

'Girl?'

I would have shrugged if my shoulder had allowed. 'Despite what your man says, I am not a liar and I have no knowledge of the lady's cows or where they are now.' This was said with fingers crossed because, as you know, Reader, I have been known to bend the truth somewhat when it suits me.

The sheriff was unimpressed by our protestations of innocence. 'If you tell me what you've done with them, I'll be lenient. I'd say you were both looking at a capital offence at the moment; I could reduce it to transportation but only if you prove that you repent your larcenous ways.'

He meant to hang us! As far as I know he had no evidence we had done anything wrong – he couldn't just sentence us to death on a suspicion.

'I don't take kindly to threats, sir,' I said stiffly. 'As I explained, we don't know where the cattle are. If you were a gentleman, you would stop these useless questions and fetch a doctor to look at my shoulder. I think I've broken something.'

The sheriff beckoned to a couple of his men who had hung back during our discussion.

'Take them back to Bonnington House for questioning. Tell Lady Ross-Baillie that I'll return soon. First I have to find out if we've caught any more of these damn cattle thieves.'

So much for the sheriff keeping an open mind about our guilt.

'But, sir,' protested Rabbie, 'my sister isna lying

about her injury. She needs a doctor. She canna ride all the way back to Lanark with a broken shoulder.'

'She should have thought of that before she took up with the Bruces. I'll have a doctor look at her when she is safely in my custody.'

The sheriff waved us away and turned his horse to pursue the rest of his men.

The two who stayed behind pulled us roughly to our feet. I suppressed a whimper of pain. By now I had guessed I must have snapped my collarbone and my left arm was out of action. Frankly, Reader, the thought of riding with all my bumps and bruises made me feel faint.

'What are we going to do wi' the lass?' the shorter of the two men asked his ginger-haired companion.

'She'll ride in front o' me. She willna slip away in her condition. Put the lad on his horse but tie his hands.'

So trussed up like Christmas geese and separated, Rabbie and I began the long journey back the way we had come.

*

After an overnight stop at an inn near Hamilton, we trotted up the drive to Lady Ross-Baillie's estate late the following day. After so many wearisome miles, I was back where I started on the land bordering the mill. Bone-weary and half delirious from the laudanum the men had given me to dull the pain, I was too far gone to care. The journey could have been worse. The sheriff's officers had surprised me by being unexpectedly kind, allowing me a straw pallet to sleep on at the inn. I had been grateful as I would have got no rest with my shoulder otherwise. The innkeeper's wife even found me a strip of linen to make a better sling and strapped my arm to my side to help the bone set in the right position. But no amount of consideration could prevent the discomfort of riding so far and I was ready to collapse when we dismounted in the stableyard.

I'd spent the last few hours cursing the stupidity of the Bruces for picking on a friend of the local sheriff to steal from – talk about tweaking the tiger's tail – so I was not in very good humour with anyone who bore that surname.

'Ye'll stay in one o' the servants' rooms until Sir Charles Laud gets here,' announced the ginger-headed man. Turning us over to the butler with a brief explanation, our guards departed.

Our accommodation up in the attic was a vast improvement on the last few nights. We were shown into a small room under the eaves with one tiny bed and a mattress on the floor. A tray of bread and cheese had been set on a stool for us. There was even a jug of water for washing. All I needed now were dry clothes, but that was too much to expect. The brace of footmen who had escorted us to our prison turned the key as they departed, leaving us alone.

I lowered myself to the bed with a groan.

'Are ye all right, Catherine?' asked Rabbie, helping me out of my damp shoes.

'It's Cat, Rabbie.'

'Och aye? The name suits you.'

'Our mother called me Maudie. Can you believe it? Maudie sounds like a ribbon-and-lace kind of girl – the sort who would cry if her frock gets muddy. I'm not planning to change back to it.'

Rabbie poured a beaker of water for us both. 'Maybe she thought ye'd be that kind o' lass.'

I snorted. 'And pigs might fly.'

'Maybe ye would have been, if she hadna left ye.'

I was stunned that he had just admitted that I had told the truth all along.

'Perhaps I would've been,' I replied with a catch in my voice, 'but we'll never know, will we?'

'It was cruel to abandon ye like that. I think I hate her for it,' he said fiercely.

'Nan thought she might've intended to send for me if she'd lived.'

'But still . . .' He shook his head.

'Yes, but still.'

We lay in peace for a few minutes, resting after our long ride across the lowlands. I could still feel an echo of the jolting trot of my last mount as if I were riding on my bed.

'Will they hang me, Cat?' Rabbie's voice sounded so thin and uncertain.

I reached over the side of the bed and grasped his hand. 'No, of course not! I won't let them.

I haven't told you much about me, but I've been in worse fixes than this and got out. And I have powerful friends – my adopted family, I suppose you'd call them. They'll step up to defend anyone who belongs to me.'

'Ye're sure? Ye are nae lying to me?'

'I'm positive.'

'Good.' He let go of my fingers and I heard him turn on his side. Swiftly, his breathing turned into the regular rhythm of sleep. He'd trusted my word – trusted his big sister enough to put his worries aside. It was the most precious gift he could have given me. I just hoped I would not let him down.

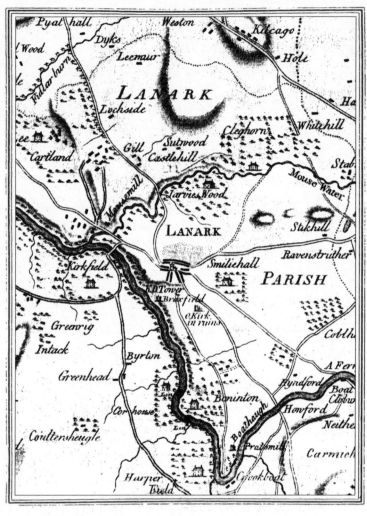

Act V – In which the sheriff confronts
Cat Royal and her merry men . . .

ACT V

SCENE 1 – THE SHERIFF'S COURT

We were woken early the next morning by the same footmen who had escorted us to our prison. Now better rested, I had enough wit to notice the smart blue and gold livery, white wigs and gloves – a gaol with very superior wardens.

'You are to come with us,' the short one with a hooked nose announced. 'Lady Ross-Baillie and the sheriff are waiting for you in the library.'

'Allow us a moment to tidy ourselves,' I replied, rolling carefully off the bed and propelling them out of the door before they could think to protest. I closed it quickly on them.

'Rabbie, we need to decide what we're going to say,' I whispered, trying one-handed to tie back my hair in a ribbon.

Rabbie stepped up to take over the task for me.

'Aye, I'll tell them ye had naethin to do wi' any reiving.'

'You'll do no such thing as it's as good as a confession that you were involved! No, we've got to stick together on this. We are both innocent – at least for today.'

'But ye didna ask to be wi' us when we were caught.'

'I don't think I'll even mention the kidnapping – that won't help your case any.'

'It wasna kidnapping.' He tugged my hair a little too hard. 'We were just keeping ye close.'

'That's what you were doing, was it? I thought Willy threatened to kill me if I tried to escape – and to skin you alive if you let me go. But we haven't got time for that now. I need to get a message to Bridgit to tell her where we are. She can contact my friends for us.' I gave my face a quick lick and a promise with the water in the ewer. Noticing that Rabbie was looking decidedly unkempt, not at all reputable, I wetted the end of my shawl and attacked before he could stop me.

'Get off me, ye daft quean!' He batted me

away but gently, taking care not to harm my injured shoulder.

Seeing his weakness, I approached again. 'It's only a little water!'

'It's cold!' he squawked as I got him full in the face and rubbed hard.

The commotion attracted the footmen's attention. The door flew open and our guards rushed in, expecting to break up a fight. Rabbie and I froze in surprise, water dripping from my shawl on to the back of my brother's neck until he thought to push it away.

'No scrapping!' warned the larger of the two footmen, yanking Rabbie back by the collar. 'We know what you Bruces are like.'

'We were washing, not scrapping,' I said primly, holding my improvised washcloth up as proof, 'and for your information, I am not a Bruce.'

The footman shrugged as if nothing I could say would possibly persuade him against his fixed opinion of us. 'We've waited for you long enough. Come along.'

Squeezing out my shawl, I spread it over

the stool to dry as if I had all the time in the world. When you are a prisoner, you have to make the most of your small gestures of independence.

'Hurry up, miss,' huffed the footman.

'I'm coming, I'm coming,' I said breezily. 'Keep your wig on.'

Rabbie snorted and ducked the clip round the ear that the footman aimed at him.

The house was a lot warmer on the lower floors, thanks to the fires in the family apartments. Through open doors I could see a pleasant parlour, a dining room and a music room – this house, though nowhere near as fine as Frank's Boxton – was luxury on a grand scale.

'Tell me about the lady,' I muttered to Rabbie as we approached a pair of double doors.

'Widow, tough old bird nae matter how she pretends she's not, very rich,' he replied in a rapid whisper. 'Fiercely protective of her property, land and cattle.

The footmen opened the doors and stood back to let us pass.

'The prisoners, my lady,' Hook-nose announced.

We entered a book-lined room with large windows facing out on to a snow-covered lawn. Stubs of rose bushes in a border below the window hinted at last summer's splendour now buried in ice. Frost feathered the corners of the window like Brussels lace. I dragged my attention from the superb view to the two people waiting by the fire.

Seated in a winged armchair was an elderly lady with fluffy white hair, somewhat like the raw cotton Bridgit had fed to the carding machine. Her arthritic hands were clenched on the bone handle of a walking stick. Dressed at the height of fashionable mourning – a purple satin gown with black edging – she gave not a flicker of emotion as we came in.

Our old friend Sir Charles Laud, the Sheriff of Lanark, stood opposite her, hand leaning against the mantelpiece as he kicked a log that threatened to tumble off the grate. He looked as well turned out as he had in his riding gear: this time dressed in a navy blue coat, yellow silk waistcoat and unwrinkled breeches. His valet should be commended.

'Your arm?' Sir Charles asked without introduction.

'I believe it is my collarbone, sir,' I replied, 'as I told you when I begged for your assistance.'

'Has it been looked at by a doctor?'

'No, sir.'

Sir Charles frowned and shot a glance at the lady. 'Godmother?'

She held up a shaky hand. 'I'll see to it, Charles dear. I did not think we should disturb Dr Gordon last night as it was clearly no emergency.'

He turned back to me. 'Are you in pain?'

'It is tolerable, sir,' I replied sourly.

He gave a nod, dismissing the matter for the moment. 'To business then. Lady Ross-Baillie wishes to know what you have done with her prize cattle. Twenty head, wasn't it?' He turned to the lady for verification.

She nodded and dabbed a lace-edged handkerchief to the corner of one eye.

'We tracked them to your tower house,'

continued the sheriff, 'then lost them on the moss, so there is no good denying that you had them.'

I glanced at Rabbie, but he was examining his boots.

'I don't know what makes you think that my brother or I would have a clue about the lady's cows. I'm a London girl born and bred and wouldn't know the front end from the back of one – except to stand well clear of both just in case, if you follow me. What would I want with Lady Ross-Baillie's cattle?'

Sir Charles bared his teeth in a humourless smile. 'I have no idea – that's for you to tell me. You are a surprise, I admit that, but your so-called brother is less of a mystery. He's well known in these parts for his reiving – his cousins have been sentenced in absentia many a time.'

That wasn't good. I was hoping to do this by casting the cloak of my innocence over my guilty brother, but if he was already condemned that would not work.

'I ken naething about the lady's cows,' muttered Rabbie. 'I'm sorry she's lost them.'

'Sorry!' The lady gave a tinkling laugh that reminded me of a chandelier jingling in the wind. 'That is very kind of you, young man.' She opened an ivory fan that hung by a silver chain from her belt and waved it before her wrinkled neck. 'But I would prefer to have my property returned to me rather than hear your regrets. I've been in a flutter ever since my headman told me that brigands had raided the home farm. Palpitations. My nerves in shreds. I will not be able to rest until my sweet girls are returned to me.'

Sweet girls? Those red shaggy monsters from the barn could only be termed so by a very disturbed individual. I narrowed my gaze at the lady, wondering what her game was.

She turned in wet-eyed appeal to the sheriff. 'It is not just the theft of my poor creatures – it is the attack on my peace of mind. I have barely slept since dear Sir John left for a better place. This, I fear, will deprive me even of the little rest I have.'

Oh she was a fine actress, this one. I could sniff out a fellow thespian playing tragic heroine, no problem. The tears were about as genuine as Chatterton's poems. While I had no time for thieves like the Bruces, I had even less time for rich widows determined to see my brother and me hanged.

I held up my right hand, 'Lady Ross-Baillie, Sir Charles, I really must stop you there. This has gone far enough. My friend the Earl of Arden will be amused to hear that you mistook me for a cattle thief, but I fear he may think the joke has been prolonged beyond the bounds of good taste if you do not release my brother and me immediately.'

'Earl of Arden!' Sir Charles said disdainfully. 'The ghillie warned you had a talent for invention.' He kicked the log again, sending a shower of sparks up the chimney. 'He says you are a mill worker – fooled him once but not again.'

'Not invention, sir. I am as I claim – a family friend of the Earl of Arden and his parents, the Duke and Duchess of Avon. I am also a protégée of the famous Mr Sheridan. If you wish to check these claims, you only need write to any one of them for confirmation. Better still, talk to Mr Dale at the mill. He knows something of the reasons for my presence in the area. That way there need be no delay.'

Swayed by this list of impressive character witnesses, Sir Charles creased his brow in doubt, questioning his initial impression of me. This did not suit Lady Ross-Baillie: she wanted her cows back and all commoners kept in their place, dangling at the end of a noose.

'I cannot abide the girl's litany of lies, Charles.' She flapped at me with her handkerchief. 'I know the duke from my days in London – he's a fine man. It is beyond the bounds of credulity to think this ragamuffin has anything to do with him, despite her refined talk.

'I've no doubt she was some servant in their household and learned to ape her betters. Yes, yes, that explains it. No young lady would behave or dress as she does.' She dabbed her eyes delicately. 'But none of this is taking us a step nearer to getting my cows back and punishing the offenders.' What a performance. Lady Ross-Baillie would make Judge Jeffreys look merciful, but it was all tied up in a bows-and-bonnet package so people didn't see her ruthless streak.

Thus reminded of his first loyalty, Sir Charles's brow cleared and he gave his godmother a little bow. 'Quite true, your ladyship. I am beginning to suspect the girl is somewhat addle-pated. But we know enough about the boy to proceed to court. I understand we can already charge the girl with trespass, if not cattle thieving. But I have a favour to beg: might I leave them in your charge until the next sitting of the sheriff court?'

Lady Ross-Baillie did not look overjoyed at this prospect. 'But Charles, I am not sure I would feel entirely safe with two thieves under my roof. Why not keep them in gaol?'

Sir Charles gave a gruff laugh. 'The kindest thing that can be said of the town prison is only those that feel inclined to stay do so. I have told the provost that we need to build a new one as the old is like a Swiss cheese. No, I want at least one Bruce to face justice; I can't risk the boy absconding. His cousins may be in the area already and would have no trouble breaking him out of the gaol.'

Lady Ross-Baillie pursed her lips. 'Very well.

I'll make arrangements to secure them here.'

'And the doctor?'

She waved the handkerchief. 'Yes, yes, that too.'

'Thank you, my lady. As ever, you are generosity itself.' He bent over to kiss her hand.

I was dismayed by how easily she had swayed him from giving me a hearing. 'You mean you are not going to ask Mr Dale to verify my story for me?'

'Why waste his time and mine?' Sir Charles checked his pocket watch, tutting over the hour.

'Because I'm telling the truth. At least let me write to my friends to prove it to you!'

'Oh, very clever. I see your mind: you mean to tell the Bruces to come and save you. Not on my watch, young woman. The Bruces will remain ignorant of your presence here to save Lady Ross-Baillie any trouble. Now, I've had quite enough of your talk. I'm a busy man. You should be grateful I have provided for your comfort. After next week, you will look back on this as paradise.'

Lady Ross-Baillie gave a smug little smile and thumped her walking stick on the floor. The footmen returned on her summons.

'Take the young persons back to their room and make sure they do not leave for any reason,' she said sharply.

With a bow, the footmen marched us back upstairs.

Behind locked doors again, I kicked the stool over and let out a frustrated growl.

'Have you heard the story of the boy who cried wolf?' I asked.

Rabbie nodded miserably.

'Well, that's me. The one time I tell the truth about my noble friends no one believes me!'

'So, ye were no spinnin' a tale?'

'No, I was not!' I hit the wall with my good hand, sending a jolt of pain up my left side.

Rabbie tugged on my skirt. 'Sit down, Cat, before ye hurt yerself.'

I slumped on to the bed. 'We've got to get word out of here one way or another. That man has made up his mind about us. He won't give us a fair trial.'

'Did ye really trespass?'

'I might've done.'

'Well, I canna say the sheriff isna fair. I ken what I did.' Rabbie scrubbed his hands through his hair, making it stick up in brown spikes. 'But I dinna want to hang.'

I patted the bed beside me, inviting him to sit. Once in hugging range, I ventured to put my good arm around his shoulders. 'You won't. I promise you.'

'At least the most he can do to ye is give ye a fine for trespass.'

'Yes, and if I'm out of here first I'll come back for you. Sir Charles the dandy won't know what's hit him when I bring in my reinforcements.' I squeezed his arm. 'Who knows, I might even get the duchess involved – then he'll really be sorry.'

'Why would a duchess be interested in the likes of me?'

'Because you're my brother.'

He gave a slight nod. 'That I am. I didn't want to be, but now I'm glad.'

I shoved him in the ribs to prevent a dip into

maudlin sentiment which would suit neither of us. 'Just because I've got powerful friends?'

He chuckled. 'Nae, because ye're a bagrel lass for me to tease.'

'Bagrel?'

'A bit on the wee side o' tall.'

'Lout.'

'Skinnymalink.'

'Clumsy oaf.'

'Midget.'

I laughed. 'That's the exchange of pleasantries over. Now all we need is a plan to get us out of here.'

True to her word, Lady Ross-Baillie allowed the doctor to visit mid-morning. I had not realized when she mentioned his name that I had met him before – it was the same doctor who had signed the death certificate for my poor aunt during the influenza outbreak. A stout party with bushy sideburns, little hair on top and a bulbous nose, he made a reassuring visitor in the sickroom. He was so vividly present with his large frame and booming voice, I felt that any illness would not dare stay when he came in.

'Well, lass, let's take a look at yer arm,' he announced with the genteel tones of an Edinburgh-trained man, his accent less broad to my ears than that of the locals. 'How did ye do that to yerself?'

'Riding accident,' I explained.

His eyes lit up with recognition when he heard my voice. 'The London lass, is it? I remember ye looked after that poor family in Long Row. What in mercy's name are ye doing locked up for cattle stealing?'

I was relieved he remembered – that saved me a lot of trouble. 'It's all a terrible mistake, sir,' I explained. 'But Sir Charles won't let me appeal to my friends for help. He caught me riding with the Bruces and assumed the worse.'

Dr Gordon's eyes flicked to Rabbie.

'Yes, that's why. Believe it or not, you are looking at my long-lost brother. Our family reunion went a touch off course when we both got arrested.' Not to mention the kidnapping and general hostility from the first meeting.

'I'm sorry to hear it.' His large hands felt warm on my skin as he gently felt the breakage. 'This appears to be as well as can be expected. I'll leave ye some laudanum for the pain. Keep it strapped up and in a few weeks it will be as good as new. It isna a serious break.' He tipped his head to Rabbie. 'Yer brother, ye say?'

'Yes. It took me a while to find him but that's my brother.'

The doctor began packing his equipment away. 'And ye need to contact yer friends?'

'Yes, sir. The dominie in the mill school and Mr Dale can vouch for me. I'm no thief.'

'But yer brother –'

'– Is only twelve,' I stated firmly. 'If we get out of here, I'll make sure he doesn't get into trouble again.' I shot a look at Rabbie, who was listening carefully to our exchange. 'I promise.'

'I need no one else to vouch for ye, lass. Ye showed yer kind heart nursing that family. Who do ye want me to speak to?'

Yes! My spirit did a little victory caper. Here

come the cavalry, Sir Charles – you'd better take cover!

'Bridgit O'Riley. She will probably be staying with Mistress MacDonald.'

'Aye, I ken the lady. I'll call in on my way home. Good day to ye.'

When he left, I let out a whoop of joy. Rabbie looked at me as if I had cracked.

'What's got into ye, ye daftie?'

I threw one arm wide. 'Rejoice with me, Rabbie the Bruce – we are going to beat the sheriff. The merry men are coming!'

'What are ye blethering about?' He couldn't help but smile.

'Just you wait and see.'

The week of incarceration passed almost pleasantly, apart from the inevitable niggles of being in close quarters with someone for too long. I'd wished for a chance to get to know my brother and now we had nothing else to do but talk and amuse ourselves. In addition to his life history, I discovered that he could cheat at cards (thanks to a pack begged off the hook-nosed footman), couldn't carry a tune and had smelly feet. I found the last point rather comforting as I felt it was exactly the kind of thing one should know about one's brother. He heard the tales of my travels, admired my singing, told me I was useless at *vingt-et-un* and laughed at my attempts to persuade him that ballet was a superior form of dance. After he almost split his sides when I performed one-armed my piece from the Paris Opera, I admitted grumpily that you had to be there to understand.*

The day of the court hearing finally arrived. As we prepared for our appearance, I wished I had some clean clothes to make a decent impression. I'd been washing out our clothes piece by piece with the soap and water we were allowed, but still we could do with a good bath and complete change. After protesting at my fussy ways, Rabbie had submitted to me removing a layer or two of grime from his person. I told myself that he secretly approved and was just objecting as a point

* If you wish to be there, Reader, I refer you to *Den of Thieves*.

of honour. On the other hand, perhaps I had worn him down so that he had decided giving in was preferable to the torment of my nagging.

We were taken in a closed carriage to the courthouse in Lanark, the sheriff doubtless fearing that we would slip away otherwise. Rabbie had been shackled, but in deference to my injury and lesser charge, I was left free.

'Ye are certain yer friends will be there?' Rabbie kept asking, nibbling on a hangnail.

'Yes, I am,' I replied.

'How can ye be so very sure?'

'You'll find that out when you meet them. You couldn't ask for better, more loyal friends. We've been through so much together.'

I kept from him my worry that just perhaps Dr Gordon had failed to find Bridgit. But no, I wouldn't go down that path. If the doctor had let us down, my brother might find himself facing a trial for his life and I'd promised him that wouldn't happen. I had to have faith.

We were taken round the back of the grey stone courthouse and led into a cheerless room to wait. I could hear a murmur of voices from the front of the building and wondered if it was market day. Intrigued by the unexpectedly lively atmosphere, I asked the man left behind to guard us what the cause was.

'They've come to see a Bruce finally get what's coming to him,' he replied, giving Rabbie an unfriendly grin. 'Long overdue to my mind.'

I seethed. The jolterhead.

Swallowing my anger but promising myself we'd get even, I turned my back on our guard and cudgelled my brains to think through the new problem. I had not considered what the locals might make of our trial. It would put a dent in my plans for a triumphant acquittal if the sheriff felt he had to bow to public pressure for justice. But how to make an obviously guilty boy come out smelling of roses?

'The court is ready for ye now,' announced an usher, appearing at the door. He escorted us to a door leading to a set of wooden steps. My stomach twisted with a feeling uncannily like stage fright. Rabbie grappled for my hand and held on tightly. I took a steadying breath.

'It will be all right, you'll see,' I reassured him.

We climbed the short flight of stairs and emerged out into the dock in the courtroom itself. A buzz of excitement hummed around the chamber on our appearance, drowning out individual voices. With our backs to the public gallery, all I could see at first was the sheriff sitting in his raised chair and a flock of black-clad officials flapping round the court like scavenger crows on a battlefield. I twisted to look behind but two attendants flanked us, hemming me in. Had I misjudged things so badly? Perhaps my friends had not had time to come – the message had gone astray – they'd been powerless to intervene. The possibilities flashed through my mind. I'd become used to relying on my adopted family of Syd and Frank; maybe this was one time when they would not be able to help me out of the fix in which I found myself.

A court official began to read through the preliminaries, asking us to confirm our names and relationship.

'Ye claim that ye are Rabbie Bruce's half-sister?' one of the crows asked.

'Yes, sir. We had the same mother.'

'But ye were born out of wedlock?'

I hadn't anticipated this. Knowing how sensitive Rabbie was about our mother's good name, he now had to listen to it being dragged through the mud before the citizens of Lanark. He squeezed my hand a bit too tight for comfort, but I had no recourse but to tell the truth. At least I could make it clear that my brother had no such stain on his name.

'Yes, sir. I was born before she married Rabbie's father.'

'And how do ye ken this?'

'I was told the facts recently by my aunt, Mrs Mary Moir of Long Row, New Lanark.'

'Mrs Moir being the sister of your mother?'

'That is the usual requirement for an aunt, I believe.'

There was a titter of laughter from the gallery. I was growing quietly more and more frantic. Surely if my friends were here by now they would have let me know their presence?

'So ye are related to the Bruces by the marriage of your mother?' the crow continued.

I frowned. I'd not thought of it that way. 'I suppose you could say that.'

'So your testimony on behalf of yer brother is likely to be prejudiced?'

Of course it was.

'No!' I lied.

The crow turned to the sheriff. 'The matter before the court is simple, yer honour. Rabbie Bruce is charged with involvement in the theft of twenty head of cattle from the farm of Lady Ross-Baillie. His sister is charged with being an accessory to the crime and trespass on the same Lady Ross-Baillie's land, no doubt for the purpose of scouting the lie of the land in advance of the actual theft.'

'What? That's a fib!' I couldn't believe it! They'd twisted my most innocent actions to fit their idea of what a Bruce would be up to.

Sir Charles gave me a reproving stare. 'Contain yourself, Miss Royal, or I will have you removed from the courtroom.'

Rabbie looked across at me, his face ashen. 'I dinna think it's going well,' he whispered.

'Don't worry,' I said with more bravado than conviction, 'my friends will come through for us.'

'I canna see them; can ye?'

'No conferring in the dock!' barked Sir Charles.

The guard shoved us apart.

'Now to the charges,' Sir Charles continued sternly. 'Call the first witness.'

SCENE 2 – MERRY MEN

'I call on Mister Archibald Brown to take his place in the witness box,' announced the sheriff.

As the ghillie stepped up to take his oath, there was a noise outside the courtroom.

'There's nae room!' I heard an official bellow. 'Go back to where ye came from.'

Sir Charles halted proceedings and gave a nod to a man to find out what was happening. When he opened the door, the exchange outside came through to the courtroom loud and clear.

'Ye canna keep us out: our cousins are in there!'

With a thrill of joy, I recognized Ian Moir's voice raised in anger. Cousins – not cousin. So they knew about me too!

'My man, I think ye should reconsider the wisdom of barring me from the court,' a second voice suggested pleasantly.

'Mr Dale, I didna see ye there,' blustered the official. 'O' course, sir, step in and welcome.'

'With my people as well.'

'But there's nae room in the gallery, sir. I didna lie about that.'

'Then we'll take the seats at the back of court kept for the town officials. There is always room down there.'

Before anyone could stop him, Mr Dale entered, followed by a string of familiar faces from the mill: the Moirs from the father down to little Jeannie, the dominie, Mistress MacDonald, my dormitory companion Annie, the good doctor and the overseer. Bringing up the rear were Jamie and Bridgit. Catching sight of my anxious face, Jamie waved and Bridgit gave me a reassuring smile.

Sir Charles stood up, forcing everyone else in the room to rise. 'Mr Dale, what an unexpected pleasure,' he said awkwardly, giving the factory owner a bow.

Mr Dale continued down the aisle to the front. 'Sir Charles, I'd like to offer myself as a character witness for the two young people you have on trial.'

'That is very kind of you – quite unnecessary though as the evidence is very clear.' The sheriff bent lower and dropped his voice. 'Surely you know the Bruces, sir?'

'Aye, that I do. But I know the girl has nothing to do with them. Under my employ she proved herself a good worker and a fine teacher, both of letters and the scriptures.'

Sir Charles could not contain a disbelieving snort.

'She isn't the kind of lass who'd get mixed up in reiving,' continued Mr Dale. 'I fear you are labouring under a serious misapprehension.'

'Me, sir?' The sheriff clearly thought Mr Dale had taken leave of his senses.

'Aye. She came to Scotland with the worthy purpose of tracing her family and it looks to me as if she has achieved it.' Mr Dale gave a nod to Rabbie.

'But she was found trespassing on Lady Ross-Baillie's land,' Sir Charles countered.

'Like half of my workers do, I suppose you mean?' chuckled Mr Dale. 'I understand from those she was with that she went on the Sabbath to see one of God's wonders, Corra Linn – hardly a hanging offence. I have suggested to Lady Ross-Baillie on numerous occasions that it is a sin to stop the minds of common people being opened and improved by viewing the mysteries of our Creator. She lets the rich gentry see the Linn, so why not those who, I would argue, need it more: the poor at her very gate?'

There was a sharp gasp of outrage from Sir Charles's right. I noticed for the first time that Lady Ross-Baillie herself was present, tucked discreetly in a corner under the gallery so as to be out of sight of vulgar eyes.

'This is hardly the place to debate property rights,' grumbled Sir Charles. He waved to the man taking note of proceedings. 'Please note Mr Dale's name as a character witness.' He turned back to the factory owner. 'Could I trouble you to take a seat?'

'Only when you've added the names of Dominie Blair, Mistress MacDonald and Overseer Shaw,' Mr Dale said evenly.

Sir Charles gave a jerky nod, as if the gesture ruptured something in his neck, and Mr Dale turned to take a seat, giving me a ghost of a wink as he did so.

'Now, back to our first witness,' announced Sir Charles, his feathers ruffled. With Mr Dale present, he was no longer undisputed cock of the walk. 'Mr Brown, please tell the court –'

He got no further for there was a renewed commotion outside the door.

'What now?' he groaned.

'Get out of the road! We've not come all this way to 'ave a runty Scot stop us goin' where we want.'

'But you canna –' squeaked the official.

'We *canna* what?' Syd Fletcher asked menacingly. I could just picture him looming over the poor man, backing him up against the door.

'Er, go on in, sir.'

Syd threw the doors open with a crash and strode into the court, taking charge as if it were a tavern in Covent Garden. At his back were Nick and Joe looking suitably threatening as officials moved to intercept them then thought better of it.

'All right, Cat?' Syd asked loudly, his eyes

sweeping the room for further threats.

I'm not ashamed to admit I had tears in my eyes when I answered. 'Yes, Syd. We're all right.'

'That your brother?' He cocked an eyebrow at Rabbie.

'Yes.'

'Don't look much like you.'

'I know, but he's mine.'

Syd gave a nod. 'All right, we'll spring 'im too.'

I choked. 'What?'

Syd grinned. 'All legal like – don't want to get in trouble with no Scottish law.'

'Of course not,' I chuckled. Not that that would stop him. Knowing Syd, he'd try legal, then try something else.

'This is descending into a farce!' barked Sir Charles. 'Who are you, young man?'

'I'm character witness for Cat Royal. Known her since a baby, I 'ave. No one knows 'er better than me.'

It was evident to all present that Sir Charles was beginning to wish he hadn't got up that morning. 'In that case, you must wait your turn with the others.' He pointed to the seats at the back of the courtroom. 'And stop intimidating my men!'

'What? Me?' asked Syd innocently, clenching his fists and baring his teeth in a mirthless smile. 'I'm 'armless – mostly.'

Nick and Joe gave me two identical grins and retreated with Syd to their seats. It might have been just a trick of the light, but I could swear that the official who'd stood nearest Joe was now short of a watch chain and accompanying ticker.

Sir Charles thought it time to remind his rebellious audience of the solemnity of the occasion and of his own importance.

'I will not allow the proceedings to be interrupted again – not for anything or anyone,' he lectured us. 'I will severely punish the next person who –'

But he was destined not to finish. A crow-attendant fluttered to his side and whispered in his ear urgently. Sir Charles's eyes widened.

'What? Here?' he stuttered.

Oh, I was just loving this! It was better than a

first night and a full house. I had a delicious sense of anticipation. Poking Rabbie in the ribs, I whispered.

'We've had Friar Tuck,' I nodded to Mr Dale, 'Little John,' I gestured to Syd, 'now, if I'm not mistaken, it's the turn of King Richard.'

He looked at me blankly.

'Haven't you ever heard the tales of Robin Hood?'

He shook his head.

'Just hold on to your hat: it's about to get exciting.'

Sir Charles was checking the arrangement of his cravat nervously. 'Let them in then,' he muttered to the official. 'Quickly!'

The door opened for a final time. Sir Charles shot to his feet again, producing the ripple effect around the courtroom as everyone else rose. I had an inappropriate desire to giggle.

'Your grace, this is an unexpected honour! And your lordship, so kind of you to come.'

Walking down the aisle came the statesmanlike figure of the Duke of Avon, his midnight blue coat the last word in elegance, his cane tapping at every pace. At his shoulder, and striding in time with ease, was his son, the Earl of Arden, neatly turned out (for Frank, that is) in a claret jacket and gold silk waistcoat. Frank sought me out and gave a smile – he was enjoying this as much as me. A tall, scholarly looking man followed, carrying a pile of papers.

'Sir Charles,' replied the duke in his quiet but firm voice. The hubbub in the public gallery died down as we strained to hear every word. 'So kind of you to make time for us. I have brought my advocate from Edinburgh, Mr Walter Scott, to advise our family friend Miss Royal. I trust that meets with your approval.'

Sir Charles gave a nod. Dazed, he looked like one of the subjects of Mesmer's experiments. 'So she didn't lie,' he said, half to himself.

Lady Ross-Baillie gave a whimper of distress. She had not for one moment believed my claim to know a duke – but she could be forgiven her scepticism. Not many Covent Garden waifs gather such friends in their career.

'Miss Royal, lie?' laughed Frank. 'Of course

not. She's the soul of honesty and ladylike deportment.'

With his back to Sir Charles, I hoped I was the only one who noticed that Frank had his fingers crossed.

'It seems to me that this unfortunate matter need not go to trial,' continued the duke. 'I've consulted Mr Scott here and he thinks the process has been most irregular. He pointed out that the defendants were not given access to legal counsel and no jury was summoned to deliberate the more serious charges. It is almost as if the guilty verdict has been decided in advance on the strength of reputation alone, but I'm sure that cannot be the case.'

Sir Charles flushed, the picture of a culpable man. The duke took out his watch, giving the impression that this had taken up enough of his valuable time already and it would be better for the future of all concerned if they did exactly as he said. 'May I suggest that we adjourn today's hearing and retire to discuss the matter as gentlemen? I can vouch for Miss Royal and am willing to extend the same protection to her brother. My family owes her a great debt and we would be most grateful to you for giving us the chance to repay it.'

Oh, well done the duke! I cheered him on silently. Reading between the lines of his polite speech, he was telling Sir Charles that his court was a shambles and that if he didn't let us go he'd earn the undying displeasure of one of the Britain's most illustrious houses.

Sir Charles tugged on his cravat and glanced up at the public gallery. It appeared the people's desire to hang a Bruce had been completely distracted by the fascinating spectacle on the courtroom floor. It wasn't every day that the little town of Lanark saw their sheriff out-bigwigged.

'I suppose . . . I suppose . . .' began Sir Charles.

'But what about my cows?' protested Lady Ross-Baillie, annoyed that her concerns were about to be so easily brushed aside.

The duke turned to bestow a brilliant smile on her. 'Why, Lady Ross-Baillie! It has been a while since I last had the pleasure of seeing you. You are looking as beautiful as ever.' He gallantly moved to kiss her hand. 'May I present my son to you?'

Frank gave an accomplished bow. Lady Ross-Baillie fluttered and blushed under the combined flattery of the House of Avon.

'I will make sure you are recompensed for your loss,' murmured the duke. 'I would never leave a lady in distress.'

'Of course you would not,' she beamed at him.

The duke straightened up from their private conference. 'What is it to be, Sir Charles?' he asked in a brisker tone.

Sir Charles glanced to Mr Dale, the local celebrity, then to the London troublemakers ready to enforce our freedom, and finally to the duke with his formidable legal counsel. He knew that he was beaten.

'The case is adjourned, pending further investigation,' he announced. 'I release Catherine Royal and Rabbie Bruce into the custody of the Duke of Avon. That is if you are willing, your grace, to stand as guarantor for them?'

The duke gave me a warm smile. 'I am.'

Sir Charles knocked a gavel on a board. 'Court is suspended.'

As he swept out, I could swear I heard him mutter, 'Thank God.'

I was ready to jump over the edge of the dock to hug my friends, but instead we were hustled back to the cheerless room. Rabbie's irons were struck off while we waited for the papers to be signed, confirming our release.

'I'm impressed,' admitted Rabbie, giving me a delighted grin. 'I had my doubts, but deep down, I believed that ye could do it.'

'I did nothing. It was all the work of my friends – and family.' I added the last with a catch in my throat. I couldn't wait to see the Moirs.

'Ye are free to go,' announced the guard unhappily, opening the door on to the back yard.

And there they were – all of them, even the duke.

Frank was the first to reach me. 'You idiot, Cat! I let you go to Scotland and you take up cattle thieving just to make my hair go grey before I'm twenty.'

'Mind my arm,' I squawked as he hugged me.

Frank realized for the first time that I had a sling under my shawl. 'Sorry. Are you all right? That was stupid of me.'

Syd altered his usual crushing embrace to a gentle squeeze. ''Ow did that 'appen?' He gave Rabbie an assessing look, wondering if he were to blame.

'I fell off a horse – my fault entirely,' I said quickly, not wanting to sour my brother's relationship with my best friends from the outset. 'Frank, Syd – may I introduce Rabbie, my brother?'

'Humph!' said Syd. 'Bridgit told us all about you, you mangy rascal – kidnappin' Cat and gettin' 'er into your trouble.'

Before Rabbie could open his mouth to retaliate, I stepped on his foot.

'All things for which he is sincerely sorry, I'm sure,' I said quickly. 'But you're missing the point, Syd. He's my *brother*. Isn't that wonderful!'

'Yeah, Kitten, I know. Congratulations.' He sized Rabbie up again. 'Big lad. I s'pose we could make somethink of 'im when we get 'im 'ome.'

Rabbie was not warming to my friends as I had hoped, but then they didn't exactly like him either. A familiar state of affairs. 'I willna be going away wi' ye,' he sneered.

Bad move to sneer at Syd. Rabbie found himself dangling from his shirtfront and lifted to Syd's eyes. 'Tough luck, mate. You should've thought of that before you got yourself in gaol.'

'What do you mean?' I asked. Syd seemed convinced Rabbie was going back to London with me.

Frank gave me a half-smile. 'Conditions of your release, Cat. My father's agreed to take you both back with us and to ensure that your brother stays out of trouble.'

'Nae!' protested Rabbie. 'Put me back in there. I'll talk to the man!'

'Too late. You had a choice between swinging for a thief or becoming the ward of a duke. We took the liberty of choosing the latter for you. Welcome to the family, Rabbie.' Frank goosed him in the ribs to deflate his outraged stance then ruffled his hair.

Rabbie turned to appeal to me. 'Cat, tell them I canna leave here.'

I bit my lip. I could guess how this must seem to him – something like an avalanche in the Highlands sweeping away all his familiar landmarks. 'I'm afraid I don't think you have much choice, Rabbie – not for now at least. And I'll be with you, don't forget that.'

Rabbie scowled but had the good sense to recognize he was up against a brick wall. He gave a curt nod. 'As long as ye promise ye'll no leave me,' he muttered.

'I promise.'

Syd and Frank moved aside so that I could curtsey to the duke and thank him for his assistance.

'Not at all, Miss Royal,' he said pleasantly. 'Considering our past history, it was the least I could do to settle the great debt our family owes you. And I'm delighted you've found your brother so unexpectedly.'

'Thank you, your grace. He's very grateful to you too.' I nudged Rabbie who murmured something which I hoped the duke construed as thanks. It sounded a little too much like curses to me.

Bridgit and Jamie came up next. I half-strangled Bridgit with my enthusiastic greeting.

'Thank you, thank you, thank you!' I exclaimed.

She laughed. 'To be sure, it was nothing: just a letter and a word in the right ear. You made lots of friends in New Lanark, Cat.'

'That ye have, Snippie,' grinned Jamie.

'I hadn't realized until today. Thanks, professor.' I felt someone nudge my hand. 'Jeannie!'

'Hello, Cousin Catherine,' the little girl giggled. 'I'm very glad ye're one o' us.'

Ian and Dougie joined her and both gave me a kiss on the cheek.

'Time to come home, cousin, and tell the family what ye've been up to for the last fourteen years or so,' said Dougie.

'Jamie says we'll no believe ye when we hear the full tale,' added Ian, picking Jeannie up to give her a lift on his shoulders. 'So we are primed to be amazed.'

'I'll do my best,' I promised, following his lead as he guided us out of the yard to the waiting carriages. 'I wouldn't want to disappoint my audience.'

EPILOGUE

HIGHWAYMEN

My friends and family (is it not a miracle that I can write that?) spent Christmas together at Kinlochrie, one of the duke's Scottish estates near Stirling. The duke himself returned to London, leaving Frank in charge of his extensive and unconventional guest list of mill workers and London market boys, but he managed admirably. We played games, burned a massive yule log in the parlour hearth, and ate and drank to our hearts' content. My friend Professor Jamie discovered the library and only rarely came up for air. He struck up a friendship with the steward over something he called 'steam engineering' – whatever that is – so we left them to their discussion of gaskets and pistons. On a less learned note, Syd identified both Dougie and Rabbie as promising boxers and spent the day after Christmas taking them through their paces on the back lawn, providing us all with much entertainment and only one bloody nose.

Remembering what Mrs Moir had told me about her side of the family, Rabbie and I sought out our mother's grave in Stirling where she had lived as a girl. We made what I like to think of as our peace with our mother on New Year's Day. Standing hand in hand by the plain headstone, we agreed that neither of us had been given the chance to know Jesse Stirling Bruce, so it was best if we put the most generous interpretation on her actions. Official family story was to be that she had meant to return for me. Her sin had been carelessness, not cruelty. She'd lived fast and messily (sounds familiar, Reader?) but not with any intent to harm her own children. My last soap-bubble dream about my mother perhaps, but this time I vowed that it would last.

Bidding the Moirs farewell at New Lanark with

promises to write and return soon, the London-bound party set off for the south in two carriages. I manoeuvred things so that Bridgit shared one with Syd and the boys, leaving Frank, Rabbie and me in the other.

'What was all that about?' Frank asked, gesturing to the vehicle travelling to our rear.

'A little bit of diplomacy,' I replied. 'Reconciling the nations and all that.'

Frank snorted. 'Why don't I trust you?'

'Because you know me so well?'

'You shouldn't try and matchmake. It'll be a disaster, you mark my words.'

'O ye of little faith.'

'That's right. I'm not stupid and I know your potential for creating mayhem.'

Rabbie had fallen asleep soon after our departure. He was currently leaning against the side of the carriage and snoring.

'What are you going to do with him?' Frank asked, now looking seriously at the rumpled twelve-year-old I had taken under my wing.

I sighed. 'I really don't know. I'm a bit short of

plans for myself too but I'm sure we'll muddle through. We get on all right most of the time.'

'I've got to go back to Cambridge – you know that, don't you? I won't be on hand to help.'

'Yes I wouldn't expect you to waste any more time on my brother and me, Frank. I'm so deeply in your debt, I can't imagine how I'll pay you back.'

'By not telling me that you are a waste of my time – I won't allow it.'

Our pleasant bickering was interrupted by the sudden slowing of the carriage.

'What's the matter?' I asked. 'Sheep on the road?'

Frank put his head out of the window and ducked back in again quickly.

'Worse – highwaymen.' He felt in the door pocket and pulled out a pistol. 'I hope John Coachman remembered to load this.'

I shook Rabbie awake. 'It's best just to give them what they want.'

Frank nodded grimly and hid the pistol under the tail of his jacket.

'What's happening?' Rabbie asked blearily.

'Get out o' the carriages!' demanded one of the highwaymen. 'All o' ye!'

Frank reached for the door handle but Rabbie held him back. 'It's my cousin Malcolm,' he explained, flashing me a regretful look.

'What! Did you ask him to come for you?' I asked accusingly.

'Nae! I didna ken about this, I swear.'

'Get out or I'll shoot the coachman!' bellowed Malcolm.

'Lovely,' muttered Frank. 'More of Cat's extended family.' He jumped into the mud and held out a hand to help me down. Rabbie splashed into an ice-crusted puddle, slipping so that he had to grab on to my skirts to remain standing.

We had stopped on a bleak stretch of road high above the Clyde Valley and now all of us were standing outside the carriages exposed to the elements. A bitter wind blew from the north, cutting through my layers of shawl and cloak. Snow scattered, stinging all areas of exposed skin, settling in drifts against the stone wall. A landscape of black, white and grey sky, it felt like the anteroom to Hell. Six of the Bruce boys, all mounted, surrounded the two carriages, guns levelled at us. Malcolm spurred his horse forward. Behind, I sensed Syd, Bridgit, Nick and Joe move to stand at our backs. Syd pushed Bridgit and me into the centre of the boys.

'We're here for the lad.' Malcolm jerked his head at Rabbie. 'Come away, Rabbie.'

Frank tightened his grip on the hidden pistol. 'He can't go with you. If he is caught again, they'll hang him. If you've Rabbie's best interests at heart, you'll let him go with his sister. Besides, my father gave his word to the sheriff and I would not have him proved false.'

Willy pushed his horse forward, splashing mud on Frank's boots and breeches. 'Shut it, lad, or we'll slit your throat. We've nae love for Sassenach lords in these parts.'

Malcolm gave a snort of laughter. 'And I dinna care about yer faither, yer lordship. I only want my cousin.'

I felt Rabbie stiffen beside me. He was faced with a choice between a life he knew and the one I had offered him. It must have been both pleasant and painful to hear that he was wanted back at the tower house. I swayed towards him, putting my hand on his arm.

'What do you want to do, little brother?'

He grimaced, his brown eyes filled with longing. He wanted both, of course – the familiar and the adventure.

'What's keeping ye, lad?' asked Malcolm. 'Say yer goodbyes to yer sister. We best make all speed homewards now we've held up his lordship.'

'Do you want to go with him?' I asked quietly. 'I won't blame you if you choose your cousins, but it will be dangerous. You won't be able to show your face in Lanark – perhaps you'll have to hide out in the Highlands like they planned.'

Rabbie rubbed the back of his hand across his nose.

'I'll write to you.'

'I canna read,' he mumbled.

'Well, one of the others could read my letters to you. And . . . and maybe you'd come and see me in London some day.'

He looked doubtful.

'No, you're right.' I sighed. 'If you stay, I suppose it's unlikely we'll meet for a very long time. If ever.' I swallowed down my fear that he wouldn't get a second chance escaping the noose.

'Och, Cat, I dinna ken what to do.'

The Bruces were getting impatient. Willy shouted, 'Hey, Rabbie, we canna wait for ye. Come, or we'll leave ye behind!'

My brother startled me by drawing me close to put his arms around my shoulders and rest his head against mine. He seemed to be breathing me in, looking to my strength to steady his.

'It's all right,' I whispered. 'Whatever you decide, it's all right.'

Rabbie let me go and stood up straight.

'Malcolm, can ye say goodbye to Nan from me? I'm no going wi' ye – I'm staying wi' my sister.'

Rockets, Catherine wheels – my heart held a private little celebration all of its own.

'Staying with her? Are ye sure?' queried Malcolm, doubting what he was hearing.

'Idiot!' muttered Willy.

'Aye. I've only just found her; I'd be daft to lose her again so soon.'

Malcolm stared at Rabbie, then at me. My brother put his arm around my shoulder, careful of my mending injury, presenting a united front. A reluctant smile broke across Malcolm's face.

'Aye, maybe ye would be. She certainly keeps strange company. Ye'll have an interesting time.' He gave a whistle to the other men – a signal to depart.

Willy nudged his horse alongside Malcolm. 'Ye're letting him go?'

'Aye. But he kens where we are if he needs us. Is that no true, lad?'

'Aye, Malcolm,' nodded Rabbie, his voice a little thicker than usual.

Willy spat at my feet but wheeled his horse round. 'Ye'll regret it, Rabbie Bruce.'

'God be wi' ye!' Malcolm said in farewell. 'And with that kittlin sister of yers.'

With a shout, the Bruces urged their horses away. They galloped off uphill and across the moor, whooping and twirling their hats until they disappeared in the fog that drifted in from the north.

Frank gave a whistle of appreciation at this flamboyant departure. 'They've got style. They may be brutes but they definitely have style.'

Syd rubbed his chin regretfully. 'But it would've been a good scrap if it 'ad come to a fight.'

'Next time,' promised Rabbie, 'I'll let ye at them.'

'Ready to head south?' Frank asked, gesturing back into the carriage.

'I am,' I admitted. 'What about you, little brother?'

Rabbie helped me into my seat and sat down beside me. 'Aye, I'll come home with ye, sister, as long as ye stop calling me "little".'

'Well, you are.'

The carriage surged into motion again.

'Only in age, but no in feet and inches.'

'But it's age that matters –'

'Are you two going to argue all the way to London?' Frank interrupted with a groan.

Rabbie and I exchanged a look.

'We'll give it a good go, won't we, brother? We've got a lot of time to make up for sibling squabbles.'

'Aye, we'll give it our best shot,' agreed Rabbie.

We fell silent, waiting for Frank to be lulled into a false sense of security. I winked at Rabbie.

'I want something to eat,' he said with a creditable whine.

'You should've had something before we left,' grumbled Frank.

'I did, but I'm still hungry.'

'Too bad.'

We waited several beats before it was my turn.

'I'm bored. Are we nearly there yet?'

'No!' bellowed Frank.

'Half way?'

'No.'

'An incey-wincey tiny bit of the way there yet?' I wheedled.

'No, no and no!' Frank then noticed that my lips were twitching and that Rabbie had his handkerchief stuffed in his mouth. 'Oh, for heaven's sake! It was bad enough when there was just one Cat Royal – now there are two chips off the same block I swear none of us are safe!'

Curtain falls.

CAT'S GLOSSARY

ADDLE-PATED – foolish, confused

ARSY-VARSY – upside down

BACK-SLANGED – made a run for it

BANBURY TALE – invention

BEDLEM – Bethlehem Hospital, home to unfortunate lunatics

BUFFLE-HEADED – fool (and there are plenty of those around Covent Garden)

CARLTON HOUSE – residence of HRH The Prince of Wales

CAST UP YOUR ACCOUNTS – nothing to do with money and everything to do with being sick

CATTLE – sometimes meaning horses (don't ask me why)

CHATTERTON'S POEMS – brilliant forgeries by a genius who died young

CLEVELAND BAYS – breed of horses suited to carriages

CORRA LINN – wonderful waterfall in the Clyde Valley

CURRICLE – death trap – sorry, Frank's spanking

new carriage

DASHER – flashy young woman

FIRST STARE OF FASHION – to be right up to date with fashion trends

FLAT – a gullible person

IRISH ASSURANCE – proverbial quality of the Irish; bold, shameless

JOLTERHEAD – idiot

JUDGE JEFFREYS – judge famed for his merciless judgements

LIGHTSKIRT – woman of loose morals

ORIEL WINDOW – a window partly projecting from the building, similar to a bay window

MAKE A CAKE OF YOURSELF – not that I ever do this, you understand, but to make yourself look foolish

MESMER'S EXPERIMENTS – Franz Mesmer, famous for his exploits with hypnosis and channelling of animal spirits (he was barmy if you ask me)

MULE – nothing to do with donkeys a machine for spinning and winding

PATTENS – overshoes

PIECER – child-worker who fixes broken threads

RACK RENTED – forced off land by unfair rises in rent

RATTLEPATE – empty-headed fool

ROUND GOWN – simple, round-necked dress

SAVE YOUR BREATH TO COOL YOUR PORRIDGE – a phrase warning you not to waste the effort

SHIPS OF THE LINE – Royal Naval fighting ships

TACHED – thatched

TENTER – woman working in carding room

TIGER – a groom (yes, i know, ridiculous, isn't it? why not call a groom a groom?)

TOOL – drive a carriage

A SUPPLEMENT TO DR JOHNSON'S DICTIONARY BY CAT AND JAMIE

AGLEY – astray, off course

BAGREL – a touch on the short side

BLETHERING – chattering

BRAW – fine, handsome

BRIGANER – bandit

BUMBAZED – bewildered

BUTTERY-LIPPIT – smooth-tongued

BY-START – illegitimate offspring

CANNA – can't

CANNY – clever

CHAP – to knock

CHUCKIE – chick

CLACK – gossip, insolence

CLAMJAMPHRY – rubbish

CLASHING – idle talk, gossip

CLOOTS – clothes

COULDNA – couldn't

DAFTIE – mad person, fool

DAIDLING – dawdling

DIDNA – didn't

DINNA – don't

DISTRACKIT – distracted

DOESNA – doesn't

DOMINIE – schoolmaster

DOUCE – respectable

DOWIE – ailing

DREICH – dismal

FAITHER – father

FASHED – bothered

FLECHES – fleas

FOND – gullible

GANG – go

GHILLIE – gamekeeper

GLAIKIT – stupid

GLEG – quick

GLEG-TONGUIT – quick-tongued, glib

GOWK – fool

HAIL – healthy

HALLOCKIT – hoyden, tomboy

HEN – girl or woman

HEN-HERTIT – lily-livered

ILL-DEEDIE – wicked

ILL-LIKIT – unpopular

ISNA – isn't

JUMMLED – jumbled

KEEK – look

KEN – know

KITTLE – fickle, unpredictable

KITTLIN – kitten

LASSOCK – little girl

MAISTER – master

MITHER – mother

MOSS – moor, bog

NAE – no

NAEBODIE – nobody

NAETHIN – nothing

NO – not

PIBROCH – bagpipe music

QUEAN – girl

RACKLESS – reckless

RAMSTAM – devil-may-care, rash

RAUCLE – stern, uncouth

REESE – flattery

REIVERS/REIVING – thieves, thieving

RICKLE – heap

SAIR-WORK – hard work

SAPSIE – weak

SASSENACH – English person

SCHOOLIE – teacher

SKELPING – beating

SKINNYMALINK – thin person

SNECKING – stealing

SNIPPIE – sharp-tongued person

SOOTHLAN – southern

THE DAY – today

THE MORN'S NICHT – tomorrow night

THE NICHT – tonight

THRAWN – stubborn, pigheaded

TON – High society, the kind of people waiters do not try to hide behind screens.

TROON SCHOOL – play truant

UNCHANCIE – risky, unlucky

UNCO – strange, odd

UNKENNIN – ignorance

WEANS – young children

WHEEST – hush!

WI' – with

WIFIE – wife

WIN OFF – get off

WILLNA – won't

WOULDNA – wouldn't

WUDSCUD – wild boy or girl